Finding Joy in Sugar Plum

A Kentucky Christmas

By
M.J. Schlotter

For Jesus—the reason we celebrate Christmas—and for my hometown, Lawrenceburg, Kentucky— you will always hold a special place in my heart!

Chapter 1

Parked on the street in her silver compact, Sophie stared blankly through the windshield at the passing freight train. *The last time she had been home*, she recalled wistfully, *had been five years ago.* Fumbling in her purse, Sophie pulled out the letter that had brought her back. Crinkled from being held and smudged with tears, she held it shakily between her fingers. *She had been so filled with pride... so stubborn... and so determined not to be stuck in her hometown, that now, even though she had spoken to him on the phone and booked the first available airline ticket home, she had been too late.*

Sophie hurriedly brushed the tears from her cheeks and took a deep breath before pulling the keys from the ignition. She could not stay in the car forever; she had to face reality and the reason she was here. Opening the car door, a frigid blast of December wind snagged Sophie's long brown curls, and as she slammed the car door shut, the wind continued grabbing at her; its icy fingers finding their way through her winter clothes. As she pulled her charcoal-gray peacoat tighter against her body, Sophie's dark-brown eyes gazed at the brick steps and large white Corinthian columns decorating the entrance of *The Sugar Plum History Museum.*

A chill, that was not from the wind, scurried up Sophie's spine. As a child, she had always had the dream of reopening and running the long-abandoned museum. It had been the dream that had inspired her to pursue not one, but three degrees in history, and the dream that her Grandfather, the man who had raised her, knew was her most desired ambition. But after earning her doctorate in history, her longtime dream quickly became overshadowed by the lure of opportunities to teach and lecture at prestigious universities, and the prospect of writing the top books in her field. But none of that mattered anymore.

When her Grandpa had told her, the town was planning on reopening the old Carnegie library and turning it into the town's history museum and tourism office, he had been so excited. *"Sophie, it's your dream!"* he had gushed, his face filled with the excitement of a child on Christmas morning. *"Just think, all those years earning your degrees. It's like it was meant to be! You can run it! I can see it now, Dr. Sophie Marten, Ph.D., curator of the Sugar Plum History Museum!"*

Recalling her Grandpa's words, caused Sophie's heart to ache. *Instead of sharing his joy*, she thought, feeling ashamed, *she had conveyed nothing of the sort*. The hurt she had seen within her Grandpa's eyes as she told him she no longer desired such a foolish childhood dream and was instead going to accept the post she had been offered at Harvard, was something she was sure she would remember and regret for the rest of her life.

If only her Grandpa had told her sooner that he was sick, Sophie thought sorrowfully. *She would have been home and swallowed her pride in an instant. She would have told him that university lecturing and writing academic books had brought her no joy; that she was sorry, and that he had always been right in knowing what would truly bring her heart happiness.* When she had spoken to him on the phone, Sophie had somehow known that it would be the last time she would get to talk to him, but she still had hoped to see him one more time in person. When she had tried to apologize, her Grandpa had cut her off, telling her there was nothing to apologize for and that he would hear none of that. *Knowing that she was coming home for Christmas was all that he needed,* he had said. As Sophie walked up the steps and slowly turned the knob on the old wooden door, she knew that although her heart was home, it was heavy, even though her Grandpa would want her to be happy.

The soft jingle of a bell sounded as Sophie stepped into the museum, and her nose was met by the warm, tickling aroma of cinnamon. Walking further into the room, her eyes fell upon the cheery twinkling glow emitting from the Christmas tree that stood next to a display of brochures detailing Sugar Plum, Kentucky's various sights and two prestigious bourbon distilleries. It was two weeks until Christmas, and this was the time of year when anticipation and holiday cheer should be bursting forth which each breath she drew. *But this year,* Sophie thought wistfully, *her favorite season would be filled with memories and thoughts of ghosts of Christmas pasts.* Surveying the room, Sophie gazed at the numerous artifacts displayed on wooden shelves and various types of antique furniture. The quaint and cozy interior, she found, offered her a warmth she had not realized for which she had been longing. It was as though a part of her that had become dormant was suddenly ignited with a spark of life. Taking the curator position in town had indeed been a pay cut, *but the way her heart felt at ease...*Sophie knew her decision to come home was worth more than gold.

Walking towards one of the windows, Sophie saw light fluffy snowflakes beginning to fall. As she stood gazing out the frosty glass, a couple of school buses drove past along the road, and Sophie smiled as she thought about all the kids at school hoping they might get dismissed early. *It only took a dusting of snow*, she laughed to herself, *for the kids' dreams to come true*. So distracted was Sophie as she gazed out the window at the snow beginning to fall more steadily, that she did not hear the soft quiet thud of approaching footsteps.

"Good afternoon. May I help you?" a woman asked brightly, causing Sophie to quickly tear her gaze away from the snow and turn seeking the speaker.

"Yes," Sophie smiled, looking at the middle-aged woman standing in front of her. "I am supposed to meet with a, Mrs. Ellen Webber, this afternoon," she replied.

"Oh!" the woman exclaimed, her blue eyes sparkling, as she hurriedly tucked a strand of silvery-blonde hair that had escaped her bobby pins behind her ear and extended her hand. "I'm Ellen Webber. That means you must be Dr. Sophie Marten! It is so nice to meet you, Dear!" she beamed, shaking Sophie's hand heartily.

"It's very nice to meet you too," Sophie replied, returning Ellen's smile.

"We are so glad you decided to accept the curator position," Ellen continued. "Your Grandfather, God rest his soul, came in here singing your praises almost every day. He was so proud of your accomplishments. *My Sophie, she got her history degrees, you know, hoping one day to open this museum up again,* he'd say," then catching sight of Sophie's face, her smile slightly faltering, Ellen gently added, her words full of compassion, "I'm so sorry for your loss, Dear; I truly am."

"Thank you," Sophie said, nodding her head and smiling warmly at Ellen.

"How about we have a nice cup of peppermint tea and get better acquainted?" Ellen suggested with a motherly smile. "Then after that, I can take you on a tour and help you get settled in."

"That would be wonderful," Sophie remarked appreciatively, as she followed Ellen further into the museum.

"Here we are," Ellen remarked, opening a door then gesturing Sophie inside. "It's not much, but I think you'll find it to be a comfortable office," she continued, a smile beaming upon her face.

As Sophie walked into the small room, her eyes quickly surveyed her surroundings. An aged wooden desk stood before her, with stationary and other office essentials neatly arranged on its top. The worn and sturdy wooden chairs that were pushed against it, matched it perfectly, and Sophie could almost see herself stepping back in time when she sat down to begin her work. A small bookshelf stood against one of the walls, housing a fair number of leather-bound volumes that most likely would give off a faint dusty aroma as their pages were turned. Sophie smiled to herself, that was a smell that made her heart flutter. Of all the years she had spent in university archives, there was nothing quite like the scent of antiquated parchment. *The dusty aroma somehow made the paper sources seem alive*, Sophie laughed to herself, knowing her words would sound extremely silly to someone who did not love history. Opposite the bookshelf, Sophie noticed a small window opening out onto the street. *Yes*, Sophie mused, *she would be extremely happy here!*

"This will do very nicely," Sophie uttered, stepping closer to the desk and turning on the small decorative stained-glass lamp that sat upon the workspace; the light casting from the lamp filling the room in a warm soft glow. *The only problem*, Sophie thought with a smile, *would be prying herself away from such a cozy office.*

"I'm so glad you like it!" Ellen replied jovially. "You just make yourself comfortable now, and I'll be back shortly with the tea," she added, before excusing herself.

Left alone, Sophie sat down at the desk and again pulled the letter from her purse. Gently unfolding the paper, she held it under the lamp light.

My Dear Sophie,

I know you and I no longer see eye-to-eye about the history museum— I guess I'm just being an old sentimental fool— but enough. I do not have the right to try and tell you how to live your life. I'm willing to never speak about it again, and I hope you'll find it in your heart to forgive me for being so persistent. I just didn't want you to give up on a dream you'd held for so long, and I couldn't believe it was no longer a dream of yours.

I have always been proud of you, Sophie. After your parents passed away and you came to live with me, I guess I've always seen you as that little girl and was blind to the accomplished young woman you've become. If teaching and doing research at a university is what makes you happy, then that is what will make me happy too. After you left five years ago, I wish we had swallowed our prides and tried to mend things sooner. Our occasional phone conversations just weren't the same, since we were both tiptoeing around the elephant in the room, too afraid to hurt the other's feelings even more. Please, Sophie, come home for Christmas this year. I've not been feeling well, and I would really love to see you again. You will always be my little girl at heart; forgive me for trying to make you stay that little girl instead of letting you grow. I love you, Sophie, I always have, and I always will.

  Love,

  Grandpa

  Sophie rested her elbow on the desk and put her chin in the palm of her hand. Looking down at the inky lettering of her Grandpa's words, Sophie smiled. "Thank you for bringing me home, Grandpa," she whispered.

Chapter 2

"Here we are, Dr. Marten," Ellen said cheerfully, returning with two steaming mugs of tea and a tin of ginger snaps.

"You can just call me Sophie," Sophie replied, taking the mug of tea she was offered, as Ellen set the tin of cookies between them, and then took a seat in the chair on the other side of the desk.

"Sophie it is," Ellen smiled warmly, lifting her tea bag up and down before taking a sip from her mug. "I don't know about you, but I love peppermint tea. Even though it's warm, it's oddly cool and refreshing. Kind of an oxymoron I dare say," she laughed. "I also find it tastes like Christmas in a cup, and reminds me of it year-round," she added, her eyes dancing happily as she continued to sip her tea.

"Thank you for the tea," Sophie said, her voice grateful as she took a sip from her mug. "I've never thought of peppermint tea quite in that way before. It's a rather lovely description," she mused. "I believe you're absolutely right. Peppermint tea is unique in both of those ways."

Ellen smiled. "I'm glad you think so. Sometimes I can get *too* poetic," she chuckled. "So, Sophie," Ellen continued, leaning back against her chair and opening the tin of cookies. "What was it like teaching at a university and living up east?"

Sophie set her mug down in front of her and helped herself to a ginger snap. "Living up east was nice," she admitted, taking a bite of her cookie. The sharpness of the cinnamon and bitterness of molasses was a sensational compliment to her taste buds. Swallowing her bite, Sophie continued. "Harvard was extremely close to Boston, and since I'm a historian, it was basically a kind of academic paradise. The winters, though, were definitely more brutal," Sophie added. She recalled once having to dig her car out of five feet of snow and hike across campus in frigid temperatures. Just thinking about it made her shiver.

"If you don't mind me asking," Ellen began, polishing off her cookie, "why would you give up living and working in such a historical place to come work here?"

Sophie swallowed the sip of tea she had just taken and held Ellen's gaze. *Would this woman she had just met believe her when she told her she had been unhappy at her presumable dream job? Even her own words— since I'm a historian, it was basically a kind of academic paradise—* Sophie realized, made her sound like an idiot for having left.

"Would you believe me if I told you I wasn't happy?" Sophie asked hesitantly. She watched as Ellen opened her mouth to reply. *Here it comes*, Sophie thought, *the laugh and the, "You've got to be joking," statement*. But Ellen did not laugh. Instead, she merely nodded and smiled understandingly at Sophie.

"You can't run from your dreams," Ellen declared knowingly. "Even when you think you've forgotten them, they have a way of reminding you they're still there, and that they're still a part of who you are."

"I thought teaching at a renowned university seemed like it was the right path to take," Sophie shared. "When I graduated with my doctorate, everyone asked me where I was going to be lecturing and researching. It just seemed like that was what I was meant to do," she added flatly. "Then after the excitement wore off and Grandpa and I had our disagreement...I found that what I thought would make me happy actually left me feeling empty. Does that make any sense?" Sophie asked.

"Honey, that makes complete sense. You felt empty because your dream had been and always was to run this place," Ellen declared matter-of-factly, offering Sophie a smile.

"You would think writing a bestseller on the linguistic heritage and influence of Gaelic in American history would make one happy," Sophie huffed.

"Sophie, did you enjoy writing that book?" Ellen asked, her eyes peering transfixed at Sophie from over the brim of her mug.

"Well...I mean...no," Sophie admitted, feeling like a failure.

"You see," Ellen said, leaning back in her chair and taking a sip of tea, "you weren't happy, because you were not doing what you, deep down inside, *really* wanted to do. You were doing what others *expected* you to do," she concluded with a smile.

"Well, if that's the case, then I've wasted over five years of my life," Sophie uttered dejectedly.

"Nothing is ever wasted," Ellen assured Sophie, setting her mug on the desk and holding Sophie's gaze. "Everything we do is all part of our education. Everything we do helps us achieve our dreams, even if it only serves to help us realize it's not what we are actually supposed to be doing."

"How can you be so wise?" Sophie asked in amazement, as she continued to stare at Ellen with awe.

Ellen laughed. "I'm not really. Although, I'd have loved it if my kids had heard me described as wise when they were teenagers," she added, her eyes dancing merrily.

Sophie smiled. "Well, I for one think you are being entirely too modest," she complimented, as she took another cookie from the tin. "I guess dating, Nathan, then had a purpose too?" she asked somewhat to herself.

"If dating him helped you realize that you needed to be here," Ellen remarked thoughtfully. "Then yes. I'd say there was a purpose."

"I guess I thought dating him would make me happy enough that I would forget how miserable I was at work," Sophie shared. *Why was she so candidly sharing her personal life with a practical stranger? Was it because now that her grandpa had passed away, she had no other family? Or was it because Ellen was so easy to talk with and was so wise and not judgmental?* Whatever the reason was, Sophie felt compelled to continue. "I know now that was selfish of me, but I didn't know it then. Nathan worked in the English department. We seemed like a perfect university couple...," Sophie's words trailed, and she stared off into space. *At first, she really had thought she was in love with Nathan, but when you're in love with someone, you drop everything you're doing to spend time with them; you don't try and fit them into your schedule.*

"So, what happened?" Ellen asked, drawing Sophie back

from her thoughts.

Sophie turned her attention again to her companion. "When I told Nathan, I wanted to leave higher ed, he told me I was making the biggest mistake of my career, and that if I left, it was over between us."

"Classy," Ellen tutted, tapping her fingers against her mug.

Sophie nodded poignantly, feeling relieved to finally be sharing this with someone. "I knew then that I wasn't the only one who had been lying to themselves. We both were *in love* with a made-up image of love."

"And there is your purpose," Ellen affirmed. "Dating Nathan made you realize what *real* love should look like."

"Yes. Yes, I believe it did," Sophie agreed, feeling a sense of complete assurance for the first time since she'd arrived.

Chapter 3

After finishing their tea and taking a quick tour of the few rooms in the museum, Ellen brought Sophie back to her new office. Seeing what was to be her workstation once again, and glimpsing the snow falling beyond the windowpanes, Sophie was again delighted by the coziness of the room and the entire museum. Stepping into her office with a smile, Sophie felt a weight lift from her chest. *She might actually, for the first time, enjoy her job!* she pondered. *And the degrees she'd spent years earning, quite possibly had found their purpose!*

"Well, I've got to get back to manning the station, and trying to answer questions from tourists," Ellen said brightly. "Although, if they ask me anything too historical, I'm coming to get you," she declared with a grin, before leaving Sophie to begin organizing her office.

As Sophie began unpacking the items from the boxes she had retrieved from her car, she felt like settling in was going to go smoothly. She pulled out a framed photograph of her Grandpa and her and placed it on one of the corners of her desk. Staring at the photo, its faded coloring and clothing choices clearly from the 90s, Sophie smiled. This had always been one of her favorite photos. She was probably seven or eight in the picture and wearing a smile with several missing teeth. She was standing in front of the history museum with her Grandpa holding a sign that read, *"I'm gonna open this place!"* The photo had hung on their refrigerator for as long as

Sophie could remember. *"To help you always visualize your dream,"* her Grandpa had told her. She had forgotten about the picture, until her Grandpa had mailed it to her a couple of years ago. *Had that been when she had first started questioning her career decision?* Sophie wondered.

Leaving the photograph on her desk, Sophie unpacked a few more items, and then decided the rest could wait. Before she could give her mind fully over to the task of moving in, Sophie knew she had to finalize her Grandpa's funeral arrangements for tomorrow. Even though it was chilly outside, she decided to walk. The brisk air would do her good, and besides, walking in the falling snow was always something she enjoyed. The museum was not too far from Main Street, where Sophie knew she would find one of her favorite shops— *All Thymes and Occasions: Bouquets and Gifts*. The local florist shop, in Sophie's opinion, was one of Main Street's crown-jewels. As she walked towards the flower shop, Sophie was delighted to see that downtown Sugar Plum had become a vibrant and thriving business sector.

Walking along the brick and cobblestone-edged sidewalk, Sophie's eyes were met by a plethora of signs promoting eating and shopping local. Even with the frigid temperature, downtown was bustling! Sophie pleasantly observed a tour bus parked along the street and several small groups of tourists clustered along the sidewalks examining brochures about the town, before they stepped into the local shops to look for souvenirs and get warm. Gazing at the luminous decorative snowflakes and silver bells spanning above her head from one side of the street to the other, Sophie found her footsteps lightening with each step as she continued to walk. The people she passed on the sidewalk smiled and greeted her with cheerful hellos, and she glimpsed the friendly exchanges of locals running into one another as they carried out their daily affairs. Slowing her pace, Sophie's eyes became mesmerized by the Christmas lights that twinkled brightly, decorating the trees and lampposts lining the street, and she found herself thinking how beautiful and welcoming a small-town can be where everyone seems to care about each other.

With her eyes continuing to take in the sights, Sophie allowed her mind to wander. *When she was a girl*, Sophie recalled, *there seemed to only be a few shops downtown*. She remembered when the local drug store, with its novelty collectables, candy, and friendly employees, had been one of the street's highlights. But when the pharmacist had retired and the shop had closed, other shops seemed to routinely emerge and disappear in silent tributes of hope and melancholy defeat. Main Street had been dying. But now, seeing several store fronts dedicated to selling local Kentucky wares, a tea and coffee shop, and a variety of local restaurants with tables and chairs along the sidewalk, Sophie could not keep from smiling. Reading the words written on a chalkboard-sign outside the front of a shop, Sophie's feet stopped. Downtown Sugar Plum now had a bookstore! Sophie couldn't resist, she had to take a quick step inside.

Pushing the glass door ajar, the bells hanging on the other side of the knob chimed brightly, as Sophie stepped inside *Bourbon Barrel Books*. The fragrant aroma of a bourbon and vanilla scented candle delighted Sophie's senses, as she gazed upon volumes of books housed along the walls in large wooden bookshelves. *Where to begin*, Sophie thought, her mind in literary heaven as her eyes rested upon the decorative holly boughs and vintage wooden sliding ladders running along the shelves. There was something about a bookstore that always made her instantly happy— it was magical. Listening to the Crooner Christmas music that was playing softly throughout that shop and having decided to peruse the section labeled *Holiday Classics,* Sophie was just about to pull out a copy of *A Christmas Carol* when...

"Good afternoon! Is there anything in particular you are looking for?" a woman's voice asked.

"No. I'm honestly just browsing," Sophie replied, as she turned to address the young woman who stood a shelf away. Gazing at the speaker, her thick ebony hair flowing over her shoulder in a loose braid, Sophie noticed she seemed to be positively glowing.

"Well, if you decide you need help finding anything, please don't hesitate to ask. You're one of my first customers," the woman continued excitedly, her brown eyes dancing lively and a smile upon her face.

"Did you just recently open up shop?" Sophie asked.

"Yes. Today is actually our grand opening," the woman shared. "I'm Vivian Fernsby by the way," she added, walking towards Sophie and extending her hand.

"It's nice to meet you. I'm Sophie Marten, the new curator for the town's history museum," Sophie introduced, shaking Vivian's hand.

"Oh! When I read about the museum reopening, I thought

that was such a wonderful decision. I'm not originally from here, so I've visited the museum a couple of times already, and both times I've learned something new about Sugar Plum's local history," Vivian gushed.

"That is the exciting thing about history," Sophie remarked. "I grew up in Sugar Plum, but I know as I work on archiving and cataloging displays, the town will continue to teach me something new. I guess I'm just overly passionate about history," she laughed.

"I completely understand what you mean," Vivian agreed. "I absolutely love books! Something about the beauty of the written word, I guess. I devour them faster than I can get my hands on them. I've always wanted to open a book shop, and my husband, Jack, and I decided to finally give it a shot before this little one arrives," Vivian shared, patting her stomach gently.

"Congratulations to you on both accounts," Sophie complimented, noticing for the first time Vivian's small rounding belly. Sophie's heart fluttered with happiness for Vivian. *This time of year was the perfect reminder that all babies are truly blessings*, she thought with a smile. "Do you know what you're having?" Sophie asked, observing the joyful anticipation on Vivian's face.

Vivian laughed. "No. We're that couple that drives all of our friends and relatives crazy. We're waiting to be surprised," she smiled. "It just seems more exciting that way. It won't be long now, though, only four more months to go."

"Excuse me, you wouldn't happen to have a copy of *The Night Before Christmas* would you by chance?" a man asked, walking through the door.

Vivian turned. "Why of course," she replied cheerfully. "I'll take you to our children's section. It was very nice to meet you, Sophie. I hope you'll stop by again or come by when we're open for the Main Street Christmas Bazaar," she added.

"It was nice to meet you too!" Sophie replied brightly, as Vivian turned to leave and help her new customer find his book. *She definitely would be back, but now she really needed to get back on task*, Sophie thought.

Stepping back outside, Sophie began walking again towards the flower shop. She had only gone a few more feet, however, when another shop caught her eye. Pausing for a moment, Sophie peered into the window of *The Sugar Plum Bistro*. The wooden tables and chairs with their crisp and festive red and green cloth tablecloths, white folded napkins, and glowing candles wrapped in holly, beckoned invitingly. And Sophie watched with eagerness as a waiter brought a tray filled with delicious looking food piled generously on plates to a table of customers. The sight of Kentucky Hot Browns, fried chicken with mashed potatoes and mixed vegetables, and bowls of steaming soup, made Sophie's mouth water. Her stomach grumbled rather loudly, and Sophie could not help but wonder what it would be like to eat at the charming café. Sugar Plum was embracing its *Bourbon Trail* location, and becoming a trendy, yet quaint, must see town for tourists. Sophie's heart fluttered. It was so wonderful to see the town she loved so much prospering and making a name for itself.

Finally, arriving at *All Thymes and Occasions*, Sophie pulled open the large wooden door and stepped inside. Even though she had not been in the shop for years, its fragrant scent of spices and flowers was the same enchanting aroma she remembered. As she walked around the shop, Sophie studied the various arrangements and knickknacks on display. Her Grandpa had always been a fan of roses, she recalled thoughtfully, gazing at an arrangement of the lovely crimson blooms. *"They are beautiful, but their thorns keep you humble, reminding you that all life deserves respect,"* Sophie heard her Grandpa's voice telling her a truth of wisdom. She would purchase a few simple arrangements of roses; he would like that, and then maybe some greenery with holly as a way to acknowledge that she had come home for Christmas. The tears began to well up in her eyes at this thought, and Sophie knew she had to find a florist and place her order before she started crying.

Reaching the counter, Sophie rang the bell and waited.

"Hello. How may I help you?" a woman asked cheerfully, as she appeared from the back of the shop.

"I'd like to…," Sophie began.

"Sophie Marten!" the woman exclaimed excitedly.

Sophie stared at the lady in front of her, her short brown hair pulled slightly to the side with a decorative silver and gold snowflake hairpin, and her blue eyes beaming brightly. *Her face looks so familiar,* Sophie thought, *but I can't seem to place her name...*

"It's me, Karah. Karah Loughty," the lady remarked, a broad smile upon her face.

It was as if a light switch turned on, and Sophie felt so ashamed. *How could she have not recognized Karah?* They had gone to school together for years and played on the high school's tennis team. Looking at Karah now, Sophie couldn't believe she had not known it was her. Seeing her again, it was as if Karah had not changed a bit!

"Karah!" Sophie smiled with embarrassment. "Gosh, I'm so sorry I didn't recognize you."

"Don't worry," Karah laughed. "We haven't seen each other in at least ten years. How are you doing? Are you living in Sugar Plum now or are you just home for Christmas?" she asked happily.

Sophie's smile faltered. "I'm doing well," she replied. "I just accepted the curator position here at the local history museum, so I'm home now. I do need to order some flowers though, my Grandpa passed away."

"Oh, Sophie. I'm so sorry," Karah said, her voice empathetic. "I forgot.... he was your only family."

"Yes," Sophie breathed. "Not only does it make spending the holidays more difficult, but I didn't get to see him in person before he passed away. I had hoped to apologize, because he wouldn't let me over the phone," she shared.

"Sophie," Karah said gently, walking out from behind the counter and giving Sophie a hug. "Your Grandpa loved you, and he would not want you beating yourself up about something you didn't apologize for."

"I know. He said pretty much the same thing when I called him," Sophie admitted, as Karah continued to embrace her. "I guess I just needed to hear someone else tell me that, though."

Releasing Sophie, Karah smiled. "I was about to step out for lunch. What do you say we order your flowers, and then go grab something to eat?"

"That would be wonderful!" Sophie replied, looking forward to catching up with Karah.

With the flowers ordered and the shop locked up for lunch, Sophie and Karah stepped outside. The snow had started to let up, but the wind was still fiercely cold. Karah tugged her scarf tightly about her neck and up under her nose.

"Alright, I'm ready to brace the arctic," Karah laughed, her mouth hidden beneath her scarf.

"You look like you're expecting sub-degree temperatures," Sophie laughed. "If you think this is cold, you should spend a winter in the Boston area," she added, as they continued making their way towards, *The Tulip Poplar*—- a local bakery and confectionery on Main Street— named in honor of Kentucky's state tree.

"Yeah, I don't think I would survive," Karah remarked shivering. "The 30s and 20s, with the occasional single digits, is just about as much as I can handle. I dare say if my family was not all living here, I'd move to the beach. Yeah, that sounds wonderful!" Karah declared, her eyes bright just thinking of the prospect.

"Speaking of your family, how are they doing?" Sophie asked, pulling her coat tighter as a gust of wind whirled about her.

"Chrissy's married with a couple of kids, and mom and dad are both enjoying retired life. It will be nice seeing them all on Christmas," Karah shared.

"It sounds like they're all doing well," Sophie remarked, suppressing the slight feeling of envy that welled up within her knowing that Karah had a family to spend time with during the holidays.

"Yeah, they are. But I know, even though we'll be celebrating Christmas, they will all start pestering me about when I'm going to get married," Karah continued, rolling her eyes. "Gotta love family," she added with a smile. "Ever since the guy I dated in college dumped me, and I moved back to town a few years ago, they've been worried I won't meet anyone working in the flower shop. There's this guy here in town though..." Karah looked at Sophie and then stopped talking. Brad, the guy she had been about to mention, had been smitten with Sophie in high school. *With Sophie back in town, would Brad's old feelings be rekindled? Sophie had not dated him back in school, but what if she wanted to now?* Karah suddenly felt like someone had punched her in the stomach. As she continued walking, Karah felt dazed. Sophie was a friend, and she felt guilty thinking of her as competition.

"Karah?" Sophie inquired, her voice penetrating Karah's thoughts. "So, who's this guy?" she asked, her voice full of interest.

Karah turned and looked at Sophie and saw the sparkle of anticipation in her eyes. "Oh, no one really, just someone my folks are trying to set me up with," Karah lied. *Why did she feel the need to lie?* Karah scolded herself. *She was not behaving like herself at all!*

"Well, I hope it works out for you," Sophie said, genuinely happy for her friend. "I'm thinking about swearing off dating for a while. My last relationship turned out to be a complete disaster," she admitted with a laugh.

Karah hesitantly returned Sophie's smile. Even if Sophie had decided to take a break from dating, Karah doubted Brad would feel the same way once he saw Sophie again. Just like she had been in high school, Sophie was still lovely and had a kind and bubbly personality. *There was no way she would ever stand a chance with Brad,* Karah thought sadly.

"Oh, I'm so glad we're finally here! I'm freezing!" Sophie exclaimed, extending a hand and opening the door to the bakery.

Relieved to be able to talk about something else, Karah followed Sophie inside. "If you haven't eaten here, you're absolutely going to love it!" she gushed.

Loosening her scarf and gazing around the eatery, Sophie admired the retro-artsy decor. How she wished she had more of a gift for interior design. Some people have such a knack for knowing how to put things aesthetically together. *The owners of this establishment,* Sophie thought admiringly; as her eyes roved over the brightly colored cushions in an array of decorative patterns lining the seats of cherry stained chairs, *were definitely blessed with such a talent!* Gazing around the bakery, Sophie's eyes continued taking in the coziness of the shop. The black-and-white photographs lining the walls depicting Sugar Plum's earlier decades, tugged at her historian's heart; and the wooden tables, with their varying stained-glass lamps or candle arrangements softly glowing, were a wonderful contrast to the vintage inspired black-and-white tiled floor and stark espresso colored walls. But nothing, Sophie realized, her stomach gurgling loudly, compared to the delicious aromas that wafted from behind the counter, and the mouthwatering display of assorted chocolates and confections!

"I don't even know what to begin to order," Sophie uttered, overwhelmed by the variety of options. "Everything sounds so delicious! And the smell...How do I even begin to decide what to try?"

"Well, one of my personal favorites is the sweet-potato quiche. You can't go wrong with that," Karah suggested matter-of-factly. "I keep telling myself I'm going to try something different every time I come here, but the quiche—it's fresh basil...sharp white cheddar...It is so amazingly good! I just can't break away from it," she laughed.

"Oh, yum! That does sound delicious!" Sophie exclaimed, imagining the savory and decadent flavors making up the savory pie. *She better order something soon*, she laughed to herself, *or her stomach was bound to start eating itself!*

"Good afternoon, Ladies," a portly gentleman with salt-and-pepper hair spoke brightly, as Sophie and Karah approached the counter, adorned in shimmering silver garland and Christmas lights. "What can I get started for you all?" he asked.

"I'll take a slice of the sweet-potato quiche and a glass of lemonade please," Karah responded without hesitation.

"And for you, Miss?" the cashier inquired, turning to look at Sophie.

"I'm going to have to try a slice of sweet-potato quiche too. Except, I will have a glass of water and a cup of coffee," Sophie replied happily, looking forward to tasting her new culinary experience. "Oh, and I'll also have a couple of bourbon balls," she added, her eyes drifting over the smooth dark-chocolate and pecan topped candies beneath the glass display case.

"Excellent choice," the cashier remarked with a smile. "Of all the candies we have, the bourbon balls are my favorite. Here you are, Ladies, your glasses for the fountain machine and a number for you table," he continued, as he handed Sophie the table number along with her glass. "The coffee mugs are next to the coffee pots by the drinks, so help yourself. A waitress will bring your food to your table when it's ready. Oh, and here are your candies," he added, retrieving a couple of bourbon balls and wrapping them in wax-paper. Enjoy!"

"Thank you," Sophie and Karah replied, before heading towards the fountain machine.

With their beverages in hand, the women walked towards a table near one of the front windows looking out on Main Street.

"If you don't mind, I'm going to pop in the restroom for a sec," Karah said, after setting her lemonade on the table.

"Alright, I'll get my coffee then wait for our food," Sophie replied, setting their number on the table and heading towards the coffee pots.

Perusing the selection of coffees, Sophie finally settled on one flavored with chocolate and hazelnut. *Something sounding that appetizing had to surely taste as amazing as it sounded,* Sophie thought with a smile. With visions of melted chocolate with a hint of hazelnut dancing in her mind, Sophie placed her coffee mug beneath the percolator and watched as the dark chocolatey colored liquid began filling her cup. *It definitely smelled like chocolate and hazelnut,* she smiled, feeling her fingers warming as the steaming liquid neared the top of her mug. After stirring in some cream and sugar, Sophie headed back to the table to wait for Karah. Leaning back in her chair, Sophie sipped her coffee, listening to the acoustic Christmas melodies playing softly in the background. As she gazed absentmindedly out the frosty window with its icicle lights twinkling warmly against the glass, Sophie smiled, soaking up the warm feeling her coffee gave her as she watched the cars driving by on the street. Expecting a waiter or waitress to be bringing out their orders, Sophie was startled when she heard the seat in front of her scrape against the floor and a man's voice begin speaking.

"Well, either my eyes are deceiving me, or Sophie Marten is back in town!" a masculine voice declared jovially.

Sophie turned her attention away from the window and stared at the man sitting across from her, his bright blue eyes illuminated by his broad grin, and his sandy-blond hair glowing in the lamp light.

"Brad Devanston!" Sophie exclaimed in surprise.

"That's *Mayor* Brad Devanston," Brad remarked enthusiastically, his grin broadening.

"Wow! Mayor!" Sophie exclaimed, shaking her head in admiration. "I can't believe you're still here! I thought you were going to move to New York and work on Wall Street."

"That was the plan," Brad chuckled. "But after starting a degree in finance, it just didn't seem like the right fit. Ultimately, I ended up switching to political science, and then got elected mayor a few years back," he finished with a shrug.

"I always knew you'd end up doing something important," Sophie smiled, taking another sip of her coffee. "You were always so popular and received top grades when we were in high school."

Brad's expression glowed with the compliment. "Well, enough about me," he said, leaning back in his chair. "I read about your grandfather's passing," he continued gently. "I'm truly sorry for your loss. He was a great man. I'll be there for you at his funeral tomorrow."

"Thanks, Brad," Sophie replied, smiling appreciatively as she saw the compassion in Brad's eyes. "That means a lot."

They remained staring silently into each other's eyes for a few moments before...

"Two slices of sweet-potato quiche," a waitress voiced with a smile, setting a plate in front of both Brad and Sophie. "Let me know, Dears, if y'all need anything else," she added before turning to leave.

Sophie could not wait to try the quiche. Her mouth was practically salivating just thinking about the first bite. *If it tasted as amazing as it smelled...* she might have to go back and order another slice. How she wished Karah would get back soon, so they could eat.

Brad stared at the plate in front of him. *It was just his luck*, he thought dejectedly. *Was the timing between he and Sophie always going to be off?* Then, clearing his throat, he forced himself to speak. "Are you expecting someone?" he asked hesitantly.

"Oh," Sophie uttered with a laugh, realizing the waitress had placed Karah's plate in front of Brad. "I ran into Karah at *All Thymes and Occasions*. She's in the restroom, but when she returns, she is going to want that slice of quiche so don't eat it, no matter how appetizing it smells!" Sophie finished with a grin.

"Well, that's excellent!" Brad remarked enthusiastically. Then catching the strange look Sophie was giving him, he quickly added, "I mean that it's *excellent* that you should run into such a good friend on your return to town. So, are you planning on staying in town for a while?" he asked casually, his face brightening as he held Sophie's gaze.

Sophie thought she saw a glimmer of hopefulness in his eyes, as she set her coffee mug on the table. Keeping her hands wrapped around the warm porcelain, Sophie smiled. "Well, as a matter-of-fact, I'm the new curator for the history museum," she shared happily.

"That's great!" Brad exclaimed, his eyes brightening as he held Sophie's gaze. "You always did love history."

"Yeah," Sophie said, a grin flashing across her face. "My senior superlative was *most likely to be found in the library*, remember?" she laughed. *It felt so good to laugh! Brad always had a way of making her laugh,* Sophie remembered, as she continued to smile at him. Brad's eyes were dancing merrily as she held his gaze. *Had he always been so attractive?*

"Ha-ha, yeah!" Brad chuckled, "How could I forget that!"

"Hi, Brad," Karah interrupted, smiling and taking the seat next to Sophie.

"I believe this is yours," Brad said, passing the plate of quiche across the table.

"Thanks," Karah replied, feeling her breath catch in her

throat. *Did Brad know how handsome he was?* "I see you've noticed Sophie is back in town," she commented. *Why couldn't she have thought of something better to say to him? Why did she have to state the obvious?*

"Yes," Brad said, smiling at Sophie. "It would have been hard not to have noticed."

Sophie felt her cheeks grow warm at Brad's compliment, as the blush she could not suppress quickly spread across her face. She and Brad had been good friends back when they were in high school. He had asked her out once, but she had told him going out would just make things awkward between them; and she did not want to ruin their friendship. *Had she been wrong in never giving him a chance?* Sophie considered. *Why was she suddenly beginning to feel like the room was becoming quite stifling? The way Brad was looking at her now...was it only because he hadn't seen her since graduation?* Sophie was relieved when Karah started speaking again.

"So, Brad, has the town's Christmas parade been finalized yet?" Karah asked, her eyes excited and full of interest as she waited for a reply. She saw Brad's gaze momentarily linger on Sophie's face. *The way Brad was gazing at Sophie,* Karah realized with a sinking heart, *was exactly as she had feared.*

"Oh, yes," Brad answered, turning his attention to Karah. "It's going to be this coming Saturday, a week from Christmas. An announcement should be in this week's edition of *The Sugar Plum Gazette*," he added with a smile.

"Excellent!" Karah exclaimed cheerfully, hoping to keep

Brad's attention. "I do love seeing all the floats, and the high school marching band playing Christmas carols. If you're not already in the holiday spirit, you *will* be after the parade!" she gushed, her face full of elation.

Sophie smiled at Karah. Her friend truly was one of the happiest people she had ever known. A true optimist, Karah was always able to see the bright side to everything. Even though Sophie had not seen Karah in years, chatting with her now was like no time had elapsed between them.

"Well, Ladies," Brad said, glancing at his watch. "I had better let you two finish your lunch and get back to the office. I've got a pretty busy schedule this afternoon. There's a budget meeting and some proposed ordinances that need reviewing. There's never a dull day when you're the mayor," he chuckled. "I'll see you later," he added, casting a smile at Sophie and rising from his chair.

After watching Brad depart, Sophie and Karah turned their attention back to their lunch. Cutting a bite of her quiche, Sophie brought the savory morsel to her mouth. The buttery and flaky crust was delicious, but the blend of sweet-potato, spices, and cheese... was absolutely scrumptious!

"Okay," Sophie declared, slicing another mouthful with her fork, "this has got to be the best quiche I have ever tasted!"

"I told you that you couldn't go wrong in ordering it," Karah replied happily. "I'm glad you find it as tasty as I do."

"It's a shame this place was not here when we were in high school," Sophie remarked, her taste buds enjoying another bite. "I think I would have had to come here at least once a week."

"I know what you mean. So much has changed. I for one would have been a frequent partaker at *Peppermint's Tea and Coffee*. No worries though," she smiled, "I'm totally making up for it, now! I wouldn't be surprised if they named a drink after me based on how often I'm there," she laughed.

"I have so many fond memories of growing up in this town," Sophie reminisced. "And hanging out with you and Brad in high school, those were truly some of the best times of my life."

"I know," Karah agreed. "Do you remember when Brad thought it would be funny to hang paper streamers in all the hallways of the school as a senior prank, and we helped him make it happen?" Karah asked, her face bright with laughter.

"How could I forget that!" Sophie laughed. "He was always instigating some kind of shenanigan. Who would have ever thought that he'd grow up to be Mayor?"

As they continued reminiscing about all of the fun times they'd had growing up in their small-town and devoured the decadent bourbon balls Sophie had purchased, the lunch flew by far too quickly. Before she knew it, Sophie found herself having to bid Karah farewell. She still had to go to her Grandpa's house and get settled in at the farm.

"I'll be there tomorrow, Sophie," Karah said, wrapping Sophie in a hug as they left the bakery. "If there's anything you need, don't hesitate to ask."

"Thanks, Karah, I truly appreciate that," Sophie replied, giving her friend a warm smile.

As she drove out of town, Sophie watched the pavement turn

into the familiar country road which she loved and could probably drive blindfolded. The various turns and swerves were sure to make someone unaccustomed to them car sick, but to Sophie, they were what gave the road its character and life. Following the wind of the road further out into the country, Sophie couldn't resist rolling down the windows despite the freezing temperatures. Breathing in the frigid winter air, Sophie filled her lungs with its pure, unpolluted crispness. Being in the business of the east coast, she had forgotten just how much she missed this unspoiled country air. *I guess*, she realized, *people just don't appreciate what they have until it's gone.*

When her eyes began to water from the cold, Sophie reluctantly rolled the window back up. She was getting closer now and could see the final bend in the road approaching in the distance. A few minutes later, she turned on to the long driveway leading to the house where she'd grown up. The gravel driveway crunched beneath the wheels of the car as Sophie drove along, twisting and turning, through a forest of trees. Although the tree limbs were currently bare, when they were donned in their summer foliage, the trees made the driveway appear as if it were some secret and magical lane dreamed up from a fairytale. Turning a bend into the clearing, Sophie caught the first glimpse of her childhood home. The white-sided and black-shuttered cape cod stood surrounded by rolling pastures lined with black-plank fencing. The herd of beef cattle her Grandpa had kept, were lazily wandering by the pond, and as she neared, Sophie saw her Grandpa's weather warn rocker sitting on the front porch next to the one he'd made for her. *Everything was exactly as she remembered*, she thought with a smile, *that is almost everything...* As she continued to draw near, Sophie's eyes rested on the unfamiliar black truck that was parked next to her Grandpa's old pick-up. Seeing the truck, however, was not the true cause of her alarm. As she pulled up next to the truck, Sophie's heart began to race, for a light was clearly visible and radiating from the kitchen window!

Someone was inside the house! Keeping the motor running, Sophie pulled her cellphone out. *No service! Not a single bar! There could be a burglar inside right now, and she had no way to call the police! Why wasn't her Grandpa's dog Ivy barking? Settle down,* Sophie told herself. *If a burglar was indeed inside, they most likely would not have turned on a light. Be rational, Sophie,* she scolded herself, *it's probably just a neighbor who has been looking after the farm until you arrived.* Turning off the ignition, Sophie stepped out of the car holding her pepper-spray just in case. As she mounted the wooden steps leading up to the porch, Sophie felt the hairs on the nape of her neck begin to prickle. *Okay, just open the door,* she told herself, taking a deep breath.

Fumbling with the house key, Sophie finally got it in the lock and slowly turned the doorknob. Holding her pepper-spray in front of her and moving it back and forth as if she were fencing, Sophie cautiously stepped inside. Her footsteps echoed loudly against the wooden floorboards, and she could feel her heart pounding within her chest as she strained to quiet her breathing. Nothing appeared to have been disturbed, but Ivy had still not appeared to great her. *Had the burglar seduced his or her way inside by offering the shepherd-lab mix a hamburger? Yes, that's all it would take,* Sophie realized, thinking of her Grandpa's loveable four-legged companion. Ivy might look ferocious, but Sophie knew she wouldn't hurt a fly.

"Whoever you are, I just want you to know I'm armed!" Sophie hollered, leaving the door open behind her and startling herself with the sound of her own voice.

She heard a pot rattle in the kitchen, and the sound of heavy footsteps walking towards her. Sophie's heart was pounding, a drum spiraling out of control, within her chest. *Pepper-spray, seriously? Why had she never thought to get her permit to carry a concealed weapon?* Still berating herself for her choice of weaponry, Sophie's attention was directed towards a man in his mid-thirties stepping into the foyer with Ivy at his heels! Sophie continued to hold her stance as the stranger, dressed in a hunter-green and navy-blue checkered flannel, advanced towards her, his hands held slightly up in the air and a disarming smile present upon his face. Sophie stared at the man. *His dark-brown hair... his neatly trimmed beard...who was he?* Sophie had no idea.

"Yes, I see you are *armed*," the man spoke, his deep-green eyes brightening as he held Sophie's gaze. "You must be Sophie."

Shocked, Sophie dropped the pepper-spray causing the man to laugh and Ivy to bound forward wagging her tail in excitement.

"I'm sorry. But if you could see your face…," the man chuckled.

Quickly recovering, Sophie bent down and retrieved the can of pepper-spray. Brushing Ivy's licks from her face, she wielded the can at the man. "You have exactly two seconds to tell me who you are and why you're in my house!" she bellowed.

Chapter 4

Sophie glared at the man waiting for his reply. He was not acting like a burglar, but still... *Who the heck was he, and what was he doing in her house?*

"I'm Grant Bakesfield," the man said, still smiling.

"Is that *name* supposed to mean something to me?" Sophie uttered, still confused.

"No, probably not," Grant chuckled. "When you decided to leave five years ago, your Grandpa realized he was going to need some help with the farm. I've been renting a room from him for the past four years and helping him out before and after work."

"Why didn't he tell me?" Sophie inquired, reluctantly deciding the man's story was sounding legitimate.

"From what I've gathered, the two of you didn't talk as frequently anymore," Grant replied evenly.

Sophie glared at him. "That is none of your business," she snapped, her words terse as she continued to aim the pepper-spray in Grant's direction.

Grant shrugged. "He sure did talk a lot about you, though."

That was the final straw. Sophie was not going to be judged by some stranger in her own house! "Thank you for helping my Grandpa. I truly mean it," Sophie uttered. "I would appreciate it, however, if you would find new lodgings as soon as possible."

"Of course," Grant smiled, turning back towards the kitchen.

"After Christmas, I'll start looking. Now, will you kindly lower that spray before you accidentally spray one of us? Come along, Ivy," he added, turning to leave.

"Excuse me?" Sophie exclaimed in disbelief, lowering the spray and following Grant. *How could Ivy be such a traitor?* she glowered, watching the dog she had known since she was a pup lick Grant's hand affectionately when he pet her. "Why can't you start looking today?" Sophie demanded.

"Well, that's a funny thing. You see," Grant began, stirring the pot on the stove, "your Grandpa had me sign a contract that I would keep renting a room here until the first of the year."

"Surly, that can be voided now that he's...he's no longer here," Sophie remarked, her words catching in her throat.

"That's the *funny* thing I was talking about," Grant continued, "he had me sign it at a lawyer's office. So, it's a legit legal document that can't be broken."

Sophie felt her mouth fall open. *Why on earth would her Grandpa do something like that? This was absolutely ridiculous! She was not going to live with a total stranger until New Years! There had to be some way around this contract. Some way to...*

"Would you like some burgoo?" Grant asked, interrupting Sophie's thoughts.

"What?" Sophie inquired, having not entirely heard him.

"I said, would you like some burgoo?" Grant repeated.

Sophie gazed at the bubbling pot on top of the stove. She had never actually made homemade burgoo before. The meat and vegetable stew, normally tomato-based, was the town's main

38

attraction at the annual fall Festival. Sophie had tasted the stew at the festival plenty of times as part of the judging for the various booths competing to be named that year's winning recipe, but she had never actually prepared it herself.

"It's pretty good, if I do say so," Grant smiled, as if reading Sophie's thoughts. "I was on the award-winning *Sugar Plum Distillery's* cooking team this fall when we won the competition. So, don't tell anyone, but I've attempted to replicate our secret recipe," he added with a wink.

Despite being annoyed, Sophie couldn't help but return Grant's smile. The way he was looking at her and holding her gaze, was not what she had expected. *Honestly,* Sophie thought, *she had no idea what she'd expected.* "Alright," Sophie conceded. "I'll try some. It does smell delicious."

"Excellent!" Grant declared enthusiastically. "I'm not a Sugar Plum native, so you can tell me if it actually tastes authentic. Now, let's see. Yes, no burgoo is complete without a small shot of bourbon to accompany it. So, for your tasting palate, which of our two excellent local choices would you prefer? *Yuletide Spirits*, or *Sugar Plum Distillery?*"

"Since I will be saying goodbye to my Grandpa tomorrow, I think I'll have a small taste of both," Sophie replied.

Grant nodded understandingly and proceeded to pour them each a small shot from both bottles. Then raising his glass and holding Sophie's gaze, Grant spoke. "To Charlie Marten. A man of exceptional character who knew no stranger; a man who always strived to do good, and a man who loved and was always proud of his granddaughter. May he rest in peace."

Sophie raised her glass to her lips, and tilting it, drained its contents. The golden-brown liquid slightly burned her throat then slowly began warming her chest, filling her with a long warm "Kentucky hug." Tomorrow she would say goodbye and move forward, knowing her Grandpa always loved her and had forgiven her even when her apology had been unspoken.

"Now," Grant grinned, rubbing his hands together excitedly, "how about we try some of this burgoo? Here you are, Sophie," he said, handing Sophie a bowl then ladling one for himself. Taking a spoonful, he watched as Sophie took her first bite. "What do you think?" he asked, unable to bear the suspense.

The savory liquid, paired with diced vegetables and hearty chunks of beef and chicken, sent Sophie's mind reeling with memories. *The taste-- its bold spices... its perfectly simmered ingredients... it was as if she was indulging in a flavor reserved for heaven!*

"It is absolutely delicious!" Sophie exclaimed, spooning another bite into her mouth and feeling her taste buds once again explode in lively dance.

Grant smiled at Sophie, the expression on his face appearing as if she'd just given him the best compliment he'd ever received. "I'm so glad you like it," he remarked.

"I don't just like it," Sophie doted with sincerity. "I love it! It tastes exactly like I remember!" She watched Grant's smile broaden. Then raising an eyebrow, she continued, "This doesn't change anything, though. You are still finding new lodgings."

"I wouldn't have expected anything else," Grant chortled, his eyes twinkling as he watched Sophie spoon another mouthful of burgoo.

"I'm glad we are in agreement," Sophie stated businesslike, as she took another bite. "Well, since your contact with my Grandpa doesn't expire for a few weeks, or until I can figure out how to void it," she continued, "you might as well tell me a little bit about yourself, so things are not anymore *awkward* than they already are."

"Of course," Grant smiled, wiping his mouth with his napkin. "I would not want to confuse avoiding *awkwardness* with genuine *interest*."

Sophie felt her cheeks flush. Twice in one day she had blushed. *What was wrong with her? Just what exactly was Grant implying? The whole situation was entirely frustrating!*

Sensing Sophie's confliction, Grant cleared his throat. "I'm originally from Tennessee. Nashville, precisely," he shared. "When things didn't work out the way I'd planned...I needed somewhere I could start over...I needed to do something different. A friend of mine from college works as a master distiller at *Yuletide Spirits*, and he suggested moving to Sugar Plum and working at one of its distilleries. It just so happened that a job in marketing was open at *Sugar Plum Distillery*, and as it happened, things worked out in my favor," Grant finished, taking a sip of water.

"What didn't go as planned?" Sophie inquired, resting her spoon on her napkin and reaching for a slice of cornbread. *Was Grant in some kind of trouble? Surely, her Grandpa would not have allowed a criminal to lodge with him, would he? But then...her*

*Grandpa had always been one to believe in second chances…*Sophie waited hesitantly for Grant to reply.

"Another time," Grant continued flatly, his abruptness causing Sophie to abandon the cornbread in her hand and stare transfixed into his gaze. As Grant watched Sophie continue staring at him, he observed her expression begin dubbing him as suspicious. Lifting a slice of cornbread from the plate, he broke it between his hands and took a bite, noticing Sophie's gaze never breaking. He had to give her more information. He could not just leave her to concoct scenarios damaging to his character. But, Grant knew, he could not give her the full truth...at least not yet. "Jack, my friend who suggested I move here," Grant continued, "knew your Grandpa from church. And when he found out Charlie needed someone to help him out around the farm and that I needed a place to stay, Jack introduced me to him," Grant finished, taking another bite of cornbread and hoping that Sophie would be satisfied with his response.

Sophie continued to stare at Grant from across the table. He had intentionally avoided answering her question, she realized in agitation. *Why was he being evasive? Just what was he hiding? She was not going to let him off that easy*, she decided. *No, if she was going to be forced to share her home with him until New Years, she was entitled to know why he had moved from the city to a small-town where he only knew one person.*

"*Why* did you move to Sugar Plum, Grant?" Sophie asked directly. There was no way now that he could avoid answering her question without either telling her the truth or lying.

"To work at one of the distilleries," Grant repeated, his voice decisive.

"*That's* not what I mean, and you know it," Sophie uttered, hearing her voice rise.

"Well, like I said," Grant stated, his tone implying the course the conversation had taken was now over, "that is for another time. Now, if you will excuse me," he remarked, rising from the table. "I am going to bed."

Placing his bowl and plate in the dishwasher, Grant then departed from the kitchen with Ivy following in suit, leaving Sophie glaring at his departing back and feeling even more miffed.

Chapter 5

Sophie had not slept well. Even though she was back in her old bedroom, she had tossed and turned all night. Not only had she been unable to keep Grant's lack of openness from entering her thoughts, but much to her chagrin, his bright-green eyes, dark-brown hair, and the rest of his perfectly chiseled features kept invading her mind. *What was wrong with her? She must surely be suffering from some kind of mental ailment*, she concluded, because sane people did not dream about annoying and evasive strangers they just met even if they were extremely handsome.

With the soft glow of morning light slowly creeping through the window, Sophie realized that sleep was to remain elusive. Stretching her arms above her head, she slowly sat up. Pushing back her quilt, Sophie shivered as her extremities were met by the drafty chill of early morning. She reluctantly stood up, abandoning her warm bed, and donning her robe and slippers, proceeded to walk out into the hall towards the bathroom. Reaching the bathroom door, Sophie noticed a beam of light creeping up the stairs, and the smell of bacon and eggs wafting in her direction. Either she was not the only one who had not slept well, or Grant was an extremely early riser. Not liking the prospect of encountering her houseguest in her pajamas, she continued into the bathroom instead of descending the stairs towards the delicious aroma.

It was now 7 o'clock, and there was nothing more for Sophie to do to get ready. Staring at her reflection, the reality of the next few hours struck her. Her dark-black dress, falling gently just below her knees, cast a somber mood within her. On any other occasion her dress, with its stylish bow drawn up about her waist and her matching black pumps and earrings, would look flattering; but that was not how she felt. Sighing, Sophie grabbed her gray peacoat and descended the stairs. Walking towards the kitchen, she heard Grant rattling pots and pans. She was not in the mood for conversation and hoped he would just leave her to her thoughts. As Sophie entered the kitchen, Ivy wagged her tail in happy acknowledgement as she continued to lay beside Grant's feet. Looking up at Grant, however, Sophie soon found herself distracted. Instead of being dressed in a flannel shirt and jeans like yesterday, Grant was wearing a suit and tie; and having heard her walk in, turned holding a plate laden with breakfast and a cup of coffee in his hands. Smiling, Grant walked towards her, and Sophie was sure her legs had turned to jelly as she suddenly forget what it was she'd just been thinking.

"I thought you might need a nice breakfast this morning," Grant said, placing the plate and mug on the table. "I've got bacon, eggs, and some jelly toast here. If you want some fruit, I can get you a banana or an orange," he continued, holding Sophie's gaze.

"Thank…Thank you," Sophie stammered, regaining the use of her legs, and taking a step towards the table.

"You're welcome," Grant replied with a smile, pulling the chair out for her. "Days like today are never easy. All we can do is try and make parts of them enjoyable."

Sophie nodded at Grant, not trusting her words to reply.

"If you'd like some time to yourself… I'll leave you to your breakfast," Grant offered.

"No… I think I'd like the company," Sophie responded softly, and watched as, retrieving his cup of coffee, Grant sat down across from her.

Despite how she currently felt, Sophie couldn't help but smile as she watched Grant carefully light two purple candles and one rose colored candle on the Advent wreath in the center of the table. *Joy,* Sophie mused. *She'd been so distracted, that she'd forgotten this week, the third week of Advent, had been Gaudete Sunday. Waiting for Christmas, there was a light of joy in the darkness. There was no better week*, she thought, feeling her heart flutter slightly, *to lay her Grandpa to rest.* Watching the candlelight flicker softly upon the evergreen garland surrounding the wreath, a sense of peace enveloped Sophie.

As he observed Sophie gazing contentedly at the candlelight, Grant felt even more determined to help her smile again, on such an emotional day, and continue to remember the joy of the Christmas season. Taking a chance, he asked, "So, we're…what a couple of weeks away from Christmas now? Do you have a favorite Christmas memory?"

Swallowing the bite of toast she'd just taken, Sophie turned her gaze from the Advent wreath and thought for a moment. As long as she could remember, Christmas had always been her favorite holiday. *Could she actually choose just one favorite memory?* And then, she remembered.

"I was seven," Sophie recalled, with a smile. "My Grandpa and I had just gotten back from cutting down our Christmas tree off our farm and were ready to decorate it, when my Grandpa couldn't find our box of ornaments." Sophie saw that Grant was hanging on her every word. "We looked everywhere. I told Grandpa that I thought we put the box in the basement last year, and then his face turned red and he got really quiet. *Was the box an old computer paper box?* he asked. I told him, yes, and then I watched as his face grew even redder. He then proceeded to tell me that he believed he may have accidentally tossed it when he was cleaning out the basement over the summer," Sophie laughed. "At the time, I was so upset and so was he, but then he had a brilliant idea. We ended up making salt-dough ornaments. We cut out shapes using cookie cutters, and then made homemade egg-based tempera paint." Sophie's eyes sparkled as she continued to recall the details. "We then hung up strands of popcorn, and using pipe cleaners from my art box, twisted candy canes. That was probably my favorite

Christmas tree we ever decorated," she finished with a smile.

"That's a wonderful memory," Grant said. "I've never made homemade ornaments before, but it sounds like fun."

"You should definitely try it," Sophie beamed. "You know," she continued, "I think that Christmas really taught me something."

"Taught you what?" Grant asked, taking a sip of his coffee.

"It taught me to keep things simple, you know, not get so wrapped up in all the commercialization...what *people* say you *need* to do or must have in order to obtain the *perfect* Christmas. Simplicity allows you to relax and just spend time with your loved ones and *really* celebrate the purpose of the holiday," Sophie reflected. "The first Christmas took place in a stable, after all, and if that's not a message to keep things simple and focus on what's important, I don't know what is," she continued thoughtfully.

"Well, it sounds like that Christmas really was a perfect Christmas then," Grant smiled.

"Yes, yes it was," Sophie nodded fondly.

"Well," Grant said, "we'd better get going. I can drive us if you like?"

"Thanks, that would be great," Sophie remarked. "And thank you again for breakfast and for helping me remember such a wonderful memory."

"It was my pleasure," Grant smiled, clearing the

breakfast dishes and loading them in the dishwasher.

Grant and Sophie drove to the church in silence, the somberness of their destination weighing heavier with each passing curve they rounded. Sophie gazed out the window, distractedly watching the passing mile markers, and was surprised when she saw that they were pulling into the church parking lot. As she stared at the brick building, a sense of homecoming wrapped around her. As a kid, she'd grown up attending Mass at Saint Nicholas Cathedral. She had made her first communion and confirmation there, and before she'd left town, she had hoped that one day she'd get married there as well. Sophie was drawn from her thoughts, when Grant opened the passenger door and offered her his hand.

"Thank you," Sophie murmured, placing her hand in Grant's. Beneath his strong calloused grip, she felt a tenderness she had not expected as he gently helped her from the truck.

As Sophie gazed into Grant's eyes, the brisk winter breeze lightly snagging his hair, it felt for a moment as if they were the only two people in the world. *The way Grant looked at her...the kindness he had shown her from the first moment they met even when she had not been that cordial...* Sophie felt the slight flutter of her heart. *How could his gaze seem to see her so well? How could...*

"Sophie!" Sophie quickly turned in the direction of her name, and saw Brad walking briskly towards her.

"I just wanted to...who's this?" Brad asked, his tone

becoming protective, as he caught sight of Grant and Sophie standing inches from one another, their hands still clasped together.

"This...this is Grant Bakesfield," Sophie replied, quickly pulling her hand from Grant's, her cheeks reddening. She had completely forgotten she was still holding his hand.

"Mr. Bakesfield," Brad breathed, nodding and offering Grant his hand.

"Grant, please," Grant returned with a smile, shaking Brad's outstretched hand.

"And, *how* do you know, Sophie?" Brad inquired, his words, Sophie recognized, full of suspicion.

"Well," Grant replied with a smile, "I actually just met Sophie yesterday. I was friends with her Grandpa, Charlie."

"I see," Brad said, sounding unconvinced. "It was nice of you to drive Sophie here. I don't want you to have to go out of your way, though," Brad continued. "Since I've known Sophie for *years*, I can give her a ride home," Brad uttered, holding Grant's gaze.

"Of course," Grant replied, clearly reading the message being conveyed.

"Grant, don't be ridiculous," Sophie remarked. "Thank you, Brad, for the offer. I do appreciate it, but you see, Grant's been renting a room at the house, so it makes more sense for him to drive me back."

"Wait, what?" Brad sputtered. "He's been...he's

staying at the house now?"

The suspicion that had painted Brad's face mere seconds ago was quickly dashed. *Was that shock, or was that jealousy?* Sophie detected.

"Apparently after I left, Grandpa decided to rent out one of the bedrooms to someone who would help him out around the farm," Sophie shared, shocked by how nonchalantly she was expressing what had and what still annoyed her.

"I don't mean to sound *indelicate*," Brad remarked coolly, regaining his composure, "but just how long is he staying at your house?"

"Till New Years," Sophie replied.

Turning his attention from Sophie, Brad rounded on Grant, his eyebrows furrowing in frustration. "Till New Years? Why can't you move out tomorrow?"

"I signed a contract with Charlie. I'm unable to move out till New Years," Grant said.

"Surly, under the circumstances, that can now be voided," Brad uttered, his eyes continuing to assess his competition. *Just what exactly were Mr. Bakesfield's motives?* he thought.

"I'm afraid not," Grant replied, with a shrug.

Brad could not believe it. There had to be some way around such a preposterous contract. "Don't worry, Sophie, I'll take a look at the contract, and we'll get things straightened out," he declared, shooting a final glare at Grant before steering Sophie towards the church.

"Really, Brad, it's alright," Sophie stated. "Yes, it is unconventional, and I initially and still find the arrangement bothersome, but.."

"It's not alright," Brad interrupted, as they climbed the concrete steps towards the sanctuary. "Sophie, you don't know anything about this, *Mr. Bakesfield*. What if he's not who he says he is? I mean, did your Grandpa do a thorough background check on him before he let him move in?"

"Enough," Sophie exclaimed, as they reached the doors. "Now is not the time to discuss this."

"Fine," Brad conceded, opening the door. "But I'm driving you home."

"Fine," Sophie snapped, her eyes momentarily lingering on Brad's face before she turned and walked inside.

Sitting in the front pew, sandwiched between Brad and Karah, Sophie stared at the crucifix hanging behind the altar, and even though she felt like crying, she was filled with a sense of peace. Even though she had not gotten to say she was sorry or say goodbye in person, Sophie knew none of that really mattered to her Grandpa. Sophie knew her Grandpa had lived a full and wonderful life. He had enjoyed the carefreeness of childhood, the romance of finding the love of his life as a young man, raised a family, and achieved many dreams. Yes, he had also had his share of heartaches, but he had lived. And with each day he had walked the earth, Sophie knew he had sought to make it a better place, and to brighten the lives of those he encountered. Like the sunlight now shining softly through the many stained-glass windows surrounding her, Sophie knew her Grandpa had been a kind and soft presence in the lives of all who had known him.

Throughout the funeral Mass, Sophie found that her sadness ebbed until it was no longer present. Death, and the loss it brought would always be sad, but the funeral Mass, Sophie realized, was truly a celebration of life, not death. The sacredness of life until natural death was not just a human dignity, it was holy. When the Mass concluded and they arrived at the cemetery, Sophie's heart was at peace as she dropped a rose upon the casket. Her Grandpa would not want her to be sad; her Grandpa would want her to live her life feeling the sweet embrace of happiness and remembering him with smiles and fondness. Sophie smiled, and her heart beat softly with such a thought.

As she stood shaking the hands and thanking the remaining friends who had come to pay their respects, Sophie's eyes lingered upon Grant. *Why had her Grandpa not told her about him in his letter or on the phone when she had called?* Sensing that he was being watched, Grant turned and met her gaze. Sophie hurriedly lowered her eyes, embarrassed at having been caught, and felt even more flustered when she realized Grant was walking towards her.

"I just wanted to say," Grant said, his voice deep and soothing as he stopped in front of Sophie, "that your Grandpa was one of the best men I've ever had the privilege of knowing. Not only did he offer hospitality to a stranger from out of town," Grant continued, holding Sophie's gaze, "but over the four years I knew him, the way he talked about you, even when you all were not on the best of terms, taught me that something I no longer believed in, existed." Then after holding Sophie's gaze a second longer, Grant turned and headed towards his truck, leaving Sophie to contemplate the meaning of his words.

"*Who* was that?" Karah asked, watching Grant climb into his truck.

"Grant Bakesfield," Sophie replied, her gaze, like Karah's, also lingering on Grant as he began to drive away.

"I've never seen him around town. How do you know him?" Karah asked, her voice full of curiosity. "It would have been impossible not to notice Grant's devastatingly good looks," she continued with a smile.

"My Grandpa knew him," Sophie remarked. "Grant's been staying and working at the farm for the past few years," she added.

"How's...," Karah began, but noticing Brad approaching, decided now was not the time to continue their conversation. "How about coming over to my place tomorrow for dinner?" she asked instead.

"That would be wonderful!" Sophie accepted, delight filling her words.

"Great! I feel like we still have *so* much to catch up about. I'll text you my address," Karah added, giving Sophie a final hug before departing.

"Are you ready to go, or do you need more time?" Brad asked, coming to stand by Sophie's side.

"No, I'm ready to go," Sophie smiled, as Brad grabbed her arm to steady her as she walked through the grass in her heels.

When they reached his car, Brad opened the passenger door, and after helping Sophie into her seat, walked around to the driver's side.

"Do you want me to drive you straight home, or would you like to stop for ice cream?" Brad offered, starting the engine.

"Ice cream does sound tempting, but I think I'd like to head home," Sophie replied honestly. It wasn't even noon, but the day already felt long and tiring.

"I understand," Brad voiced, forcing a smile as he turned onto the main road. "Will I see you at the Christmas parade on Saturday?" he asked hopefully. "There's also a Christmas Bazaar afterwards. The shops on Main Street will all be having open houses, and there will be booths set up along the street," he continued.

"Yes, I was planning on going with Karah," Sophie replied brightly. "I haven't attended the parade since high school. I'm really looking forward to it. The bazaar sounds wonderful too!" Sophie smiled to herself, as she recalled how much she'd enjoyed watching the parade as a kid.

"Excellent!" Brad exclaimed, glancing at Sophie with

a grin. "You know," he continued, "it's really great having you back in town."

"It's great to be back," Sophie said, returning Brad's smile. "I only wish I'd come home sooner."

"Yes, I know," Brad acknowledged, as he turned into Sophie's driveway. "But at least you're back now. I'd forgotten how much I *missed* seeing you around town. Seeing you again...well, it's like nothing has changed."

Sophie felt her cheeks flushing. The way Brad had said that he'd *missed seeing her* and that *it was as if nothing had changed*, she knew carried more meaning than just the friendship they had shared. She had always enjoyed spending time with Brad. They'd been friends most of their lives, Sophie reflected. Having grown up in a small-town, they shared a certain camaraderie together, a certain history—a history whose bonds could not be severed. Brad's words seemed to suggest, however, that his view of their relationship had not changed. The candle he'd held for her years ago in high school still burned, even despite them choosing to remain friends. *Could she possibly return his affection? Could she hope for, and desire, to seek more from their relationship?* Sophie pondered.

Watching Brad continue to drive, Sophie gazed at him, deep in thought. *Brad was funny, smart, and indeed attractive. Honestly, he was quite a catch. But could she ever love such a good friend romantically?* Sophie knew that she had changed from high school, and Brad most certainly had too. *Surely then, his feelings for her had only been rekindled due to seeing her for the first time in so long, right?*

"Why are you looking at me so funny?" Brad asked, catching sight of Sophie's gaze out of the corner of his eye.

"I'm not looking at you funny," Sophie quickly uttered, averting her gaze. She heard Brad chuckle softly as she stared out the windshield at the houses and farms they were passing.

"I'm going to pretend that I believe you," Brad remarked. "Sophie," he said, causing her to once again turn in his direction. "I hope you liked what you were looking at." Watching Sophie's cheeks flush, Brad smiled, satisfied by Sophie's response, then turned his attention back to the road. *Sophie was most certainly infatuated with him*, he thought with delight.

They did not have to drive much further, before Sophie glimpsed the winding gravel drive leading to the farm. After Brad's comment, she had refused to make eye-contact with him for the remainder of the ride. She was not entirely sure of her feelings just yet, and she was not ready to give Brad the wrong impression if indeed that proved to be correct. Sophie needed time to think, time to sort things out, and was relieved when Brad began slowing the car and parked in front of her house.

"Here we are," Brad declared, turning off the engine and removing his hands from the steering wheel. "Would you like me to come inside?" he asked, eyeing Grant's truck with displeasure.

"No, that's alright," Sophie replied assuredly. She was not ready to have a repeat of the parking lot conversation.

"If you're *sure*," Brad responded, his voice a bit dejected.

"I'm sure," Sophie remarked. *"Honest.* Thank you, Brad, for driving me home."

"It was my pleasure," Brad smiled, hoping to conceal his irritation. *Why did Sophie seem to be "okay" with this "Grant" fellow staying at the farm?* "I'd do anything for you, Sophie, I hope you know that," he added, holding her gaze.

"Well, maybe you could take a look at that contract my Grandpa made Grant sign," Sophie joked.

"Absolutely!" Brad exclaimed, the dejection that had moments ago been present in his voice replaced with pleasure. "I'd be more than happy to do that. You can give it to me at the parade." *So, he'd been wrong. Sophie did want Grant out of the house. This was an excellent development!* he thought happily.

"Great," Sophie responded, hoping her words sounded enthusiastic. She had not expected Brad to be so excited by the prospect. Yes, Grant's presence was somewhat annoying, but she had made her comment, although true, in jest. That, however, was unequivocally not the right joke to make. "I'll see you Saturday, then," Sophie added, opening the car door and hearing a soft crunch as her feet met the gravel.

"I'll look forward to it the rest of the week!" Brad exclaimed, flashing Sophie a grin. "See you later, Soph. And, *please*, call me if you need anything."

"I will," Sophie promised. Then closing the door behind her, she stood in the driveway and watched as Brad waved cheerfully out the window then backed the car around and drove away.

Chapter 6

When she could no longer see Brad's car, Sophie turned and headed towards the house. Her heels, making a slight click as she walked across the wooden floorboards on the front porch, reminded her of chattering teeth. Putting her hand on the frigid brass doorknob, Sophie turned the latch and stepped inside. She had not realized just how cold she had been until the warm air wrapped itself around her like a snug and toasty blanket.

After hanging her coat in the hall closet, Sophie went upstairs to change. Donning a charcoal-gray cable-knit sweater and a pair of jeans, she quickly threw her mass of curls into a loose ponytail before leaving her room. The wooden stairs creaked as she made her descent, and Sophie couldn't help but laugh to herself. After her Grandpa had caught her, the one time she had tried to sneak out when she was in high school, Sophie had tried to memorize which steps creaked only to find, much to her annoyance, that every step creaked!

Upon reaching the kitchen, Sophie found she was not alone. Grant was sitting at the table, with a coffee mug in hand, reading from a magazine pertaining to American bourbons and whiskeys. As she stepped through the doorway, he looked up, and Sophie felt herself instantly paralyzed as Grant's deep-green eyes held her captive.

"I see you're back," Grant remarked with a smile, breaking the silence. "I just heated up the kettle if you'd like a cup of tea."

"Umm, sure. Yeah...tea sounds great," Sophie fumbled. *Why did Grant make her feel like such a babbling idiot?* Regaining the use of her legs, she began walking towards the counter, as Grant stood up from the table.

"Why don't you have a seat," Grant offered. "I'll make you a cup."

"That's not necessary," Sophie muttered. *Why was he constantly wanting to wait on her? Was he hoping that being nice to her would allow him to keep renting his room even after his contract expired? If so,* Sophie declared, *that was totally not happening!*

"It's no trouble," Grant remarked, ignoring Sophie's words and reaching the kettle before she could stop him.

Seeing that Grant was not to be persuaded, Sophie shrugged and sat down at the kitchen table. She watched as Grant placed a teaspoon of loose-leaf Indian Chai into a tea infuser to seep. While she waited, Sophie glanced at the article about bourbon tastings Grant had been reading. Even though she had grown up in a town that was home to two prestigious distilleries, Sophie really did not know a whole lot about bourbon. Yes, she had toured and tasted at both local distilleries, as well as a few other distilleries in nearby counties that were part of the Kentucky *Bourbon Trail*, but Sophie found she could never truly discern the different flavors and subtleties that were the mark of true tasters. She always wished she was more perceptive and able to detect the uniqueness and subtleties of each blend, but much to her annoyance, Sophie never could get past the initial burning sensation of the first sip. *Some Kentucky girl she was!* she laughed to herself. *Now bourbon balls on the other hand,* Sophie thought with a smile, *were a treat she absolutely loved*! *Maybe, she would try and make some homemade ones this Christmas,* she thought, feeling her mouth beginning to salivate just thinking of the delicious bourbon chocolates.

"Here you are," Grant said, jarring Sophie from her thoughts, as he set a steaming mug of tea in front of her. "You'll want to let that steep a couple more minutes before you drink it. Until then, you can have one of these," he added, handing her a caramel candy wrapped in a waxy paper.

"Oh!" Sophie exclaimed excitedly, holding the candy in her hand and smiling. "I haven't had one of these in years!"

"You like them then?" Grant chuckled, "Well, it's a good thing I have a whole box."

"You know, these are made right here in town," Sophie stated happily, unwrapping the candy.

"Yes," Grant replied, "I learned that. And after tasting one, I have to say I'm pretty much addicted to them," he laughed.

"Oh, I totally agree," Sophie smiled, taking a nibble. She closed her eyes, savoring the first flavorful bite. *The sweet caramel coating covering the light and fluffy marshmallow...*She imagined was like tasting an edible cloud--- *simply divine!*

Polishing off the delectable confection, Sophie pulled her cup of tea towards her and removed the infuser. Stirring in a bit of milk and sugar, she raised the mug to her lips and felt the hot and spicy liquid warm her throat.

"Chai is my favorite tea," Sophie remarked fondly, over the brim of her cup.

"Yes, your Grandpa told me it was," Grant admitted quietly, taking a sip from his mug.

"What *else* did my Grandpa tell you?" Sophie asked curiously and somewhat annoyed, since he'd mentioned nothing to her about Grant.

Grant set his tea on the table and stared thoughtfully. Sophie could see the contemplation on his face as he continued to look at her. *Why had her Grandpa shared information about her to Grant, yet had failed to reveal anything about his house guest to her? Her Grandpa had always had a purpose in everything he did*, Sophie recalled. *So, what then was his purpose for keeping such a secret?*

"Well," Grant finally said, his words breaking the silence as he began unwrapping a piece of candy. "Charlie told me that you have one of the kindest hearts he's ever known, that your strong spirit and mind reminded him of your Grandma, and oh, he may have mentioned you liked these," he smiled, popping the soft confection into his mouth.

Sophie stared speechlessly at Grant. She never knew her Grandpa had seen those qualities in her, he had never told her. *Why had he been compelled to confide them to Grant?* Sophie felt conflicted. Looking at Grant as he sat across from her, his eyes bright and attentive, Sophie suddenly began to question if she looked alright. *But that was sill. She didn't care what Grant thought of her, or did she?*

Setting his mug on the table, Grant stood up. "I've got to head to the barn to feed the cows. Would you care to join me?" he looked at Sophie expectantly.

"Of course," Sophie replied, rising to her feet. She was in charge of running the farm now after all, and once Grant moved out...she'd have to handle things all on her own. "I'll grab my boots and coat and meet you outside."

Grant nodded and left the room. *How was she going to manage things on the farm and her job at the museum?* Sophie hadn't really thought about that. Her Grandpa had always run the farm as his job. He had raised beef cattle, pigs, chickens, and grown the grains to feed them when she was growing up. Sure, he'd hired farm hands seasonally during the busy times, but even with Sophie's and their help, her Grandpa had always done most of the work himself. Even though her Grandpa had downsized the farm to just cattle for the last ten years, raising cattle was not an easy task.

Finding her old rubber boots where she had left them in the

mud-room years ago, Sophie shoved her feet inside and then buttoned up her coat. Grant had been pulling the weight since she had arrived, but it was now time for her to start showing him that she was capable of keeping the farm running. A blast of cold air smacked her in the face as she opened the door. Sophie saw Grant, with Ivy trotting happily before him, only a few yards ahead of her. As she began following them towards the barn, Sophie took a deep breath, filling her lungs with the cool winter air. It was so good to be home! The familiar smell of hay and manure met her as Sophie stepped inside the dimly lit building. To some, the stable's odor might be rank, but to Sophie its pungent aroma was rustic and homey. Some of her favorite memories had taken place in this barn, Sophie recalled. *The many times Karah had come over to stay the night and they'd laid up in the hayloft on a quilt telling ghost stories...watching baby calves be born with her Grandpa and the vet...sitting on the hay bales and drawing pictures of the animals lost in thought...*

"Alright, are you sure you're ready to muck out stalls?" Grant asked, handing Sophie a shovel and looking at her seriously.

"Yes," Sophie snapped, taking the shovel from his hand. "I've cleaned out many stalls before."

Grant chuckled. "I know you have. I just wanted to make sure city life hasn't softened you up, that's all," he added with a grin.

Sophie glared at Grant. *The nerve of him! Just who did he think he was, insulting her like that? She'd show him she knew how to clean out a stall*! Walking briskly towards the nearest stall, Sophie heard Grant continue chuckling to himself. *It's like he's purposely trying to annoy me,* she thought to herself. Shoveling up the soiled hay, Sophie began dumping it into an empty wheelbarrow. The stall wasn't that big, but even so, Sophie began to work up a sweat. Wiping her brow with the back of her hand, she stood the shovel up and leaned against it. *One stall down,* she smiled satisfied, just *about ten more to go.* Sophie leaned her shovel against the wall, then lifted the wheelbarrow. She had just started to push it towards the door, when she felt her feet start to slip out from beneath her. The wheelbarrow wobbled. *She was going down!* Sophie struggled to keep the wheelbarrow from toppling over on its side, mortification flooding her thoughts. *She was going to land on her butt and look like a complete idiot!* It was as she continued to think about her pride and how Grant would find her incompetent, that Sophie felt a pair of hands grab her under the arms and catch her a mere inch from the ground.

"Are you alright?" Grant asked, lifting Sophie up on to her feet.

"I'm fine," Sophie muttered embarrassed, feeling her cheeks flaming despite the cold.

"It's easy to lose your footing in the mud. Just last week, I lost my footing out in one of the pastures when I was feeding the cattle and slid halfway down the hill. I got covered in mud," Grant shared. "How about I take the wheelbarrow out this time?" he offered.

"Alright," Sophie conceded. "But I've got it next time."

"That's fair," Grant smiled, taking the handles from Sophie and steering the wheelbarrow towards the door.

Then swallowing her pride, Sophie blurted, "Thank you for catching me."

"No problem," Grant grinned, before disappearing around the door.

Chapter 7

till embarrassed by her near manure fiasco, Sophie pulled her boots off in the mud-room and began unbuttoning her coat.

"I wouldn't take off your jacket just yet if I were you," Grant remarked from the hallway.

"And why not?" Sophie retorted, as she felt her cheeks beginning to thaw. "It's freezing out there and warm in here, and we're finished feeding the cattle and cleaning the stalls." *Just who did Grant think he was anyway, trying to boss her around?*

"Well, if you take your coat off, you're going to be mighty cold on the ride to the feedstore," Grant replied, popping his head around the corner of the mud-room door and smiling.

"Oh. I didn't realize we were already out of feed," Sophie uttered in disbelief. *Had she really forgotten how much cattle ate?*

"We're not out, but we are running low. With it being winter, I'd rather be well stocked in case it snows," Grant said. "I'll be out in the truck. You can come out when you're ready," he added, before departing.

Pulling her boots back on, Sophie wondered if she was going to be able to run the farm all on her own. The thought of selling it, however, was something she would never consider. She would just have to get back into the swing of farm life. *Being away for five years had made her soft.* After putting her hands back in her gloves, Sophie locked the door and walked towards Grant's truck.

"Alright then, let's get going," Grant said with a grin.

Watching the farm disappear out the side-view mirror, Sophie turned her attention to Grant knowing she couldn't very well ignore him for the entirety of the trip.

"I know you said you will be staying at the farm until the first of the year, but when are you going to start looking for new lodgings?" Sophie inquired. "I'm not going to renew your contract you know," she added firmly.

Grant gazed at Sophie from the driver's seat. "I will start looking soon enough. Don't worry," he chuckled. Then smiling he added, "I won't be imposing past the duration of my contract."

Sophie felt her cheeks flush. *Why did Grant's smile have the ability to disarm her? Every time she wanted to be mad at him, he was somehow able to make her forget her frustration with a simple flash of his teeth. It was downright infuriating!*

Sophie turned her attention back to staring out the window and watched as Grant turned down a small side-street. Driving along what seemed almost like an oversized alleyway, the brick and wooden structure of Sugar Plum's old farm store emerged into view. *If you didn't grow up here,* Sophie thought with a smile, *you would probably never know*

this old store existed hidden in the midst of downtown.
Seeing the store, with its burlap bags of feed and loads of hay
bales lining the length of its large wooden front porch,
caused a wave of happiness to rush over Sophie. How many
times she had come to this store with her Grandpa she did not
know; it was almost like her second home. Not only had they
come here to buy feed for the animals they raised and farm
equipment, but Sophie remembered buying rabbit food and
salt licks for her pet rabbit too. Every time she bought a new
salt lick, she would ask her Grandpa if she could lick it first
before giving it to her rabbit, and he would always oblige her
request. Just thinking of that made Sophie laugh. Why on
earth she had ever wanted to do such a silly thing she did not
know.

Sophie heard the door slam beside her and watched as
Grant walked around the front of the truck and opened the
passenger door.

"Shall we?" Grant asked, offering Sophie his hand.

"I can get down myself thanks," Sophie replied
curtly, as she unfastened her seatbelt and climbed awkwardly
out of the cab, stumbling slightly. *Okay, taking Grant's hand
would definitely have been helpful, but she was not going to
let him know she had been wrong to refuse his assistance,*
Sophie thought, her cheeks red with embarrassment as she
refused to acknowledge the gaze Grant was casting in her
direction.

Climbing the wooden stairs up to the porch, Sophie

burst through the door without waiting for Grant. The soft jingle of a bell sounded, announcing her entrance, and Sophie proceeded to walk across the creaky old floorboards further into the store. Everything was just as she remembered! The smell of sweet corn permeated throughout the air, and the shelves of animal feed and farming merchandise filled the building.

The live Christmas tree, smelling of pine and decked with small circular white salt licks and burlap ribbon, stood near the register, and there, gathered around the large potbelly stove talking and keeping warm, were some of the fellow farmers Sophie had known practically her entire life!

"Well, all be darned. If it isn't Sophie Marten!" one of the men hollered, rising from his chair and walking towards Sophie.

"Hi, Mr. Carroll," Sophie exclaimed cheerfully, as the elderly man enveloped her in a bear hug.

"It's good to see you, Girl, it's been too long," Mr. Carroll smiled, his light-blue eyes warm and cheerful as he released Sophie from his embrace.

"Now, Hank, don't go monopolizing all the hugs," one of the other men said, arriving next to Mr. Carroll.

"I've got a hug for you too, Mr. Floyd, don't you worry," Sophie grinned, causing the old farmer to smile brightly.

"We're awful sorry about your Grandpa. Things around here won't be the same without him," Mr. Floyd remarked, his voice filled with sincerity.

"Thanks, Mr. Floyd, Mr. Carroll," Sophie replied, squeezing both men's hands softly. "I know how much he loved coming down here and talking with you all."

"If there is anything we can do for you, you just let us know, okay," Mr. Carroll said gently.

"I will. Thank you both," Sophie smiled.

"Now, Sophie, are you going to tell us why Grant Bakesfield is standing over there watching you with a foolish looking smile plastered on his face?" Mr. Floyd asked protectively, eyeing Grant with both curiosity and discernment of his intention.

"Oh," Sophie uttered sheepishly. *She had not even considered that her fellow farmers would know Grant. But of course, they did. Grant had, after all, been helping her Grandpa on the farm. Did that mean they knew he was staying at the farm? What would they think about him staying there now?* She turned and looked at Grant, an expression of panic flashing across her face.

"Hi, Mr. Carroll, Mr. Floyd, it's good to see you both," Grant said, crossing the room and shaking the hands of both men.

"It's good to see you too, Grant," Mr. Carroll replied with a smile. "I know Charlie was mighty appreciative of your help on the farm these past few years."

"What are your plans now, young man?" Mr. Floyd asked with interest.

"Come now, Bud, we both know Grant here is a respectable young gentleman," Mr. Carroll chuckled.

"Even so, that doesn't mean he can avoid answering the question," Mr. Floyd countered, looking at Grant expectantly.

Was this really happening? Sophie wanted to crawl into a hole. Mr. Carroll and Mr. Floyd were giving Grant the third-degree about his intentions towards her and she was not even dating him!

"I'm helping Sophie get some hay for the cattle and am going to stay on at the farm to help her get settled for a while," Grant remarked casually.

"There. See Bud, he's being a gentleman," Mr. Carroll smiled, his eyes twinkling with amusement.

"Well, Gentlemen, if you'll excuse me. I have some hay bales to load up. Merry Christmas!" Grant remarked, excusing himself with a grin.

When Grant was through the door and safely out of earshot, Mr. Floyd turned towards Sophie with a smile. "That's a nice young fellow you have there, Sophie."

Sophie stared, suddenly flustered, at Mr. Floyd. *Had he really just said what she thought he had? Staring at him, watching him smiling at her...* "Grant is *not* my man," Sophie uttered, the color in her cheeks rising. "I've got to go. Merry Christmas, Gentlemen," she added, before hastily turning and leaving before they glimpsed the deep shade of scarlet her cheeks were continuing to glow.

As they watched Sophie leave the store, Mr. Carroll turned to Mr. Floyd. "You were right, Bud, they are smitten with each other," the old farmer grinned knowingly.

"I always am," Bud replied with a mischievous wink. "Charlie told me they were perfect for each other. All they had to do was meet," he said.

"Yes, Charlie did say that," Hank recalled fondly. "Now, how about we old timers get back to solving the world's problems and let those lovebirds sort things out for themselves?"

"That sounds like an excellent idea," Bud agreed, following Hank back over to the stove, which crackled warm and inviting within its firebox.

Chapter 8

Before heading into work, Sophie had helped Grant rotate the cattle to another pasture. She'd been trying since yesterday to forget what Mr. Floyd had implied about she and Grant, but so far it had been useless. *Why had it bothered her so much? It wasn't like his words had been true...?* Hopefully work could distract her, Sophie thought.

Listening to the sound of Christmas music softly playing, Sophie quickly threw her hair into a messy bun on top of her head and began examining the box of letters that had just arrived as part of an estate donation. Carefully handling the letters with her gloved hands, she scanned the elegant and loopy cursive penmanship. *Cursive was almost a lost form of art*, Sophie thought sadly, *and so was the romance of letter writing. The way sentences were composed... the very syntax and thoughtful meaning of each word choice and punctuation mark, could convey so much meaning and allow one a glimpse into the soul of the writer. Everything about writing was simply magical! If only people today would pick up a pen instead of merely sending a text message*, she mused wistfully.

As Sophie analyzed the first letter and began transcribing it, it reminded her of a time she had spent in the archives when she had been in graduate school, and she'd had the opportunity to read love letters written during the Civil War. Over the course of the correspondences, Sophie recalled with a smile, she had been able to witness the romance between a Union soldier and the young woman he had loved grow from friendship, to courtship, to engagement, and then marriage. To a historian, it was like Christmas had come early! Her only disappointment, Sophie recalled, had been that she'd only gotten to read one side of the romance; only the soldier's letters had survived. *But these letters*, Sophie smiled fondly at the parchment she was holding and the other letters before her, *held both sides of the story.*

Leaning towards her desk, Sophie held the letter in one hand and wrote in print what it said with the other. She was so absorbed in her task, that she did not hear the knock on her office door or look up when it was opened.

"I see I'm interrupting. Should I come back later?" a voice asked.

"Wait, what?" Sophie looked up, pulling her glasses off and setting them on the desk.

"I asked if I should come back later," Brad chuckled.

"Gosh, I'm so sorry. I didn't hear you come in," Sophie apologized, as she pulled her gloves off and stood up.

"I hadn't noticed," Brad smiled.

"What can I do for you, Mr. Mayor," Sophie asked brightly.

"Oh, it's not official business," Brad remarked. "I was just on my way to lunch and thought I'd drop by and see if you wanted to join me."

"Is it really lunch time already?" Sophie asked, astonished.

"Yes, it is," Brad replied, his eyes as bright as his grin.

"Brad, that's so nice of you to invite me, it's just...well, you see, I just got these letters, and they're so...," Sophie's eyes sparkled as she thought about the correspondences she was reading. Reading love letters from people who had actually lived was like reading the best romance novel ever written!

"Come on, Soph, even historians need to take a lunch break," Brad persisted. "The letters will still be here when you get back."

"Oh, alright. I guess they can wait," Sophie caved, feeling her stomach grumble.

"Great!" Brad grinned. "How does going to *The Sugar Plum Bistro* sound?"

"That sounds wonderful! I walked past it a couple of days ago, and it looked really nice," Sophie agreed, putting on her coat and grabbing her purse.

As they walked along Main Street, Sophie looked at the Christmas lights twinkling and the various storefront Christmas displays. *It really was so nice to be back home*, she thought, as a shop owner waved merrily at them as they passed by.

"What are you thinking?" Brad asked, turning to look

at Sophie.

"I was just thinking about how nice it is to be back home," Sophie admitted, a look of contentment filling her face.

Brad stopped walking and looked admiringly at Sophie. "I'm really glad you're happy to be home," he said. "Christmas time has a way of making you appreciate what you sometimes overlook, and makes you stop and see what's really important. Sophie, I didn't realize it until I saw you earlier this week, but I've missed you."

"Brad," Sophie began, starting to walk again, "when we both went away to college, we only saw each other occasionally when we were back in town. How can you say you missed me?" she asked, her tone unconvinced.

Brad gently grabbed Sophie's arm and stopped her. "Sophie, when we were in high school, I liked you, even after you turned me down the one time I asked you out. I knew you only saw me as a friend, and I enjoyed spending time with you, so I never asked you out again. But seeing you again…. seeing you after all these years…" Brad gazed longingly into Sophie's eyes. "It made me realize that I still like you— that I always have."

Sophie stared at Brad. She had not expected him to express his intentions so suddenly. Yes, since she had returned home, she had speculated that Brad might still be harboring feelings for her; she had even recently been herself contemplating if she returned his infatuation, but Sophie had not expected him to share his feelings so soon.

"Brad, I...," Sophie began hesitantly. How she hoped she could find the right words to say.

"Soph... I just...I had to tell you. If you don't feel the same way...just forget it," Brad said, releasing Sophie's arm and shaking his head as he continued walking.

"Brad, wait!" Sophie called, turning and catching back up to him. "I didn't say I don't feel the same way. Honesty, I don't know how I feel about us exactly. I'd be lying if I said I haven't thought about what it might be like to date you," Sophie admitted. "Can we just, maybe slow down a bit?" she beseeched.

Brad turned and looked at Sophie again, his eyes intrigued. "Are you saying you might return my feelings?" he asked, his words tinged with hope.

"I'm saying that I don't know how I feel. I like you Brad; I really do. I'm just not sure my *like* is or will grow into *love*," Sophie admitted.

"But you're willing to take things slow? You're willing to date me? To give me a chance?" Brad continued, not really hearing the full meaning of Sophie's words.

"Yes," Sophie agreed. "That is if you're okay with that?"

"I'm definitely okay with that!" Brad exclaimed. Then smiling at Sophie, he took her hand in his as they continued walking. *This means I still have a chance*, Brad thought, satisfied by the fact that *Grant Bakesfield* had not succeeded in asking Sophie out.

Feeling Brad's hand grasped around hers, Sophie found that she did enjoy holding his hand. Brad's grip was strong, warm, and self-assured, but also gentle. In fact, it wasn't that different from Grant's. *What was she doing? Why was she thinking about Grant when she was walking with Brad?*

"Is something wrong?" Brad asked, gazing at Sophie with concern.

"No, nothing," Sophie replied quickly. *She had just momentarily had a lapse of judgement, right?*

"Good," Brad grinned. "Well, here we are," he declared, opening the restaurant door for Sophie.

As they walked into the dining establishment, Sophie was determined to give Brad a chance. He was a good-hearted and decent man, and all the time she'd known him, he had always treated her with respect. Grant Bakesfield, and his irritatingly good looks, were not going to invade her lunch date!

"Brad! Sophie!" Karah exclaimed, catching sight of the pair as they walked into the bistro. "I only just placed my order. Would you care to join me?" she added, gesturing towards the empty seats at her table.

Sophie glanced at Brad. She glimpsed the frustration he hurriedly tried to conceal.

"Sure, Karah, we'd love to," Brad smiled politely, walking towards Karah's table as Sophie followed him.

Sophie knew this was not the lunch date Brad had been expecting, but to be honest, she was a little relieved. She hadn't been on a first date in a while, and now that tension no longer existed with the addition of Karah. Taking her seat, Sophie ordered a water when the waitress appeared, and began scanning the menu she'd been handed.

"So," Karah said, taking a sip of her water, "Brad, are you going to ride as Santa in the parade again this year?"

"Ha ha, no," Brad chuckled, "I was finally able to get someone else from the office to take my spot on the float this year," Brad shared, his face appearing anything but disappointed.

"Really?" Karah asked in surprise. "Well then, you'll have to come watch the parade with Sophie and me," she smiled, her eyes brightening.

Sophie looked at Karah and the way she was smiling at Brad. *Was it possible that Karah was interested in Brad?* she wondered. *If so, had she been wrong in telling Brad she was okay with the two of them trying to take things slow?* Sophie suddenly felt torn.

"I'd love to meet up with you both at the parade," Brad replied, turning and smiling at Sophie.

"Yes," Sophie agreed. "That would be nice."

It was now Karah's turn to read the gaze between Brad and Sophie. With a sinking heart, Karah realized Brad's affections continued to lay elsewhere. In high school, she had known Brad was smitten with Sophie. Sure, he'd been

Sophie's friend, but he'd always followed her around like a lovesick puppy. Karah sighed as she looked down at the pimento cheese sandwich that had just been set in front of her. *Not only was Brad good looking, but he was kind, charming... a real gentleman.* When he had returned to Sugar Plum after college, Karah knew Brad had dated a few girls, but nothing had ever come of those relationships. Now, having been elected mayor, Brad continued to remain the town's most eligible bachelor. Taking a bite of her sandwich, Karah continued to ponder. *Before Sophie had returned, she'd thought Brad had begun to look at her with interest the few occasions he'd stopped by the flower shop. But now,* Karah thought sadly, feeling her heart ache, *her hopes were dashed.* If Brad and Sophie were indeed interested in one another, their past history made them deserve each other. They'd be the almost high school sweethearts that finally ended up together, the perfect love story for the town; and she had no right to stand in their way.

"So, Karah," Sophie said, causing Karah to look up from her lunch. "What all does your family have planned for Christmas?"

Karah swallowed the bite she'd been chewing. "We're all going over to my parents' house," she said. "My sister and her family are going to be there, and we're going to have a late lunch and then exchange gifts with the kids. Chrissy's got three boys now," Karah smiled fondly.

"Oh, I bet you just love being an auntie!" Sophie

proclaimed longingly.

"Yes," Karah agreed. "It's a lot of fun getting to spoil and sugar them up and then send them back to Chrissy," she laughed. "What about you Brad? What are your plans?"

"Since my brother and sister and their families are coming back home this year, we all decided to rent out *The Belle of Sugar Plum* for both Christmas Eve and Day. My parents are super thrilled about this," Brad shared.

"Wow!" Sophie, exclaimed. "*The Belle of Sugar Plum!* I remember going to its restaurant for breakfast once in high school. It used to have the most wonderful blueberry crepes," she added, remembering how the fresh blueberries and cream cheese melted in her mouth.

"Yeah," Brad said enthusiastically. "We've rented out the entire bed and breakfast for both days."

Sophie shook her head in amazement. "That is so awesome! Being the history nut that I am, I'm so happy that the old schoolhouse is still a historical landmark and is continuing to be utilized in a way that allows people to share in its history."

Brad saw the way Sophie's eyes were sparkling. "Why don't you come and spend Christmas Day with my family and me? I'm sure my parents would love to see you," he continued with a smile.

"Brad, I couldn't," Sophie replied, shaking her head. "I don't want to impose on you and your family. You all should get a chance to just enjoy being together." Besides,

Sophie realized, she wouldn't be spending Christmas alone, Grant was at her house. *Did she want to spend Christmas with Grant instead of Brad then? If her Grandpa had not passed away so quickly, she would have been spending Christmas with both of them, right?*

"You wouldn't be imposing," Brad persisted. "Honestly, Soph, I'd love it if you'd come. I don't want you spending Christmas with…," he couldn't bring himself to mention *Grant* and risk getting into another argument with Sophie, especially when she'd just agreed to give him a chance. "*Please*, consider the invitation," he continued instead.

"Okay, I'll think about," Sophie smiled.

"Thank you," Brad replied, echoing Sophie's smile.

"Well," Karah uttered, getting up from her seat. "Would you look at the time. I've got to get back to the shop." *How could Sophie not leap at the prospect of spending Christmas with Brad? Was she crazy? If Brad had asked her...she would have said yes in a heartbeat!*

"Oh, gosh!" Sophie sputtered. "You're right, Karah, I've got to get back too. Let me pay my check and I'll walk out with you."

"Okay," Karah nodded.

"Don't worry about it, Ladies," Brad remarked with a grin, rising from his chair and taking both of their receipts. "Lunch is on me this time."

"Thank you, Brad, but you don't have to do that,"

Sophie said, reaching for her receipt.

"Yes, I do," Brad chuckled, pulling the receipt out of her reach. "Consider it a welcome back lunch, Soph, and Karah, it can be a Christmas gift," he added with a smile, causing Karah to blush and mumble her thanks.

"Brad Devanston, you are simply impossible," Sophie laughed with a smile.

"I'm flattered! I'll take impossible," Brad grinned. "Although, I'd prefer the synonyms *extraordinary* and *incredible*," he teased.

"You're extraordinary and incredible," Karah breathed, her eyes gazing longingly at Brad.

"You see, at least one of you has it right," Brad grinned. "I'll see you both on Saturday," he added, before flagging down a waitress to pay their bills.

Once they were outside, Karah turned to Sophie. "Brad is *so* nice, isn't he?"

"Yes, he's always been a nice guy," Sophie agreed, looking at Karah with empathy. Then before she could stop herself, she blurted, "Karah, do you like Brad?"

"That would be silly, wouldn't it?" Karah uttered, not meeting Sophie's gaze.

"That wasn't an answer," Sophie prodded.

"Alright, if you must know, no, I do not like Brad," Karah declared, turning her face towards Sophie and holding her gaze. How she hoped Sophie couldn't see the lie she had just told through her eyes. If Brad was in love with Sophie, she was not going to stand in his way, even if her own heart was breaking.

"You're sure?" Sophie asked again, not entirely convinced.

"Yes, I'm sure," Karah remarked curtly. "Now, let's just talk about something else."

"Okay," Sophie mumbled. *Maybe her intuition had been wrong.* If Karah had told her she liked Brad, Sophie would have let her have him. Sophie knew she had no right to waltz back into town and try and make something out of a friendship that might not even turn into anything if someone else was in love with Brad. *But since Karah didn't like him...Was she being unfair to Brad when she didn't know her own feelings and kept thinking about Grant, a man she was supposed to dislike for being an unwanted houseguest?*

"Well, I've got to head this way," Karah remarked, pointing a gloved hand to the left. "You're still coming over for dinner tonight, right?" she asked.

"Absolutely! I'll head over after work," Sophie replied, as she turned the opposite direction and began her walk back to the museum. *At least I've got enough letters to keep me occupied for the rest of the afternoon,* she thought, *for letters were a lot less confusing than her present situation.*

Chapter 9

Sophie had been able to transcribe twenty of the fifty letters before it was time for her to leave. Turning off her desk lamp, she grabbed her coat from the back of her office door then turned off the overhead light.

Pulling the door shut behind her, Sophie pulled her keys out of her purse and locked her office. As she walked past the front desk, Ellen looked up and smiled.

"Do you have any plans for dinner?" Ellen asked, putting on her coat and following Sophie out of the museum. "Because if not, Gerald and I would be delighted to have you over," she added cheerfully.

"Oh, Ellen, that's so sweet of you and your husband to think of me," Sophie replied graciously. "I actually do have plans, though. My good friend from high school, Karah, has invited me over for dinner."

"Oh, how wonderful!" Ellen exclaimed, satisfied by Sophie's response. "I just hated to think of you eating dinner all by yourself, especially this time of year."

Did she have a "please pity me" sign pasted on her forehead? Sophie wondered, feeling a little rejected. She knew Ellen was just being kind, but her words still hurt her pride. She had eaten dinner by herself numerous times over the years. It wasn't that terrible to eat alone. Yes, she'd hoped by now that she would have met that special someone, that man of her dreams, but being single was not an ailment requiring *pity*.

"Well," Ellen continued brightly, not realizing the impact Sophie had felt from her words. "We shall just have to have you over for dinner another night. How does that sound?"

"That would be lovely," Sophie replied, smiling at Ellen. Ellen meant well, and Sophie was happy to be working with someone who genuinely cared about her, even if Ellen had unintentionally said the wrong thing. "I'll see you tomorrow, Ellen," Sophie waved with a smile, after locking the front door.

Once inside her car, Sophie pulled out her phone and opened the message Karah had sent her with her address. Opening the address on her phone's GPS, Sophie clicked start and proceeded to put her car in drive. It turned out Karah didn't live too far from downtown. As Sophie pulled into the driveway of a little brick house a few streets away from the elementary school she'd attended, Sophie was pleased to see that Karah's Christmas spirit was in full swing. A cute wooden snowman holding a sign reading, *Merry Christmas*, stood cheerfully on the front porch, and a large red-and-white homemade Christmas wreath, resembling a giant peppermint, hung on the front door. Stepping out of her car, Sophie smiled as she continued gazing at the decorations. White Christmas lights glowed warmly, wrapping themselves lightly around the front porch pillars, and the windows of Karah's house were illuminated by the soft gleam of electric candles. *Karah's home was warm and inviting just like its owner,* Sophie thought happily. She had barely raised her hand to knock, when the front door was flung open, sending a cascade of light flooding the front porch.

"I saw you drive up," Karah said, her voice as bright as her smile. "Come on in," she added, stepping aside and taking Sophie's coat.

"I *love* your home," Sophie declared, following Karah into the foyer.

"Thank you!" Karah replied. "It's not that big, but I think it's pretty cozy," she smiled.

As they passed through various rooms on their way to the kitchen, the wooden floors creaked warmly with age beneath their feet. *Karah was right*, Sophie mused, *her home was extremely cozy*. Unlike some smaller homes that sometimes felt cramped from clutter, Karah's was tastefully decorated in a quaint and homey farmhouse style. With its soft earthy tones and subtle accents, Karah's home was elegant in its simplicity.

"Here we are!" Karah remarked, stepping into the kitchen. "Dinner is almost ready. How about some apple cider while we wait?"

"That sounds perfect!" Sophie agreed, taking a seat on one of the white wooden bar stools that stood by the island.

Karah pulled two mix-matched pottery mugs from one of the open shelves hanging beside the sink, and ladled apple cider into them. The smell of cinnamon and cloves delighted Sophie's senses as she breathed in the aroma from the mug Karah handed her.

"The Christmas season has so many wonderful smells and flavors," Sophie uttered, taking a sip of her cider. The warm apple spiced liquid was one of those holiday delights that Sophie never tired of drinking or smelling all season long.

"I know exactly what you mean," Karah agreed, lifting her mug to her lips. "I think I could smell apple cider simmering on the stove all year round and never grow tired of it. So," Karah continued, casting Sophie a questioning gaze, "now that you're here, are you going to tell me more about this *Grant Bakesfield* fellow?"

Sophie felt her cheeks grow warm, as she set her mug on the island and looked into Karah's face.

"There's really nothing more to tell," Sophie stated. *Liar!* she heard herself blurt. *Grant invades your thoughts on a daily basis...he's considerate...he's handsome...get a grip! You're supposed to be giving Brad a chance, who is every bit as considerate and handsome as Grant...but he doesn't invade your thoughts, does he?*

"Really?" Karah asked, her eyes seeming to read Sophie's thoughts. "You told me he had been staying at the farm helping your Grandpa out. What's he doing now?"

Sophie took a cracker from the plate Karah had set on the island and spread some of the cream cheese with pepper-jelly onto it. "It's crazy really...," she began. *Did she dare tell Karah the crazy truth of the situation? She had been upset by it; Brad had been upset... Did she really need to upset someone else?*

"What's crazy?" Karah persisted, popping a cracker into her mouth.

"Alright," Sophie gave in, taking a deep breath and plunging ahead. "My Grandpa made Grant sign this stupid contract that he is not allowed to move out of the farmhouse until the first of the year."

Karah's eyes widened. "So, you mean he's living with you in your house *now*?"

"Yes," Sophie replied. "It's rather inconvenient." *But was it really inconvenience she was feeling or was it something else?*

"Does Brad know?" Karah asked.

"Yes. He's not too happy about the situation, but there isn't much he can do about it. He's going to take a look at the contract for me, but there still might not be anything that can be done until the contract expires. It's not that bad really," Sophie added. "I'll admit I was initially miffed by the arrangement, but Grant's not that bad of a roommate. He's...," Sophie stared at the plate of crackers in front of her, letting her words fall short.

"Do you like him? Grant, I mean?" Karah asked, as Sophie continued to stare glassily at the plate of appetizers.

"Don't be silly," Sophie uttered, tearing her gaze away from the plate. "I barely know him. Besides, Brad and I..."

Karah felt a pang in her heart and forced a smile. "Of course. You and Brad are perfect for each other. Forget I ever said anything. Now, let's have some dinner!" Karah turned and headed towards the oven not wanting Sophie to see the dejection in her eyes.

Was it silly? Sophie wondered, watching Karah retrieve a pan of chicken and rice out of the oven. *It was true that she didn't know Grant that well, but was having him in such close proximity causing her to have feelings for him?* Sophie felt so conflicted. She was supposed to be having feelings for Brad, not Grant. Yet as Sophie tried to focus her thoughts on Brad, an image of dark-brown hair and deep-green eyes flashed across her mind. Sophie closed her eyes and hurriedly shook her head, hoping to dispel the image of Grant's face.

"Are you okay?" Karah asked, setting a plate of wild-rice and cream-sauced chicken with dried cranberries in front of Sophie.

"Umm...yes! Sorry, don't mind me," Sophie muttered, as she opened her eyes and smiled. She watched Karah continue to stare at her questioningly and skeptical, as Karah took her seat. "I promise, I'm fine. I just thought of something I...um...need to do," Sophie lied. *Well, it's not really a lie,* she reassured herself, *I do need to stop thinking about Grant!*

"Okay. If you're sure…" Karah said, her expression still incredulous but willing to let the conversation drop. "Make sure you save room for dessert. I've baked a peach cobbler. I know it seems like a summer treat, but the recipe I have calls for cinnamon and all sorts of other warm spices…. I just love it around Christmas!" Karah remarked jovially.

"Karah, you've outdone yourself!" Sophie exclaimed. "Not only is this chicken and rice amazing, but I can't wait to try your cobbler. I've missed this," Sophie continued happily. "It's so nice to be home, but it's even nicer to be in the company of my good friends once again!"

Chapter 10

Stretching as she got out of bed, Sophie threw on a pair of leggings and an oversized sweatshirt. She'd had a wonderful time at Karah's. Not only had dinner and dessert been delicious, but they'd spent the rest of the evening catching up. Sophie had forgotten how nice it was to have such a good friend nearby. *Yes, she had made friends when she'd moved away, but none of them had been like Karah.* Tossing her hair into a messy bun, Sophie left her bedroom. After a whirlwind week, today was finally Saturday. Even though it was Saturday, she had set her alarm half an hour earlier than usual. She would have a quick breakfast, do her chores, and then take a shower and get ready for the parade. Bounding down the stairs, Sophie found that once again Grant had beaten her to the kitchen. She knew she shouldn't be irked, but she couldn't help it. It was downright infuriating that he managed to look so put together so early each morning and she always appeared like she'd just rolled out of bed! *Why couldn't he sleep later so she could sneak into the kitchen before him?*

"Good morning," Grant nodded, pouring a mug of coffee and handing it to Sophie.

And to make matters worse, Sophie thought irritated,

not only is he always put together and in the kitchen, but he constantly waits on me! Being treated with such chivalry was something, though Sophie hated to admit it, she really enjoyed. *Did Grant know it was her weakness or was he just being himself?*

"Good morning. And thanks," Sophie returned, taking a sip of coffee. Grant really knew how to make a good cup of coffee. Even though he drank his black, he put just the right amount of creamer in hers. *Why was he so infuriatingly perfect?* As if she needed more proof of her assessment, Grant proceeded to pull a large stack of pancakes and tray of bacon out from the oven.

"How do you do it?" Sophie inquired, before she could stop herself.

"Make pancakes?" Grant asked. "They're pretty easy. I can show you how if you'd like."

"No," Sophie clarified. "How do you do *everything* so well?"

"I have no idea what you mean," Grant chuckled, as he put pancakes and bacon on the plates he had sitting by the stove.

"I don't believe that," Sophie remarked, pulling the jug of orange juice from the fridge and pouring them each a glass. "You're always up early. You never look like you just rolled out of bed. And you have breakfast made before I'm out of my room, even when I set my alarm half an hour earlier," she declared, returning the juice to the fridge and setting the glasses on the table.

"So, you've noticed how I *look*?" Grant inquired with a grin.

Sophie glared at him. "That's not what I mean."

"Of course not," Grant remarked, looking amused as he set the plates of pancakes and bacon on the table.

Pouring a generous amount of syrup on her stack of pancakes, Sophie cut a bite with her fork and brought it to her mouth. Once again, Grant's culinary skills impressed her. Whenever she made pancakes, not only were hers never this fluffy, but she was lucky if one of them turned out round. Not only were Grant's pancakes all round and a nice golden color, but they were light, fluffy, and buttery.

"Before you move out," Sophie said, in between bites, "you've got to teach me how to make these."

"It would be my pleasure," Grant said, his deep-green eyes gleaming with happiness.

Sophie felt her heart rate begin to increase and quickly averted her gaze. *Staring into Grant's eyes was bad! Not only did it cause her thoughts to wander, but staring into his deep-green eyes made her begin to second-guess...made her begin to feel as though she could lose herself in their warm and compassionate allure...No! She was definitely not allowed to stare into his eyes!* Chewing her pancakes in silence, Sophie tried to forget the way Grant could melt her with a mere glance.

A few hours later, after finishing breakfast and her

chores, Sophie was ready to go to the parade. She had decided to wear her favorite burgundy sweater along with a pair of skinny jeans and caramel colored riding boots. She had debated putting her hair in a ponytail and decided instead to bobby pin it to one side, allowing her long brown curls to cascade over her shoulders and gently frame her face. Reaching the coat closet, Sophie pulled her peacoat from its hanger and then grabbed her purse.

"I was thinking we should probably ride together," Grant said, walking up behind Sophie and grabbing his coat.

"Wait... *What*?" Sophie asked confused, as she turned and looked at Grant.

"Ride together to the parade," Grant continued, ignoring Sophie's baffled expression.

Finding her words, Sophie uttered, "You're going to the parade?"

"Well, yeah," Grant replied, his words sounding as if Sophie was crazy to think he would miss such an event.

"What will people think if we show up together?" Sophie asked, still mystified.

"They'll think we're being eco-friendly for carpooling," Grant stated matter-of-factly. "That is unless you want them to think something else?" he added with a smile.

Sophie glowered. "No. I don't want them to think something else, thank you very much. I'm just worried someone might get the wrong impression, might think...,"

Sophie found herself unable to suggest what Brad might think.

"Don't worry," Grant continued, pulling his arms through his coat. "I'll give you a ten-minute head start when we get there, so Mr. Devanston won't get the *wrong* idea."

"Thank you," Sophie said, sounding pleased as she opened the door and walked out onto the porch. "That's very gentlemanly of you."

"Always happy to be a gentleman," Grant returned, shutting the door behind them and following Sophie down the steps.

Opening the passenger door of his truck, Grant offered Sophie his hand and boosted her up into the cab. Once he was seated, Grant turned on the engine and backed the truck around until they were ready to head out of the driveway. "Shall we listen to some Christmas music?" he offered, fiddling with the buttons on the radio.

"Sure," Sophie replied, unable to keep the delight from her voice. "I love Christmas carols."

"Do you have a favorite song?" Grant asked, turning to look at her.

"*O Holy Night*," Sophie replied automatically, her entire face lighting up. "I think I could listen to every rendition of the song anytime of the year. What about you?" she asked.

Grant thought for a moment. *He had always liked Christmas carols too, but he had never had a favorite until this year*. The past four years he'd spent with Charlie on the farm after he'd had to leave Nashville, had helped him find a home again. *And then all he'd learned from Charlie about Sophie, without even meeting her...* Grant had found he had unconsciously made Sophie a part of his new home. *Was it weird that he'd started falling in love with Sophie from everything Charlie had told him about her? How he'd hoped, just as much as Charlie, that she'd come home this Christmas, if only to prove to him he'd fallen in love with a real person?* "I'll Be Home for Christmas," Grant finally said. "That's my favorite Christmas song."

"Oh," Sophie smiled brightly. "That's a good one too!"

Yes, Grant thought, *it definitely was a good one.*

Chapter 11

When they arrived in town, Grant was true to his word. Sophie got out of the truck and headed towards Main Street in search of Brad and Karah, while Grant remained in his seat and waited for her to disappear from view. As he watched Sophie growing further and further away in the distance, Grant felt his heart throb within his chest. *Why was he foolish enough to think that Sophie would ever feel for him the way he felt about her?* When he no longer saw her, he got out of the truck and made his way towards downtown.

Reaching Main Street, Sophie looked around the faces of the growing crowd. She was supposed to meet Brad and Karah in front of the town courthouse, but she didn't see them yet. Looking up at the courthouse, its sandy stone walls built from Kentucky River Stone, Sophie's eyes followed the large stone columns leading up to the building's Grecian styled front, and finally rested upon the large clock tower near its roof. Even though the current courthouse was the third to be built, after the two previous ones had been destroyed by fires over a hundred years ago, it was still an impressive architectural structure. The courthouse had even made a Hollywood appearance, when a motion picture was filmed in town during the mid-nineteen-hundreds. *Sugar*

Plum, Sophie thought affectionately, *truly was home to some wonderful treasures. All one had to do was open their eyes and look.*

"Soph! Over here!" Brad called, catching sight of Sophie.

Hurriedly crossing the street before the parade arrived, Sophie joined Brad and Karah on the sidewalk in front of the courthouse.

"Oh!" Karah exclaimed excitedly. "How I just love this parade!"

"I know what you mean," Sophie remarked cheerfully, hearing the first sounds of the high school marching band making its approach.

All around her, people were smiling and cheering as they waited excitedly, and Sophie couldn't help but do the same. When she was a little girl, Sophie remembered riding in the parade as an angel the year her church made a nativity float. She'd also got to ride on a "Christmas around the world" float where she and the other kids had dressed in the traditional attire of the country they represented. Seeing the floats when they were all put together, was a sight like no other!

"Here it comes!" Karah exclaimed, jumping up and down with excitement.

Sophie cheered along with the rest of the town as the marching band, dressed in Nutcracker styled uniforms and white plume-feathered caps, appeared playing lively renditions of Christmas carols. The drumline jubilantly belted out *Jingle Bells,* as the flag core sent red-and-white flags spinning in spiral waves making it appear like a sea of whirling candy canes. The entire scene was absolutely mesmerizing! After the band marched past, the line of bright and vivacious floats emerged. Decked out in Christmas lights, the floats were filled with festive Christmas scenes and music, and people throwing candy to the crowd. Interspersed within the floats, cheerleading squads and sports teams marched along, and vintage automobiles drove past merrily tooting their horns. Sophie found herself clapping as loudly as Karah and smiling from ear to ear, as she continued to watch the sights pass by with lively anticipation. The parade was simply enchanting! There was nothing quite like the unity and love both watchers and participants experienced in a small-town parade. Pride for one's hometown...happiness for the Christmas season...the emotions binding the crowd in solidarity were so strong, that even the *Scroogiest* of people would be unable to keep from feeling the elation.

Sophie's heart was drumming with delight. She had to know if Brad was enjoying the parade as much as she was. Forcing herself to tear her gaze from the carnival of sights, Sophie's eyes turned towards Brad when they suddenly froze. Instead of looking at Brad, Sophie found herself staring transfixed down the sidewalk into a pair of deep-green eyes! *Seriously? What was Grant doing so close by?*

There was an entire street, for goodness sakes! Why did he have to be only a few hundred feet away? Was he spying on her? Sophie glared at Grant, and much to her chagrin, he smiled then turned his gaze back towards the parade leaving her knees feeling slightly wobbly. *Why did Grant's smile have to be so disarming?* Sophie stood on the sidewalk, feeling flustered, until Karah's voice broke into her thoughts.

"Here he comes!" Karah exclaimed. "Oh, Brad, just think this could have been you!" she continued cheerfully.

"Well, I'm for one glad it's not," Brad snorted, a look of relief present upon his face.

"You can't possibly mean that," Karah tutted, her eyes large with disbelief. "Where's your Christmas spirit?"

"Not dressed in a red suit," Brad replied. Then catching sight of Karah shaking her head silently at his words as if he had just admitted a form of blasphemy, he quickly added, "I love Christmas. I just never really made that good of a Santa. I guess I didn't really fit the part." *Were there really certain qualifications for dressing up like Santa on a parade float? He knew how to laugh; he was rather merry. But was he as giving and selfless to others as Saint Nicholas, the inspiration for the jolly old elf? Once those qualities might have been true descriptors of him,* Brad realized dejectedly. *Had he really changed that much over the years? Had he really become so concerned with his own ambitions that he'd forgotten how to help his neighbors and those less fortunate?* Brad stared at the approaching float depicting

Santa and the North Pole suddenly conflicted by his new epiphany of his character.

With the parade and Main Street all aglow in sparkling Christmas lights and music, the crowd erupted in cheers as Santa appeared waving and riding on his sleigh. There was something magical about seeing Santa, waving and smiling merrily from his sleigh as the final float in the parade, that made the inner child of all come alive! As Sophie watched the jolly elf ride by, she found herself recalling the lyrics of *The Christmas Song*. Christmas had a wonderful way of making everyone from the very young to the very old feel merry. Christmas, Sophie realized, had a way of making everyone believe that on such a *holy* night, love, peace, and selfless generosity were still possible. When the parade concluded, although Sophie wished for more, her heart felt happy and more prepared for Christmas.

"Wasn't that simply wonderful?" Karah declared, her voice bubbling with glee.

"It definitely was!" Sophie agreed, her voice matching the pitch of Karah's delight.

"Yes, it was very nice," Brad admitted. "I stand by my earlier comment, though, that I'm happy I didn't have to dress up like Santa this year. That suit is incredibly itchy!" he laughed.

"Oh, don't be such a *grinch*," Karah teased.

"I'm not being a *grinch*, I'm just stating a fact," Brad shrugged. "I don't know about you Ladies, but a warm beverage sounds pretty good right now. How about stopping and grabbing some coffees while the vendors set the booths up for the bazaar?" he suggested, rubbing his hands together.

"That sounds great!" Sophie exclaimed. "I was so excited about the parade, I forgot how cold I am. I'm absolutely freezing!" she laughed, as a gust of wind caused her to shiver.

"Here," Brad replied, starting to unbutton his coat. "Take my coat."

"Don't be silly, you'll freeze. Besides, I'm wearing a coat," Sophie reminded him.

"Are you sure?" Brad asked, his voice serious. "I don't want you getting sick."

"Yes, absolutely. Thanks, though," Sophie added.

"Alright, since I can't change your mind," Brad said, rebuttoning his coat. "The coffee shop's not too far, we'll be there in no time," he continued, leading the way.

Arriving at *Peppermint's Tea and Coffee*, Brad opened the door for Sophie and Karah.

"This is so cozy!" Sophie smiled, stepping inside. The smell of fresh coffee grounds wafting through the air and the pleasant sounds of grinders and other barista machines, gave the little shop a warm and inviting atmosphere. "I've never been here before," she continued, as she took her place in line.

"Oh! That's right," Karah exclaimed, remembering the timeframe of her friend's absence from town. "The shop opened up a couple of years after you'd already moved away. They have great chocolate-cinnamon lattes. Who am I kidding, every drink on their menu is terrific!" Karah continued, pressing her lips together and running her tongue along them as she thought about the warm and slightly nose tingling cinnamon-infused beverage.

Sophie smiled. "That does sound amazing," she remarked, as she continued to observe the busy and homey shop. Comfy oversized cushions, and pillows looking like giant peppermints, covered the shop's three spacious window seats; while a variety of small, circular, wooden tables and upholstered chairs were nestled snugly around the crackling fire that glowed warmly within the large brick fireplace. With *Bourbon Barrel Books* only a few shops away, Sophie knew she had undoubtedly found her new lunchbreak retreats. Tearing her gaze away from the shop's decor and towards the counter, Sophie thought from the looks of the menu, that Karah seemed right. Everything did sound delicious!

"Oh, and you've got to try one of their caramel-ginger-spiced muffins. They have them every Christmas...you've just got to try one. I mean...I just don't have the words to do them justice," Karah uttered, her eyes looking beseechingly at Sophie.

"Okay, I'm trying one," Sophie laughed.

"You're going to love it," Karah confirmed with a grin.

When the barista handed Sophie her muffin, Sophie's

mouth fell open at the sight of it. She had to be gazing at the biggest muffin she had ever seen! *Seriously, there was no way she could eat it all,* she thought in disbelief, continuing to eye the delicious golden-brown muffin drizzled with white frosting and caramel and topped with a caramel candy. Besides looking like an enchanting confection from *The Nutcracker Land of Sweets*, the spiced aroma wafting from the muffin was mouthwatering. Casting an amazed glance at Karah, Sophie took a bite of her muffin. *If there was a college class dedicated to the sole craft of gingerbread,* Sophie thought, *whoever made this muffin should be teaching it! The moistness of the dough... the robust flavors of cinnamon, cloves, and ginger...it was an absolute work of art!*

"This is by far the best gingerbread muffin I've ever tasted!" Sophie declared, after swallowing her bite.

"I told you you'd love it," Karah remarked with satisfaction.

"Really?" Brad uttered unconvinced.

"Absolutely! Here, have a bite," Sophie remarked, offering Brad her muffin.

Taking the muffin, Brad took a bite. *How long had he lived here, and why had he never ordered this before?* "Wow! This is impressive!" Brad remarked. "Hang on, Soph, on second thought, I'm not sure this is good. I don't think you want to eat it," he teased, taking another bite.

"Hey! Drop the muffin and get your own," Sophie

ordered, taking her muffin back and grinning.

Brad chuckled then turned to the cashier. "I think I'm going to have to add one of these muffins to my order," he said.

With their lattes and muffins in hand, the trio headed back out onto the sidewalk.

"I've missed this town," Sophie reminisced fondly, taking a sip of her latte.

"It is a wonderful town," Brad agreed. Casting a smile at Sophie, he couldn't find any truer words. *Yes, Sugar Plum was wonderful, but now that Sophie was back...the town seemed even more wonderful*, he realized.

"Yes, it definitely is homey," Karah remarked. "Well, this is my stop," she added, as they reached *All Thymes and Occasions*. "We closed for the parade, but now I've got to get ready for the Christmas Bazaar open house that starts in ten minutes. I'll see you all later," she added, smiling at Brad and Sophie before departing.

"Where should we go first?" Brad asked, as he took a sip of his latte and bite of his muffin.

"You've got to check out the new bookstore that's opened," Sophie replied instantly. "Have you been there yet?" she asked.

"No, I haven't," Brad replied. "But it sounds interesting."

"Oh, it is! Not only does it have volumes of books, but it's got these really neat sliding ladders along the bookshelves," Sophie shared enthusiastically.

Walking along the sidewalk, they passed by local vendors who were hurriedly putting the finishing touches on their booths. The twinkling Christmas lights… the vibrant smells of evergreen and cinnamon... the lively Bluegrass-style Christmas carols filling the air... made Sophie imagine that she was walking through one of the famed Christmas markets of Europe. After stopping at the book shop, Sophie was excited to see what the rest of the bazaar had in store. Polishing off her muffin, Sophie pulled open the door to *Bourbon Barrel Books*. The smell of paper and binding mixed with the subtle aroma of a bourbon and vanilla scented candle, permeating from its candle warmer, greeted Brad and Sophie as they entered the shop.

"Isn't this fantastic!" Sophie exclaimed, loosening her scarf and gazing enchantedly around the shop.

"It is rather nice," Brad acknowledged, as he picked up a book filled with postcard photos of Christmas in Kentucky scenes, and began thumbing through it. "A shop like this will definitely be a good tourist attraction and addition to Main Street."

"Welcome to *Bourbon Barrel Books*," Vivian said brightly from behind the counter. "Oh, Sophie, it's so good to see you again! How are you?" she asked, a smile lighting up her features as she recognized her customer.

"It's great to see you too, Vivian!" Sophie returned. "I'm doing fine. How about yourself?"

"Doing well. Except I'd love it if this little one would learn to sleep at night and be active in the day," Vivian laughed, fondly rubbing her stomach.

Arriving at the counter, Sophie continued, "Allow me to introduce you to Brad Devanston, the Mayor of Sugar Plum. Brad, this is Vivian Fernsby. She and her husband own the book shop."

"It's very nice to meet you, Mr. Mayor," Vivian said, extending her hand.

"It's nice to meet you too, Mrs. Fernsby," Brad smiled, shaking Vivian's hand. "I must say, your shop is a wonderful addition to Main Street."

"Thank you," Vivian replied. "We haven't been open long, but we're getting good traffic," she shared enthusiastically.

"Well, I hope business keeps doing well for you," Brad said cheerfully. "It was very nice to meet you, Mrs. Fernsby. I'm going to browse around a bit more if you don't mind," he added to Sophie.

"Not at all. Take your time," Sophie replied, remaining at the counter.

Once Brad departed, Vivian turned towards Sophie. "Mayor Devanston seems like a really nice fellow," she said.

"Yes, he is," Sophie agreed. "He's always been a nice guy."

"Have you known him for a long time?" Vivian asked.

"Since high school," Sophie shared.

"Well, you all make a very nice couple," Vivian declared with a smile.

"Oh...well...we're not really a couple, yet," Sophie admitted, feeling the heat rising in her cheeks. *Was she no longer allowed to be in the company of a man without everyone assuming they were dating? First Mr. Carroll and Mr. Floyd had implied Grant was her beau, and now Vivian had assumed she and Brad were an item. Which, they kind of where,* Sophie admitted, *but still...*

"I'm sorry, I just assumed..." Vivian stammered embarrassed.

"Don't be sorry," Sophie remarked, feeling annoyed with how she had reacted. "Brad and I are seeing each other; we're just not entirely committed to one another yet. We were friends for a long time, so we're taking things slow to try and see if we can be more than friends," she admitted.

"I completely understand," Vivian remarked. "My husband, Jack, and I were good friends in college, and it wasn't until after college we realized we were attracted to each other and decided to give dating a try. Things ended up working out for us," she smiled. "Now, enough about all this. Are you staying for the rest of the Christmas Bazaar?" Vivian asked.

"Yes! I can't wait to peruse the booths," Sophie said, her eyes bright with excitement.

"Good! You'll have to make sure to stop by Jack's.

He does woodworking as a hobby, and he's really good," Vivian praised.

"Really! What does he make?" Sophie asked with interest.

"He carves children's rocking chairs and wooden signs mostly, but he decided to whittle and paint some ornaments this year too," Vivian shared. "If you look out the window now, you can actually see his booth on the street in front of the book shop," she added, pointing out the window.

Sophie turned her gaze in the direction Vivian was pointing and saw a man with strawberry-blond hair chatting enthusiastically with a customer. Gazing more intently, Sophie realized the man Jack was talking with was Grant! And not only that, but Grant was clasping Jack on the shoulder as if they were old friends!

"How does your husband know Grant?" Sophie wondered aloud.

"Oh, they've been good friends since college. Grant's a really great guy! It was such a shame when...Hang on. You know Grant?" Vivian asked, mystified.

"Umm...yes," Sophie murmured, shocked by the fact that she'd voiced her thoughts aloud.

"He's such a gentleman, isn't he?" Vivian continued. "Helping Mr. Marten out on the farm after his granddaughter left town. That's just the kind of man he is, always so kind and thoughtful. How'd you meet him?" Vivian asked.

"I'm Charlie Marten's granddaughter," Sophie

replied. Although Vivian had not said anything unkind, she still felt slightly humbled by her words.

"Sophie...So *you're* Sophie Marten!" Vivian realized, a smile spreading across her lips. "Jack and I have heard nothing but wonderful things about you," she continued.

"Really?" Sophie uttered surprised, and not sure if she should feel embarrassed or delighted by the fact that Grant had spoken of her.

"Really," Vivian affirmed, her eyes sparkling.

"Alright, I'm ready to go check out the booths if you are," Brad said, arriving back at the counter and distracting Sophie from her thoughts.

"I'm ready," Sophie agreed. Then saying goodbye to Vivian, Sophie followed Brad out of the shop, her mind whirling and wondering at just what exactly Grant had said.

Chapter 12

"Where should we begin?" Brad asked, taking Sophie's hand in his as they exited the book shop.

"Let's head towards the courthouse and work our way back this direction," Sophie suggested. *If she could avoid Grant for the time being, that would be wonderful*, she thought.

"Sounds like a plan," Brad agreed, as he began leading them away from the book shop.

Walking along the street, Sophie gazed at the various booths filled with their wares. *Homemade wreaths... boughs of holly and evergreen...delicious baked goods...fragrant seasonal potpourri...handmade stockings and quilts...beeswax candles...roasted chestnuts...Every booth was filled with Christmas treasures!* Stopping at the candle booth, Sophie picked up a cinnamon-spice fragrance and lifted it to her nose. Closing her eyes, she took a breath. It smelled exactly like a cup of spiced apple cider!

"This smells good enough to eat," Sophie laughed, offering the candle to Brad.

"It does smell rather appetizing," Brad agreed.

"I'm buying this!" Sophie declared brightly. "My office is currently lacking in festivity."

After paying for her candle, Sophie and Brad continued walking through the booths, and soon found themselves back in front of the book shop.

"Well, we've arrived at the last booth," Brad remarked, picking up a wooden sled ornament and examining it.

"The craftsmanship of these ornaments is exceptional," Sophie complimented, as her eyes scanned the carvings of stars, stables, snowflakes, gingerbread men, and Santas. "The time it must have taken to carve and paint these…" she wondered aloud in awe.

"Can I help you folks find something? A special Christmas gift perchance?" Jack asked, his hazel eyes filled with festive cheer.

"I'll take one of these Santas," Sophie said with a smile.

"Certainly! Let me wrap that in some tissue paper for you," Jack replied. Then wrapping the ornament carefully, he handed it to Sophie.

"I really like yours and Vivian's book shop," Sophie remarked, paying for the ornament. "Vivian said I should also check out your booth. I must say, your woodworking skills are really good," she added.

"Thank you on both accounts," Jack replied smiling. "We're happy we were finally able to open up the shop. I seem to be behind, however," Jack continued with a smile. "You apparently know I'm Jack Fernsby, but I haven't had the privilege of being introduced," he added, offering Sophie his hand.

"I'm Sophie Marten," Sophie divulged, clasping Jack's hand and watching his eyes brighten with interest.

"It's nice to meet you. I believe I just spoke to an acquaintance of yours a little while ago," Jack said, releasing Sophie's hand.

Sophie stared into Jack's hazel eyes. She had known she wouldn't be able to avoid mentioning Grant for long. "You must mean Grant Bakesfield," Sophie replied.

"Why yes, I do," Jack remarked happily. "He just so happens to be a very good friend of mine."

"Well, I've got to be going. Thanks for the ornament and have a Merry Christmas!" Sophie said quickly.

"Merry Christmas too!" Jack wished. "Oh, and the next time you happen to see Grant, tell him, Jack, says hello," he added with a grin, knowing full well that Grant was still lodging at the farm.

Sophie smiled and nodded then left the booth. *Just what exactly was Grant up to? Had he seen she and Brad together and then conspired with his friend, Jack, to mention his name and make subtle reference to the fact that Grant was still living at the farm?* Sophie thought suspiciously. She was just glad that Brad had been waiting for her outside the booth while she paid. Meeting up with Brad now, Sophie handed him the tissue wrapped ornament.

"This is for you," Sophie said. "You may have

escaped being Santa on the float this year, but I expect to see you on the float as Santa next year, Mayor Devanston," she teased with a smile.

"You're cruel," Brad laughed, taking the ornament from Sophie. "If you weren't so cute, I'm not sure I'd except this," he added, his eyes bright and full of marvel as he gazed at Sophie.

Sophie smiled back. So far Brad seemed just like the Brad she remembered.

"Where did you park?" Brad asked, turning to Sophie and resting her hand in the crock of his arm. "I'll walk you to your car."

"Oh! Don't worry about it, I can manage," Sophie replied quickly. She had been having such a wonderful time at the bazaar, that she had almost forgotten how she'd arrived in town. Having Brad see that she'd ridden to the festivities with Grant suddenly made Sophie's stomach feel queasy.

"It's no trouble," Brad assured. "Besides, it would give us more time to talk," he continued, smiling at Sophie walking beside him.

"I'm clear at the other end of the street in the parking lot by the city green," Sophie said, hoping her response might detour Brad's chivalry.

"Excellent! Then I have more time in your company," Brad smiled, squeezing Sophie's hand and gazing longingly into her eyes.

Foiled! She'd been foiled! Sophie felt her heart

flutter, and she knew it wasn't flutters of love, but rather nervous flutters. *What was Brad going to think when he saw Grant's truck? Worse, what was he going to think when he saw Grant?*

"Oh, I've been meaning to ask, did you bring the contract for me to take a look at?" Brad asked happily, oblivious to Sophie's worry.

Sophie stopped walking. *She had completely forgotten about the contract!* When she'd found out Grant was coming to the parade too, she'd become distracted. "No. I completely forgot about it," she admitted.

Brad turned and looked at her. "How could you forget about something so important?" he asked, flabbergasted. "Don't you want this, *Mr. Bakesfield,* guy out of your house?" His words were not so much of a question but rather an assessment.

"Look, Brad, I'm sorry, alright," Sophie replied, frustrated by Brad's remarks.

"I'm not upset with you," Brad acknowledged. "I'm just frustrated by the whole situation. It just makes things... *difficult*. I guess I'm just worried about you. I'm sorry, for my outburst," he added sheepishly.

"It's alright," Sophie smiled, lowering her defenses.

"Let's just change the subject," Brad continued. "Would you like to go to the high school basketball game tonight, and maybe have dinner together before?" he asked.

"Yeah, that would be great," Sophie replied, feeling

more and more apprehensive as they continued to draw closer to the parking lot. *Was she sweating? Could Brad feel how warm her hand was becoming?*

"I'll pick you up at five then," Brad continued, giving Sophie's hand another slight squeeze.

"Perfect!" Sophie uttered, subtly scanning the parking lot for Grant as they approached and offering silent prayers of thankfulness that she didn't see him. "You don't have to walk me all the way to my car. Here's good," she added hurriedly.

"Okay, if you're sure..." Brad returned with a smile. "I'll see you at five," he added, stepping closer to Sophie and putting his hands lightly on the side of her arms. "I'm already counting down the minutes," he said softly, meeting Sophie's deep-russet gaze. *Sophie's eyes were warm and beckoning, almost like a mug of hot chocolate,* Brad thought, continuing to stare transfixed. Watching the breeze gently snag her curly tresses, Brad's gaze ventured and rested lingeringly upon Sophie's lips. Leaning forward, he pulled Sophie closer to him and gently kissed her.

As Brad's lips connected with hers, Sophie was taken by surprise. She hadn't expected Brad to kiss her, at least not yet. Feeling his lips move gently against hers, Sophie's thoughts wandered. *What if Grant witnessed Brad kissing her? Why was she thinking about Grant? Brad's lips were soft and warm...but did she feel anything else? What was wrong with her? Why was her mind analyzing everything and not staying present in the moment?* When Brad released her from his embrace, Sophie's head was spinning; and despite her racing thoughts, she found herself speechless. As Brad smiled at her, Sophie observed that his face was gleaming with satisfaction. *Was her face displaying the same emotion?* she wondered, suddenly feeling faint.

"See you at five," Sophie murmured, taking a step back, her face flushing slightly.

Brad's eyes sparkled, as he nodded and flashed Sophie another dazzling smile before departing. Waiting until Brad had disappeared down the street, Sophie then turned and headed towards Grant's truck. As she walked down the steps leading to the parking lot, she saw that Grant had arrived without her seeing him. *Had he seen Brad kiss her?* Sophie felt her stomach twist in knots. *Why was she so worried about what Grant had or had not witnessed?*

"Did you enjoy the parade and Christmas Bazaar?" Grant asked, when Sophie arrived at the truck.

What did he mean by that? Sophie thought, frazzled. "Yes, I did," she smiled, regaining her composure. "I had a great time. What about you?"

"I'm glad," Grant remarked, opening the passenger door. "I enjoyed the parade and bazaar as well. It was nice of Mr. Devanston to walk you back," he smiled, closing the door behind her and walking around to the driver's side.

Darn! He had seen the kiss, Sophie realized, her heart suddenly pounding as if she was about to run a race.

"Would you like to stop somewhere for lunch before heading back to the house?" Grant asked casually, as he turned out of the parking lot.

"No, I think I'll just make a sandwich at home," Sophie replied. *Why was her heart still pounding? It wasn't as if she had feelings for Grant...?*

"Is my company that bad?" Grant joked, turning to look at Sophie with a smile.

"No," Sophie admitted. Despite wanting too, she realized she didn't really mind spending time with him. "I... I just have to get back and start getting ready," she said in a rush.

"Getting ready for what?" Grant asked with interest.

Sophie pursed her lips. She had to tell him; he was going to find out anyway when Brad arrived to pick her up. "I'm going to dinner and the basketball game tonight with Brad," she uttered, not meeting Grant's gaze. *Was she afraid her words would hurt him?*

"Oh," Grant remarked flatly, turning his eyes back to the road and remaining silent the rest of the ride home.

To say that the remainder of the ride was awkward, would be an understatement. Staring out the window, stubbornly refusing to be the first one to break the silence, Sophie felt the tension within the cab so apparently, it was suffocating. As Grant drove along the gravel driveway, Sophie was relieved to glimpse the farmhouse coming into view. Once Grant had parked the truck, Sophie opened the door and climbed down without waiting for him to offer to help her down. *She had to get out of the cab! Being next to Grant...not speaking...it had been intolerable!*

Sophie darted towards the house. She could feel Grant's gaze lingering upon her as she climbed the porch steps, but she refused to glance back. Once inside, she headed upstairs. Sophie didn't know why she felt so distraught. She had every right to go out with Brad, and Grant had absolutely no reason to be upset. She had known Brad forever, and only just met Grant. Besides, just because she and Grant were currently living together, that didn't mean they had feelings for one another. *That would simply be preposterous, wouldn't it?* Sophie thought, pulling a sweater dress out of her closet and laying it across her bed.

It was a quarter to five, when Sophie finally headed downstairs. Instead of the sweater dress, she'd opted instead for jeans and a royal-blue cashmere sweater. They were going to a basketball game after all, and she had decided the sweater dress would have been a tad over dressed for such an outing. The sweater, however, was dressy enough to make her ensemble casual, yet nice. Pleased with her appearance, Sophie sat on the window-seat in the living room and gazed through the glass waiting for Brad to arrive.

As she waited, Sophie heard Grant come in from outside. He had not spoken to her since he'd learned Brad was taking her out. Now, carrying an arm full of firewood, Grant stepped into the living room. Walking towards the fireplace, he set the logs he was carrying down on the hearth, crumpled some paper and lit it with a match, and then began prodding the kindling with a poker

"So, are you not going to talk to me anymore?" Sophie asked, when Grant continued to go about his work refusing to acknowledge her presence. Grant's occupancy at the farm... the ridiculous contract binding him here...continued to frustrate her, but when compared to not acknowledging her...Sophie was not entirely sure why Grant's silence bothered her the most.

Grant set the poker down and brushed his hands against his jeans. "No," he said turning to face Sophie. "I'll still talk to you. I'll always talk to you," he uttered.

Was it Sophie's imagination, or was there a glimmer of hurt within Grant's gaze? A knock on the door, however, caused Sophie to cease her contemplation.

"Have a nice time, Sophie," Grant said. "I'm glad you're happy," he added, holding her gaze a second longer before turning his attention back to the fire that had begun to catch.

"Thanks," Sophie replied, a bit bewildered that her words were lacking enthusiasm, as she stood and left the room.

Opening the front door, Sophie saw Brad, wearing dark jeans and a red-and-white button-up beneath his partially opened coat, standing on the porch, smiling.

"Wow! You look lovely, Soph," Brad complimented,

offering Sophie his arm and leading her down the steps.

"Thanks," Sophie smiled back. She caught a slight whiff of the spicy and rustic aroma of his cologne. "You look nice too."

"I'm looking forward to *finally* having a date on our own," Brad remarked, as he helped Sophie into her seat.

"Yes," Sophie laughed. "We haven't really had a real date yet, have we?"

"Nope," Brad grinned. "But that error is about to be rectified."

As they drove into town, Sophie caught sight of her old high school. It was hard to believe she'd already been a high school graduate for fifteen years. Seeing the familiar brick building, made Sophie feel as though it was just yesterday that she was walking through its blue and green lockered halls.

Brad sensed Sophie reminiscing. "Once a Polar Bear, always a Polar Bear," he grinned, taking a hand off the steering wheel and resting it gently on Sophie's.

They continued driving, and as they drew nearer to the school, they passed Kentucky's memorial honoring the state's fallen servicemen and women; its flags waving in the winter breeze in silent tribute for each fallen Kentucky soldier who had given his or her life during the War on Terrorism. As Sophie watched the flags billowing in the breeze, her heart leapt with pride. Her Grandpa had served in the Navy when he had been young, and she deeply respected all the brave men and women who had served their country throughout the years, especially those whose lives had been lost in sacrifice for their country. Sophie watched quietly as the memorial passed from view and was brought from her thoughts when she heard the soft click of the turn signal as Brad pulled into the parking lot of one of Sugar Plum's popular dining establishments.

"Here we are!" Brad exclaimed, parking the car. "I hope chimichangas or quesadillas work for you," he smiled.

"Oh, they definitely do!" Sophie replied enthusiastically. "You know me so well!" she smiled, causing Brad's grin to broaden.

Once they were inside and seated at a booth, Sophie removed her coat, and putting her elbows on the able, rested her chin on her hands. "So, I know you got your degree in political science and are now the mayor, but aside from the few times we ran into each other after graduating high school, what else have you been doing? Do you still like to run 5Ks and help build homes for those in need? I guess," Sophie continued, "I feel like I know the high school you, but don't really know the grown-up man."

Brad smiled. "I'm pretty much the same guy," he admitted. "Just a bit older," he laughed.

"No," Sophie persisted. "I mean it, seriously, tell me about yourself."

"Okay, what's to tell?" Brad replied, taking a tortilla chip from the basket and dipping it into the bowl of salsa.

"Let's see. After graduating college, I worked on some campaign teams for some congressmen, found that didn't really pay the bills, so I got a job as a Local Government Advisor working for the State. Working as an advisor, I realized how much I enjoyed local government, and I decided I could be of better service running for an elected position myself. So, I bought a house in town, ran for mayor, and got elected," Brad finished. "I don't run 5Ks anymore," he continued, "but I still try to volunteer when it fits into my schedule, mostly with charity events now. Being mayor has been great, but I've found sometimes, since I don't have a family of my own, people don't always take me seriously, which is irritating. Enough about me, though. What about you, Soph?" he asked, then took a sip of water.

Sophie leaned back against the booth. "I'm pretty much the same history and volunteer nut I was in high school. After getting my Bachelor's in history, I pursued a Master's in American History with an emphasis in Kentucky history. I then decided to get my Ph.D., with a minor in Scottish and Irish variations of Gaelic."

"Seriously? Why on earth would you minor in Gaelic?" Brad interrupted, unable to stop himself.

"Because immigrants from Scotland and Ireland came to Kentucky, and I wanted to examine the possibly influence their old-world language played in their adaptation to their new lives in America," Sophie stated, as if her reason had been obvious. She ignored Brad shaking his head and continued. "I ended up studying for two years abroad at Cambridge, and upon graduating was offered a position as an adjunct instructor at Harvard, and a year ago finally earned my assistant professorship. So, for the past five years, I've been writing academic books, lecturing to undergraduates, ran the Boston Marathon once and nearly died, and continued volunteering at Habitat for Humanity once a month. But now that I've got the farm," Sophie remarked, "I've been thinking of volunteering at the food pantry here in town instead."

"Wow," Brad uttered, in disbelief. "How is a guy supposed to compete with that kind of a résumé?"

"We're not competing," Sophie stated.

"I know," Brad remarked, scooping a spoonful of rice and beans onto his fork. "Just think what having a wife like you would do for my political image!" he declared aloud to himself with a smile.

"Brad," Sophie uttered, interrupting his thoughts. "We decided to take things slow, remember? Talking about marriage, and marriage just to fluff up your image, is not the definition of slow."

"Right," Brad remarked. "Just forget I said anything. We should probably get the check anyway; the game is about to tip off."

As Brad signed the receipt, Sophie sipped her water and stared at him from across the table. She didn't much like the thought of being a "trophy" wife. *Did Brad even realize how he had sounded and the implication of his words?* As she continued to watch him, Sophie began to second-guess her decision to date him. *Maybe over the years they had become different people. Maybe, they were only ever meant to be friends.*

Chapter 13

"Alright! Let's head over to the game," Brad declared enthusiastically, standing up and grabbing his coat off the back of his chair. "When was the last time you attended a game?" he asked, helping Sophie with her coat.

"Gosh, it was probably back when we were in high school," Sophie admitted.

"Well, aside from some renovations to the gym, it will probably be just how you remember," Brad concluded with a smile.

As they walked into the gym, Sophie's face lit up with excitement. The pep band was playing the same familiar school song that brought the crowd to their feet in jubilant cheers of motivation. Making their way along the side of the court, Sophie heard the cheer squad enthusiastically chanting. The wooden floor of the court gleamed shiningly, illuminated by the overhead lights, and a large painting of the school's mascot, the Sugar Plum Polar Bear, covered the center of the court growling and holding its paws up as if ready to attack. Banners recognizing championship years hung brightly from the rafters, and the sound of squeaking gym shoes and bouncing balls filled the air. Everything was exactly as she remembered! Brad glanced at her, and Sophie watched as a smile spread across his face upon seeing her delight. *A small-town girl can move to the city, but she'll always be a small-town girl at heart!* Sophie thought with pride.

"Do these seats work?" Brad asked loudly, as he gestured towards some open space a few rows up the bleachers.

"Yeah!" Sophie hollered back, climbing the steps towards the seats. "What a great view!" she exclaimed, scooting along the wooden bench next to Brad.

"Yeah, not too bad," Brad agreed. "Oh! Come on!" he hollered rising to his feet, "You gotta pass that! There we go! Nicely done!" he exclaimed, clapping his hands and whistling then sitting back down.

"I see you're still a huge basketball fan," Sophie yelled, over the roar of the crowd.

"Yesery!" Brad shouted back with a grin. "Some things never change!" Brad glanced at as watch as the Polar Bears took a timeout. "I hate to do this, Soph, but I told a member of the city council I'd have a quick word with him here at the game. Gotta love being the mayor," he grinned.

"You planned a meeting during our date? We've only been here for ten minutes!" Sophie uttered incredulously, trying to hide the hurt she felt from appearing on her face.

Brad smiled sheepishly. "Yeah, I didn't think you'd mind since it should only take a second. Plus, you know how much being mayor means to me."

"Fine," Sophie murmured, trying to comprehend what would have ever given Brad the notion that she would be okay with him scheduling a meeting during their date. It was unbelievable!

"I knew you'd understand! I won't be long, I promise," Brad smiled, standing up.
"You can fill me in on the game when I return."

As Brad descended the stairs, Sophie continued to watch him in disbelief. Yes, she knew how happy Brad was being mayor, but she had thought when he had asked her out tonight that her attention would be his priority. *Was she wrong to be upset with him? It was true that with politics one always has to uphold some kind of image, but what kind of image was presented when you ignored your date?* Sophie tried to direct her thoughts back to the game, but even though she was in a crowded gymnasium, she could not help but feel alone.

"Are these seats taken?" someone asked loudly.

Sophie looked up at the sound of the voice and about toppled off the bleachers. There, standing on the stairs looking at her with smiles, were Karah and Grant! Sophie opened her mouth to speak then closed it again. Brad had said he would be back soon, but that had now been twenty minute ago. *Had Karah and Grant arrived at the game together?* Sophie wondered. *Why did it suddenly bother her if they had? She wasn't jealous...the thought of that was simply foolish. Jealous....I mean, really...*

"Brad is going to be back in a little bit," Sophie remarked, not wanting to be the third wheel on Grant and Karah's date if that was the purpose of their presence together. She was "dating" Brad, not Grant, Sophie reminded herself, so Karah had every right to date Grant. *Why then did her heart hurt at this realization? Grant was just an unwelcome houseguest, right? It wasn't as if Grant had asked her out. But wait,* a small voice reminded her, *he did ask you if you wanted to grab a bite to eat after the parade. But that couldn't have been asking her out on a date, could it?*

"We'll just sit here until he returns then, to keep you company," Grant smiled, taking a seat next to Sophie and scooting over to make room for Karah.

"Well, don't get too comfortable," Sophie glowered at Grant. "Brad just had some quick mayor stuff to take care of and will be back any minute."

"I'm *sure* he will," Grant replied. "In the meantime, how about sharing one of these *walking-tacos* with us," he continued, handing Sophie a spoon and snack-size bag of corn chips filled with chili and cheese.

"Oh, my goodness! I'd forgotten about these!" Sophie exclaimed. "Remember, Karah, how we used to get one of these at every football and basketball game we attended and share it?"

Karah laughed. "Of course, I do! We were practically addicted to them! Who needs nachos when you've got the fabulously mouth-watering goodness of a walking-taco?"

Sophie dipped her spoon into the bag, and moments later heard the soft crunch of corn chips in her ears as the savory chili and cheese melted in her mouth. "Gosh, this is delicious!" she remarked, licking her spoon and sticking it back in the bag.

"Yeah, I ran into Karah at the concession stand. She introduced herself as one of your friends, and then she told me I had to try one of these taco things," Grant remarked, jabbing his spoon into his bag.

"So… you didn't come to the game together," Sophie stated, hoping her words sounded nonchalant.

"No," Grant smiled, his eyes twinkling as he looked at Sophie. "Would it have mattered if we had?"

"What? No, of course not," Sophie fumbled, feeling her cheeks flush. Then seeing Grant's smile broaden, she quickly turned her attention back to the game. The Polar Bears were doing great! There was a little over twenty minutes to play, and they were currently tied with their rival!

"Come on, Sophie!" Karah yelled, jumping to her feet. "We need some of that Sophienator energy!"

"*Sophienator*?" Grant sputtered, rising to his feet and gazing at Sophie with interest.

"Yeah, didn't Sophie ever tell you that was her nickname in tennis?" Karah remarked. "Not only was she an awesome tennis player, but when she cheered you on, you felt like you were awesome too!"

"Well, what are you waiting for, *Sophienator*," Grant teased, smiling at Sophie. "Let's hear you cheer on your team."

Not caring how foolish she might look now that she was a grown woman, Sophie jumped to her feet. "Okay, if I'm doing this you two are also," she shouted, turning towards Grant and Karah. "Ready?"

"Ready!" Grant and Karah exclaimed in unison.

"Okay, follow my lead!" Sophie exclaimed. Then jumping up and down, she waved her hands in the air and danced side-to-side yelling, "OH ...P… OLAR... B...EARS! POLAR! BEARS! BEARS! BEARS! POLAR! BEARS! BEARS! BEARS!" as Grant and Karah did the same.

Pretty soon their entire row was joining in, and then the rows in front of them and behind. They watched as the Polar Bears' point-guard dribbled down the court then passed the ball to a teammate who scored! But now they were only up by two. Sophie glanced at the clock, and saw that time was running out. "Come on Polar Bears! You can do it!" she yelled, as the score became tied once again. She glanced at Grant, who smiled back at her and continued to cheer. *Grant was not even from Sugar Plum, but he was cheering her school's team on as if it were his own beloved team*, Sophie thought, astonished.

Ten seconds on the clock remained...a timeout was called by the opposing team...the Polar Bears had the ball... five seconds...a shot...three..two...score! The gym erupted in unison, as the boys' varsity team pulled off a stellar buzzer-beating win over their rival. Sophie felt like she was a member of the student section at a national championship game as she turned, jumping up and down, towards Grant.

"We won!" Sophie exclaimed, her heart racing from adrenaline, as she flung her arms around Grant.

"That was an exceptional game!" Grant agreed, hugging Sophie back.

*Feeling Grant's arms around her, their strength and gentleness...*then realizing what she was doing, Sophie quickly pulled away from Grant's embrace. *What was she thinking?* "Sorry, I didn't mean to hug you," Sophie mumbled embarrassed.

"You needn't be sorry," Grant remarked softly, his eyes looking at Sophie with tenderness.

"Yes...I mean...I was out of line," Sophie rambled. "I need to go find Brad." At her words, Sophie noticed the usual sparkle of Grant's eyes dull as if a cloud had suddenly covered them.

"Well, Ladies, I must be going," Grant remarked. "Thanks again, Karah, for the wonderful concession suggestion. Sophie," he added with a nod, before taking his leave.

"It really was a great game, wasn't it?" Karah stated. "And wasn't it nice that Grant was able to join us? I'm glad I recognized him in the concession line. He really is very nice," she smiled.

"Yes, he is," Sophie agreed, feeling her heart flutter as she spoke.

"Well, I've got to get going too," Karah remarked smiling. "It was nice meeting up with you. Give me a call, and we can meet up again either before or after Christmas," she added, giving Sophie a hug.

"That would be fantastic," Sophie agreed with a smile, as she returned Karah's embrace.

With both Karah and Grant now having left, Sophie scanned the mass of faces departing the gym. Not only had Brad missed the entire game, but he'd missed most of their date. *If he'd forgotten about her that easily, would he forget that he needed to give her a ride home?* Sophie wondered, stewing with agitation. As she continued analyzing the people in the crowd, she felt extremely vexed. Not only had Brad asked her out on a date and then made other plans during it, but he had promised he would come back and then had never returned! By the time they had arrived at the game, Sophie had pushed the unsavory conversation they'd had at dinner out of her mind, but now the conversation resurfaced to add further proof of the utter disaster their date had been. Sophie was just about to pull out her phone to see if Karah could come back and give her a ride home, when she caught sight of Brad waving in her direction and bounding towards her.

"Soph! I am *so* sorry!" Brad exclaimed, leaping up the stairs two at a time and offering her his arm. "I know I said I would only be gone for a bit, but one thing led to another, and before I knew it...time just slipped away from me. *Please*...tell me you will forgive me," he added, his eyes fighting to remain hopeful. "What can I do to make it up to you?" he asked, his voice apologetic.

Sophie felt her anger and annoyance bubbling within her, but as she looked into Brad's eyes and saw the sincerity of his apology, she took a deep breath, allowing her emotions to simmer, and decided against unleashing her temper. "You can drive me home for starters," she said, forcing a smile.

"Done," Brad agreed, a flicker of relief passing across his gaze. *At least Sophie had spoken to him,* he thought, *even if it was just to convey her desire to be rid of his company. Had he completely ruined his chances with her, or had he merely bruised them?* Brad pondered, dejectedly. *He could tell from the tone of her words that Sophie was upset with him and rightly so, but seeing Sophie again, seeing how charming her company was...well, it could do wonders for his political career! Maybe after he had been mayor for a couple of terms he'd run for the State Legislature or maybe even Governor! Sophie was beautiful...sophisticated...civic-minded...everything she had been in high school, but now even more so! It was seeing her again and spending time in her company, that had reminded him that Sophie was exactly the kind of woman a man in his position needed to have by his side. Oh, how he hoped he had not entirely dashed her growing infatuation with him by his serious blunder.*

"I truly feel awful, Soph," Brad said, forcing himself from his thoughts and hoping to remain in Sophie's good graces. "I will not try to deny it. It was extremely rude and thoughtless of me to schedule business during our date. I promise I will never do it again. Will you please give me another chance to make it up to you?" he asked. He turned and looked hopefully into Sophie's face.

Sophie stopped walking and held Brad's gaze while the crowd continued to disperse around them. "I'll admit I'm angry with you, Brad. You really hurt my feelings. But I've known you forever, and because of that I can forgive you." She turned her gaze from Brad's face, and they continued walking.

"Thank you," Brad breathed a sigh of relief. "I thought that...never mind," he smiled. "I hope you were still able to enjoy the game despite my absence."

Sophie beamed, unable to keep the excitement from flooding her face. "The game was spectacular! It was nerve-racking right down to the final second! It's really a shame you missed it," she remarked, reeling in euphoria as she recalled the final minutes. "Karah and Grant ended up sitting with me, so I wasn't alone," she added.

"Oh," Brad murmured, slowing his pace as they walked across the parking lot. "Are Karah and *Grant* seeing each other then?" *Was it too much to hope that the competition he'd felt threatened by was no longer a rivalry?*

"No," Sophie remarked. "They just happened to meet

up with each other in the concession line." *Why did she still feel relieved by this revelation?*

"Oh," Brad repeated flatly, as he opened the car door for Sophie. Closing the door behind her, he walked around to the driver's side. *That's what you get for hoping,* he thought irritated. *But,* he pondered with a smile, *there just might be something I can do about Sophie's irksome houseguest that could end happily for all parties involved!* As Brad turned on the car, the chagrin he'd only moments ago been feeling began to dissipate, leaving his heart beating delightedly within his chest. *Yes, if his plan worked, he would ensure that Sophie chose him!*

Chapter 14

As Brad drove her home, Sophie's anger melted, and she began filling him in about the incredible performance of the Polar Bears. As she spoke, Brad gave Sophie his undivided attention without interruption. Listening to Sophie's words, her voice lively and bright and her face animated, Brad was mesmerized by the notion that she appeared even more lovely than she had at the beginning of their date.

"Have you decided yet if you'll give me a second chance, Soph?" Brad asked, parking the car and turning towards her when they arrived at her house.

"Yes. My Grandpa always said that everyone deserves a second chance," Sophie replied, feeling her heart increase its pulsing when Brad leaned closer to her and smiled.

"Then I can't wait to take you out again," Brad said softly, leaning closer to Sophie, his face inches from hers.

Sophie felt her heart racing as Brad's eyes held her gaze and his smile broadened. Then lifting his hand to cup her cheek, he leaned forward and kissed her! As his lips met hers, Sophie's mind whirled as a kaleidoscope of thoughts flashed before her. *Brad's lips were soft and warm and his hands gentle. Ever since he'd kissed her at the parade, she had wondered what it would be like to kiss him again, to truly be present in the moment without wondering if they were observed. And now, as Brad deepened their kiss, softly pulling her closer, Sophie noted he was a very good kisser. But even so, something was missing. If Brad was the man for her, she should feel something, something like a spark... something magical... she should have better words to describe the sensation of his lips moving gently against hers, and kissing him back, she should feel a passion that left her breathless and longing for more. Her heart should melt, her lips should feel like a thousand fireworks were erupting...if Brad was the one, the man destined for her, she should not have felt--- nothing.*

"Until our next date," Brad smiled, removing his hand from Sophie's cheek and leaning back against his seat.

Mistaking Sophie's speechlessness as a sign that his kiss had sent her soaring in love-filled delight, Brad helped Sophie out of the car feeling satisfied with his revelation. *Finally, after all these years, he had been able to kiss her not just once but twice!* And smiling to himself, Brad found he rather enjoyed it! Sophie no longer had any family in town, and she did not need to be alone. *He could offer her a new start*, Brad thought, happy at the prospect of feeling needed. They could sell the farm, buy a bigger house in town, one more suitable for the mayor, and Sophie was the perfect woman to have on his arm when he attended political functions. *She was beautiful... intelligent... and civic-minded. Yes*, Brad smiled, relishing in his daydreams once again,

Sophie would make the perfect wife!

Standing on the front porch, Sophie felt dazed and unsure as she watched Brad drive away. Her heart pounded loudly within her chest, reminding her that it was indeed capable of speaking. Hearing the clamoring of its beating, however, filled Sophie with a sense of dishonesty. For even when you wanted them to, she knew, hearts *never* lied. When the taillights of Brad's car disappeared around the bend, Sophie forced herself to tear her gaze from the road, and turning, went inside. It had been a long time since she had been on a date, but even so, she knew what it should feel like to be in love. There was a difference between the infatuation of a crush and the deep connection of love. Sophie had felt the bubbling excitement of attraction, but she had never been in love. *Maybe, she was searching for something that only existed in romance novels and movies,* she thought sadly. Love, more specifically unconditional love, must surely be a myth found only in fairytales. Hanging her coat in the hall closet, Sophie took off her shoes and went into the living room. When she stepped into the room, her attention was drawn to the fireplace.

"What are you doing?" Sophie asked in shock, catching sight of Grant sitting on the hearth with a marshmallow and roasting stick.

"I decided," Grant replied, with a smile, "that whoever wrote the lyrics to, *The Christmas Song,* had it all wrong. You shouldn't roast chestnuts over a fire. You should roast marshmallows and make s'mores. Would you like one?" he offered, holding up the bag of oversized marshmallows sitting beside him.

Sophie covered her mouth with her hand and tried not to laugh. Grant looked entirely silly, but he did seem to have a point. Roasted marshmallows did sound a lot more appetizing than roasted chestnuts. *Besides, something so innocent as roasting marshmallows was completely harmless,* she told herself. *Even if you have to sit next to Grant with his extremely good looks and pleasant-smelling cologne?* she heard a small voice ask, as she quickly forced it from her thoughts.

"Sure," Sophie said, walking over and sitting down on the fireplace. "I haven't had a s'more in years."

"Well," Grant replied, with a smile in his eyes, "you're in for a treat." Popping a couple of marshmallows on the stick, he then proceeded to roast them. "How do you like yours?" he asked.

"Flaming," Sophie grinned, causing Grant to turn and look at her incredulously.

"Seriously? You're one of those *torch it on the outside* people?" he asked, shaking his head in disbelief.

"Guilty," Sophie laughed, as Grant jokingly made a look of disgust before catching the top marshmallow on fire and blowing it out.

"Here you are," Grant laughed. "Charred to perfection!" He slid the marshmallow off the stick and onto a graham cracker. Then pressing a chunk of chocolate and graham cracker on top, handed the s'more to Sophie.

"Oh, thank you!" Sophie exclaimed, taking the s'more and holding it gently between her fingers.

"You're welcome," Grant smiled, then turned back to roasting his marshmallow. "Charred," he chuckled.

"What's wrong with charring it?" Sophie asked, licking the melted chocolate from her fingers.

"Nothing's wrong with it," Grant conceded. "It's just, if you want a really perfect and amazing tasting marshmallow, it takes patience. You can't rush it. Good things come with waiting,"

Sophie thought about Grant's statement. *Was there more meaning behind his words than just simple talk about marshmallows?* she wondered. *Was she like the charred marshmallow? Had she and Brad rushed things because she was back in town and it was almost Christmas? Was that why she was having doubts and analyzing everything? Because they had, in a sense, jumped straight into some hypothetical fire and everything was going to go up in flames?* Sophie felt the tears welling up within her eyes.

"Sophie," Grant uttered. His voice was full of concern as he lay the roasting stick across the bricks and held her gaze. "It's just marshmallows we're talking about."

"I know. I'm just being stupid," Sophie sobbed, wiping her eyes. "I'm fine now, honestly."

Grant continued to look at Sophie uncertainty, but did

not prod her to divulge the real reason she was upset. Instead, rising from the fireplace and offering her his hand, he said, "How about we make some hot chocolate and watch a Christmas movie?"

"That sounds simply wonderful," Sophie smiled, wiping the remaining tears from her cheeks and taking Grant's hand.

Feeling the warmth of Grant's hand against hers as they walked towards the kitchen, Sophie's heart began to flutter. Her hand seemed to fit perfectly within his. Grant's hand was steady and strong, and its somewhat calloused grasp was tender and supportive. *Did she dare chance a glimpse at his face, or would her thoughts betray her?* As they reached the kitchen, Sophie felt her heart flutter again, as she felt Grant release her hand and found herself wishing the walk to the kitchen was longer. This could not be happening! The way she was beginning to feel about Grant was how she was supposed to be feeling about Brad. *Was Grant purposely trying to sabotage her relationship with Brad? Did he even really like her? She had been wrong to allow herself to take his hand. It was causing her nothing but doubt,* Sophie thought in frustration.

"I'll get the baking chocolate from the pantry. If you could grab a couple of mugs from the cupboard, that would be great," Grant remarked.

If Grant was indeed trying to sabotage things, he sure was hiding it well, Sophie decided. "Sure, no problem," she replied. Opening the cupboard, she grabbed two earthenware mugs and set them on the counter.

"The secret to good hot chocolate," Grant began, placing a saucepan on the stove, "is making it with chocolate milk and melted chocolate." He smiled as he poured several cups of chocolate milk into the pan. "Here, you can cut the chocolate into pieces," he added, handing Sophie a bar of baking chocolate.

"Okay, I promise only to eat a little bit of it while I work," Sophie smiled.

"I've got no problem with that so long as you share," Grant returned with a grin.

Why did Grant have to be so charming and likeable? Sophie pondered, as she pulled out a cutting board and knife and proceeded to chop up the chocolate. Ever since she had arrived home, all Grant had ever been to her was cordial, even when she wasn't in the most amiable disposition. *Why was he so determined to be nice to her?*

"Alright, the milk is beginning to steam. It's time to start adding some chocolate," Grant instructed, pulling Sophie from her musing.

"Here it is," Sophie replied, as she brought the cutting board over top of the pan.

"Nope, not yet. It's going to cost you," Grant teased.

"Cost me what?" Sophie asked, raising her eyebrows.

"Why a piece of chocolate of course," Grant laughed.

"Oh, of course," Sophie smiled. "I'd forgotten about

taking a piece myself."

"Add away," Grant remarked, through his bite of chocolate.

Grant continued stirring the milk as Sophie slowly began adding the chocolate. It didn't take long for the chocolate pieces to begin melting, and Grant and Sophie watched as spirals of dark-chocolate began appearing within the mixture, swirling in mouthwatering wisps of delight.

"It's almost ready," Grant declared, giving the hot chocolate a final stir before removing it from the heat. "Finished!"

"It smells so delicious!" Sophie acclaimed, as she breathed in the chocolatey aroma.

Ladling out the hot chocolate, Grant handed Sophie her mug. "Cheers," he grinned, clicking his mug against hers.

"Cheers," Sophie echoed. Taking a sip of her cocoa. Sophie's senses tingled---*heaven!* It was absolutely a chocolate lover's' pure heaven! Words could not even begin to describe the impeccable blending of sweet and bitter chocolates. If the hot chocolate had not already been liquid, Sophie was sure it would have melted in her mouth!

"What do you think?" Grant asked, surveying Sophie with interest.

"It is absolutely sublime! The richness, and smoothness…," Sophie's words trailed, and she saw the delight gleaming within Grant's eyes.

"I'm glad you like it," Grant murmured happily. "So,

should we start a movie?" he asked, his voice full of childlike anticipation.

"Absolutely!" Sophie declared.

Holding her warm beverage in hand, Sophie smiled as she walked with Grant back into the living room. The fire was crackling brightly in the hearth, and as she sat down on the couch, Sophie felt content. Taking a sip of her hot chocolate, she watched Grant pull the DVD from the shelf and place it in the player. *How did he seem to know exactly what she needed?* Sophie mused, as Grant skipped past the previews. *Was she really that easy to read, or was Grant just somehow extremely perspective?* Sophie's thoughts, however, were quickly quelled when Grant turned around. The force of his smile caused Sophie to choke on the sip of hot chocolate she had taken, and she suddenly felt lightheaded. When Grant smiled, it was almost...*angelic.* As he walked towards her and sat down beside her, Sophie's heart began to flutter wildly, and she felt the heat rising within her cheeks. Captivated, Sophie was barely aware that the movie had begun, as Grant continued to smile at her side.

As the movie played, Sophie found herself unable to pay attention. Not only did she keep wondering what Grant was thinking, but she found herself fretting about the possibility that her breath smelled like a walking-taco. *What was wrong with her? Why on earth had she allowed herself to eat something like that? Her heart fluttered within her chest. Did she dare glance over at Grant, or did she keep pretending she was watching the movie? Was Grant pretending too?* The ending credits began to play, and Sophie realized she could no longer avoid Grant. She turned to look at him, and her heart began racing even faster. Grant's deep-green eyes met her gaze, and the smile that spread across his face...Sophie felt faint. She needed to get some air..."Goodnight, Grant," she uttered quickly, rising from the couch. *Too fast! If she was not careful, her knees might buckle beneath her, then what would Grant think?* Sophie thought frazzled.

"Goodnight, Sophie," Grant returned gently, rising to his feet. "I'll see you in the morning."

Sophie nodded, then before she could say anything stupid, dashed up the stairs as fast as her legs would allow.

Chapter 15

hy couldn't it be Monday yet? Sophie thought, covering her face with her pillow. She had to get out of this house, or she might possibly start falling for the wrong guy! Brad was who she was supposed to be in love with. Brad, yes he had changed, but he was still Brad, the Brad she had known for years. *Why was she even entertaining thoughts about Grant? Was she trying to sabotage herself?* Reluctantly getting out of bed, Sophie knew she could not stay in her bedroom forever. Not only was hiding ridiculous, but she had a farm to run. Descending the stairs in a pair of work jeans and a sweater, Sophie was annoyed to find that Grant had once again awoken before her. *Well*, she thought, heading to the mud-room and jamming her feet into her boots, *maybe I can still beat him to the chores.*

"Good morning," Grant said cheerfully, popping his head around the corner. "I've got breakfast on the table if you're hungry."

"Thanks," Sophie blurted. "But I think I'll take care of the cattle first."

"No need," Grant uttered. "I thought you might need to sleep in a bit, so I already feed them," he added casually. As Sophie looked up at him, the gratitude Grant had been expecting was not the emotion present on her face.

"How am I supposed to start managing the farm on my own if you keep doing things before I have a chance!" Sophie exclaimed haughtily.

"I'm sorry. I didn't mean to...look, I was just trying to be nice," Grant muttered.

"Well stop being nice. I don't want you to be nice to me," Sophie replied. *Grant had to stop being nice to her. He had to stop making her feel so special. He had to allow her to give Brad a chance!*

"Here's your coffee," Grant said, a flash of hurt within his eyes, as he set the coffee mug on the bench next to Sophie. "You can get your breakfast yourself," he added, before leaving.

Watching Grant leave, Sophie felt like such a jerk. *What had come over her? Not only had she been rude, but she had been intentionally cruel.* Feeling her stomach squirm with guilt, Sophie knew her Grandpa would have been ashamed of her behavior.

"Grant! Wait! I'm sorry," Sophie hollered, as she tugged her boots off and headed towards the kitchen. "I was rude. You've been nothing but kind to me, and I was horrible," she declared, bursting into the vacant kitchen. *Where was he? Oh, what had she done?* "Grant!" Sophie exclaimed frantically, abandoning the kitchen and heading to the living room. Arriving at her destination, relief swept over Sophie as she glimpsed Grant sitting on the sofa and tying a ribbon around a box of chocolates.

"I'm sorry I was rude," Sophie apologized, as she took a step into the living room. "I...I behaved very badly. Is there some way I can make it up to you?" she asked hesitantly, as she watched Grant pick up another box of chocolates and again tie a ribbon around it. "What are you doing?" she asked, confused by Grant's actions.

Grant paused what he was doing and looked up at Sophie, his green eyes coolly assessing her face. Her expression seemed genuinely remorseful. There was no sarcasm in her words or lack of eye-contact in her gaze. He would be a fool not to forgive her. But even so, Grant could not quell a recollection from the past from welling up within him. *Would he regret forgiving Sophie? Would he once again be blinded by love?* He watched Sophie continue to stare at him waiting for a reply. *She deserved forgiveness. No one could behave perfectly*, he knew. Forcing the doubts from his mind, Grant's eyes softened. "Yes. I forgive you," he said. *The life that flooded back into Sophie's face was worth every word he had spoken,* Grant thought, observing the smile that animated her features.

"Thank you!" Sophie gushed. "Now, will you tell me what you are doing?" she asked in interest.

Grant smiled. "I'm tying ribbons on a few boxes of chocolates to take over to the nursing home this afternoon. I called ahead to find out which residence will most likely not receive any visitors this Christmas, and the receptionist at the front desk gave me five names," he explained.

Sophie stared at Grant in amazement. *Could he be any kinder or more thoughtful? Was he for real? Surely, men like him did not exist except for in the pages of Jane Austen style novels...* Sophie held Grant's gaze, pondering his character. "How can you be so thoughtful?" she asked aloud.

"Well, I can't take credit for it really," Grant replied, his eyes dancing brightly. "My Grandmother used to visit people in the nursing home at Christmas every year. When I was in elementary school, she started taking me with her. She would pack a purse full of little boxes of chocolates, and we'd spend time talking with and giving the chocolates to those we visited. My Grandma said she read about a man who did this in a book once, and after that she began making visiting people in the nursing home an annual Christmas tradition," Grant finished.

"Your Grandma sounds like a wonderful woman," Sophie said with a smile.

"She definitely was," Grant agreed. "I'm going to stop at the nursing home after Mass. Would you care to join me?" he asked. Then teasingly, and somewhat serious, he added, "You did ask how you could make it up to me."

Sophie could not help but smile at his quirk. "Well, now that you put it that way, how can I possibly say no," she replied.

After Mass, as they drove to the nursing home, Sophie could not help but feel a little nervous. It was silly, she knew. She had volunteered with charitable foundations to build houses for those in need and assisted at a soup kitchen in college, so service work was not something she had never done before, but the idea of spending time in prolonged conversation with a total stranger was a bit daunting. *What was she supposed to talk about?* As Grant turned into the driveway and slowly made his way towards the entrance, the nerves Sophie had quietly been trying to quell fluttered within her, and she hoped Grant could not see how anxious she was becoming.

"Here we are," Grant declared, cutting the engine and unfastening his seatbelt.

"Grant, I...I'm not sure I'm going to be any good at this. I mean...I don't even know what I'm supposed to say," Sophie stammered, her eyes staring at Grant with a look of uncertainty.

"Sophie," Grant smiled. "Don't worry about what to say, just be yourself," he assured. "Sometimes just listening is more important than speaking anyway. Everyone deserves and wants to have someone truly listen to them."

"How are you so wise?" Sophie asked, staring at Grant in awe. "I mean, I've read hundreds of books through the years about various people and cultures, but you...you really *understand* what's important to people."

"I guess I just spent a lot of time with my Grandma," Grant remarked. "And she passed on her wisdom. Sometimes I think we get so caught up with our own lives that we forget the wisdom of the older generations. If you just look into the eyes of the elderly, you'll see they're willing to share their wisdom if we just give them a chance and listen. Every life has dignity and deserves to be treated with it. Now, I think we should probably head inside?" he continued with a smile.

"You're a mystery, Grant Bakesfield," Sophie uttered, opening the door and climbing out. "You're full of surprises."

"A *mystery*," Grant chuckled, grabbing the chocolate boxes off the console. "I think I like the sound of that."

As they entered the lobby, they were met by the sound of classical Christmas melodies playing softly on a player piano. Approaching the front desk, Sophie took in the sight of a large Christmas tree, adorned in twinkling lights and red garland, shimming warmly as a few of the home's residences sat in the sitting area around it, talking and playing cards.

"Good afternoon," the receptionist said brightly, as Grant and Sophie arrived at the desk. "How may I be of assistance?" the woman asked.

"Hi, I'm Grant Bakesfield. And this is Sophie Marten," Grant replied. "I called yesterday asking which of your residence might not receive any visitors this Christmas and…"

"Oh!" the receptionist interrupted. "They will be so happy to see you. My boss told me you would be coming today. It's so nice of you, Mr. Bakesfield, to come each

Christmas."

"It's nothing," Grant replied quickly, embarrassed by the compliment.

"Oh, but it's not," the receptionist continued. "What you're doing is extremely kind." Then turning to Sophie, she added, "You've got yourself a good man here, Honey."

Now it was Sophie's turn to blush. Twice now, people had assumed that she and Grant were a couple. *Was there something they were doing that was giving everyone the wrong impression? Her stomach turned in a somersault as Grant did not deny the lady's assessment and she merely smiled in response. What was wrong with her? Why didn't she correct the receptionist's assertion? Better yet, why hadn't Grant? Did she want to correct the misinterpretation?* Sophie wondered guiltily.

"If you both will just sign in here and leave your driver's licenses at the front desk, I'll give you the names and room numbers of the residence you'll be visiting," the receptionist said cheerfully.

With the list of names and room numbers and their boxes of chocolates in hand, Sophie and Grant headed down the first hallway. As they walked along, a group of elementary-age kids passed by singing Christmas carols, and Sophie's heart warmed recalling when she too had sung Christmas carols here as a kid. Listening to the kids belt the lyrics to *Silent Night*, Sophie was glad that the caroling tradition had not been abandoned over the years. Grant suddenly came to a stop beside her and raised his hand up to the door and knocked.

"Come in," a woman's voice sounded from within the room.

"Hello, Mrs. Brown. I'm Grant, and this here is Sophie. We wanted to stop by and wish you a Merry Christmas and bring you some chocolates. May we come in?" Grant asked.

"Oh, my! That would be wonderful, young man," Mrs. Brown replied, smiling brightly. "I don't get many visitors any more these days. Please, come in," she said, gesturing to the two seats sitting beside the bed.

"Thank you," Grant replied, as he took a seat and extended a box of chocolates to the elderly woman.

Taking the seat beside him, Sophie looked at Grant in amazement. He was so at ease, and so genuine with someone he had just met.

"Oh, milk chocolates! My favorite!" Mrs. Brown gushed, holding the box of chocolates in her hands. "Thank you," she said, her eyes tearing up as she turned to look at Grant and Sophie.

"You're welcome," Grant replied warmly.

"When I was a girl, my dad would give my mom a box of assorted chocolates every Christmas," Mrs. Brown recalled fondly. "My mom would then place a few pieces on a cutting board and cut them into pieces so our whole family could take turns trying the different chocolates and trying to guess the flavors of their fillings. We'd repeat it each night after dinner for the next few days. It was so much fun sitting around the dinner table talking and trying chocolates. I'd almost forgotten how much I loved that tradition," she added.

"That's a wonderful memory," Sophie heard herself saying. She had thought she was only thinking those words, but apparently not.

"Yes. Yes, it is," Mrs. Brown agreed, giving Sophie a motherly smile. "Always make traditions with your family, Dear," Mrs. Brown advised. "Because before you know it, your children will grow up, and you'll hope you've given them a good foundation as they begin their own families."

"I will," Sophie replied, holding the older woman's gaze. *Mrs. Brown's words held so much truth*, she thought, recalling all the holiday traditions in which she and her Grandpa had participated. Besides holiday traditions, they'd also had the silly first day of school tradition of packing her lunch with only items that began with the letter "F." Needless to say, that was pretty complicated, so her lunch tended to be stuffed full of junk foods, which would make Sophie smile and laugh and her teachers stare in horror. *Traditions*, Sophie mused, *brought people together. Traditions helped make a family a family.*

It was nearly six by the time they finished delivering all their boxes of chocolates. Now, sitting in the truck, Sophie turned to Grant. "Thank you," she said, hoping her voice conveyed the true depth of her gratitude.

"Thank you for what?" Grant asked, his eyebrows furrowing in question.

"Thank you for helping me to remember that listening and giving is more rewarding than receiving," Sophie replied.

Grant smiled at Sophie, his deep-green eyes twinkling merrily. "When we take the time, during Advent, to slow down as we wait for Christmas, we not only help spread hope, peace, joy, and love in our lives and hearts, but we help pass the fullness of these emotions to others we spend time with and encounter." Then turning on the engine, Grant began driving them home, as Sophie reflected on the truth of his words.

Chapter 16

"I'm glad you were able to come with me today," Grant said, when they arrived back at the farm. *In truth*, he thought to himself, *he was delighted that the assessment he had made over the years about Sophie's kindness had proven to be correct.*

"I am too," Sophie agreed, her deep-russet eyes gleaming with joy like that embodying Dickens' Spirit of Christmas Present. "I only wish I had done something like this sooner," she shared, her expression glowing with sincerity. *Grant had helped her now, in so many ways,* Sophie thought, in admiration. She only hoped that she was able to return his generosity somehow. *Maybe...maybe she could allow him to keep renting his room past the New Year instead of just kicking him out regardless of if he had found new lodgings or not. Yes,* Sophie resolved, *that would be the kind thing to do; that would be exhibiting the Christmas spirit.* It was decided then, Sophie concluded. Grant could stay until he was able to find suitable accommodations regardless of the *imposed* deadline.

"What are you thinking about?" Grant asked, searching Sophie's expression, her features lost in thought.

"Nothing," Sophie lied. Grant raised an eyebrow, implying his disbelief, as Sophie continued watching him silently.

Holding Sophie's gaze, Grant opened his mouth to speak. "It's never too late to start doing something good," he remarked, referring back to their discussion of their visit to the nursing home, instead of prying. "You don't even have to wait until Christmas. I'm sure the folks we met today would welcome a visit from you anytime," he remarked.

"You're right again," Sophie declared, her head slowly shaking back-and-forth in awe at Grant's insightfulness. "Maybe, I should make visiting the people we met today a weekly tradition. Maybe they would even let me record and transcribe some of their stories, so they could be shared and preserved at the town museum as oral history accounts," Sophie wondered aloud, her historian-eyes gleaming with excitement at the prospect of preserving the knowledge and first-hand accounts of her town's older generation.

"Now, that sounds like a fine idea," Grant approved with a grin. "I'm sure they would love getting to share what they know and have experienced with future generations."

"Do you really think so?" Sophie asked, a slight quiver of worry working its way into her excitement.

"Yes, I do," Grant assured. "Anyway, you'll never know until you ask, so don't go assuming rejection," he surmised.

"Alright, I'll ask," Sophie voiced with determination. Having recordings of people who had lived in Sugar Plum, possibly their entire lives, could be the crown jewel of the town's museum, as well as a way that she could give back to the community who had given her so much!

"Okay, *Herodotus,* before you get too excited that you forget to eat, how about we make dinner?" Grant suggested.

Sophie's mouth fell open in astonishment, and she watched as delight spread across Grant's features and his lips pulled into a smile. *How was it possible that Grant had once again amazed her? He was absolutely unfathomable!* Slowly closing her mouth, Sophie followed Grant silently towards the house, staring at his retreating back. *Grant knew the man who is considered to be the father of history. Impressive...very impressive!*

"Since it's kind of late, I was thinking about making something relatively simple for dinner. How does grilled-cheese and tomato soup sound?" Grant asked, once they were inside.

"That sounds yummy," Sophie murmured, still in shock at Grant's historical knowledge.

"Good! I was thinking of adulting them up a bit. That is if that's okay with you?" Grant remarked, his eyes holding Sophie's gaze questioningly.

"*Adulting* them up?" Sophie repeated. "What exactly does that mean? A grilled-cheese is a pretty amazing sandwich. How can you possibly make cheesy perfection any better?" she inquired, gazing at Grant with skepticism.

"By adding sautéed onions, two types of cheese, a

slice of tomato, and just a tad of mustard," Grant replied without hesitation. "Just talking about it makes me hungry," he laughed.

"That sounds... umm...*interesting*," Sophie remarked, "but I'm willing to try your *concoction*," she added, her eyes dancing brightly. Grant's company, with his many surprises, was something that was proving more and more enjoyable by the second.

"Well then, let's get cooking," Grant declared in satisfaction.

Once in the kitchen, Grant proceeded to pull out the frying pan and other ingredients. "The secret," he said with a smile, as he unwrapped the loaf of bread, "is to butter both slices of bread with just enough butter to give them that golden-toasted-look and savory flavor."

Sophie watched as Grant liberally began spreading butter across four slices of bread and then proceeded to slice an onion up into rings.

"Would you mind sautéing these?" Grant asked, setting the onion laden skillet on top of the stove and pouring a tablespoon of olive oil into the pan.

"Sure, I'll give it a try," Sophie replied. "I'm not going to guarantee that I won't burn them though," she added, pulling a wooden spoon from the utensil canister on the counter and stirring the onions.

"Don't worry," Grant encouraged. "The more caramelized they are the better they will taste. Here, add some pepper and a little bit of garlic powder to them," he instructed.

Sophie shook the spices over the pan and gave the onions another gentle stir with the spoon. The mouthwatering aroma of cooking onions tickled her nose as she listened to the sizzling sound emitting from the pan. *Even if you were not a great cook, like herself, the smell of sautéed onions made you appear to be a chef extraordinaire,* Sophie smiled to herself.

"Those look excellent!" Grant said after a while, peering into the frying pan. "Now, if you can scoop a few of them out and place them on top of the cheese and tomato I have over here, we can get the sandwiches in the pan," he remarked.

"How did you come up with this recipe?" Sophie asked, spooning onions onto the sandwiches.

"I had a great-uncle who used to like putting a slice of tomato on his grilled-cheese sandwiches, and my Grandpa used to put onion and mustard on his. I decided to combine it all one time and the result turned out to be delicious," Grant shared, as he put the tops on the sandwiches and transferred them to the frying pan.

"With a resume like that," Sophie said, "they are bound to be delicious! Is there anything else I can do to help?" she asked, thoroughly enjoying herself.

"Yes. If you wouldn't mind getting the tomato soup going, that would be great. There's a couple of cans in the pantry," Grant replied.

While they waited for the soup and sandwiches to finish cooking, Sophie found herself drawn to conversation. She suddenly wanted to know as much about Grant as she possibly could. *Why would such a kind and thoughtful man, and a man who knew his way around the kitchen,* Sophie marveled, impressed, *up and leave the city only to come to a small-town where he only knew two people? What had made Grant want to leave the life he had always known? What was he looking for? Had he found it?*

"Grant," Sophie uttered, twirling the soup in the saucepan. "There's so much about you that I feel like I don't know. I feel like you know me already so well even though we've only just met," she admitted.

Grant pressed the spatula against a sandwich in the frying pan and looked up. "I know you want to know why I left Nashville, but I'm not ready to talk about that yet. And I know that's not what you wanted to hear," he added, his voice serious, as he watched Sophie's face waiting for her reaction.

Sophie bit her lower lip and stared into Grant's deep-jade eyes. *Could she accept his answer and be content to remain curious? Surely, everyone was entitled to their own secrets and had the right to share them in their own time or never at all...* Sophie assessed Grant's expression. A subtle pain tinged the softness of his gaze, but within his eyes Sophie also read that she was entitled to know the truth, that he would share with her his reason for coming to Sugar Plum when he was ready. For her to continue to pry or begrudge him, Sophie knew, would not solve anything.

Taking a deep breath, Sophie replied. "Why don't you tell me about your favorite Christmas memory instead. Remember how I told you about mine?" Her dark-brown eyes gazed at Grant gently, as she allowed a smile to spread across her face.

"Of course," Grant agreed, a smile again present upon his face as he flipped the sandwiches in the skillet. "Let's see," he mused, resting the spatula against the side of the pan. "I think the year I got a sled for Christmas, when I was probably seven or eight, was one of my favorite Christmases," he recalled fondly, a twinkle shimmering within his eyes. "I was so excited and wanted to ride it right away, but unfortunately we didn't have a single speck of snow that year."

"Hang on," Sophie interrupted in shock. "You said this was one of your favorite Christmases...but there was no snow...you didn't get to ride your sled. How can this be..."

"Yes, I said there was no snow. But I didn't say I didn't get to *ride* my sled," Grant interrupted with a chuckle; a smile dancing across his face as he raised a hand to his chin in thought.

"Now, I'm confused," Sophie blurted, trying to make sense of the crypticness of Grant's words. "How could you possibly ride your sled without any snow?" she asked.

"My folks saw how upset I was, so while my brother and I were playing with his new train set, they snuck outside," Grant said. "When they came back in and asked me to bring my sled outside, I was flabbergasted. It was pretty apparent that snow had not fallen in the last half-hour. When I walked outside, my mouth fell open. It had to have been a priceless expression for my parents to witness. Looking past their smiling faces, I saw the mudslide they had made down the hill in the backyard. *Well, what are you waiting for? Get your brother and the two of you go mudsleding,* my dad remarked excitedly. My brother and I zipped down the hill at ridiculous speeds and got covered in mud. I still don't think I ever had as much fun as I did that day, and I know I've never been muddier," Grant finished, placing the sandwiches on plates and grinning.

Taking the plate Grant handed her, Sophie smiled at him. *What a wonderful memory. The love Grant's parents had for him had undoubtedly helped make him into the kindhearted man he was today.* "Thank you for sharing that with me," Sophie said, as they walked over to the kitchen table.

"You're welcome," Grant replied. "Now, on a more serious note, I've got to know if this is the best grilled-cheese you've ever tasted," he remarked. Then lifting his own sandwich into his hands, Grant watched as Sophie took her first bite.

As the warm buttery bread and melted cheese made

contact with her taste buds, Sophie chewed silently trying to find the right words to do such a delicious sandwich justice. *The savory blend of butter... the boldness of the variety of cheeses...the fresh juiciness of the tomato and tang of mustard...*Words could never truly describe the sensation of such blended tastes. Putting a hand to her heart, Sophie smiled at Grant as she continued chewing the bite she had taken. *Whoever said the way to a man's heart was to his stomach had it all wrong. Clearly it was the way to a woman's heart*, Sophie thought, gazing at the handsome chef sitting across the table.

Chapter 17

*T*he time she had spent at the nursing home with
*Grant...the people they had met and talked with... the
stories that had been shared...*Try as she might,
Sophie could not keep her mind from wandering. *Not
only had Sunday afternoon been an unexpected eye-
opening experience for her, but dinner with Grant....
Cooking with him... Talking with him...Focus, Sophie. It's
Monday. You're at work. You've got to focus!* Sophie chided
herself, as she finally finished transcribing and cataloging the
box of letters she had been working on before the weekend.

Turning her attention to a box of photographs,
Sophie began rummaging through the faded portraits seeking
to identify locations and people. The task, however, she soon
found to be excruciatingly difficult, since try as she might,
she could not stop herself from daydreaming about Grant and
Brad. *She had forgiven Brad for his blunderous date and
agreed to give him another chance, but...* Sophie still could
not shake the feeling that when they had kissed...*well, it just
had not been as romantic as she had imagined, and nor did
she experience the feelings she had been sure should
accompany such a display of affection. Was she merely over
analyzing things? Brad was a good guy, a guy she had
known for a long time. But was she attracted to him?* Grant,

on the other hand, seemed to cause her heart to flutter uncontrollably, and try as she might, Sophie could not suppress the secret desire that she wondered what it would feel like to kiss him! *She was a complete and utter mess!* Ellen popped into her office, and Sophie was glad for the interruption. Her coworker's appearance could not have come at a better moment.

"Sophie, I was listening to the weather, and it sounds like the ice-storm they have been tracking since this weekend is supposed to arrive later this evening. They're projecting about two inches of ice and then four to five inches of snow on top of that," Ellen shared, her face looking worried. "I sure hope it's not like the storm we had several years back," she continued. "Gerald and I lost power for a week!"

Sophie remembered, all too well, the storm Ellen was talking about. She and her Grandpa had lost power too. If there was one thing Sophie knew for certain about Kentucky weather, it was that ice-storms, when they hit, were crippling. Entire communities came to a standstill, and power outages were almost a guarantee.

"We can close up early," Sophie said, watching relief replace Ellen's worried expression. "If it turns out to be not as bad as they're predicting, we will open up tomorrow later in the day."

"Thank you, Sophie," Ellen smiled. "I'll let you get back to your work."

Even though she recalled the severity of the ice-storm

Ellen was referring to, Sophie was doubtful the storm would be as bad as the meteorologists were anticipating. Kentucky's winters were indeed a strange phenomenon. One day it could be 60 degrees, and the next day drop to a high in the 30s. Some winters the state received lots of snow accumulation, and others none. And then… there were the storms that happened every five to ten years that dumped a foot or more of snow and ice. Sophie's phone rang, distracting her from her thoughts. Glancing at the screen on her desk, she saw it was Brad.

"Hi, Brad," Sophie answered, walking over to the window in her office and gazing out.

"Hey, Soph," Brad replied brightly, on the other end. "I was wondering if you would want to come over to my house tonight and make dinner together?"

"Sure, that could be fun," Sophie replied. "But what about the storm that's projected to arrive?"

"Oh, I don't think we have to worry about that," Brad assured. "We'll probably end up only getting a dusting. You know how everyone goes crazy around here anticipating 'snowmageddon' at the first mention of snow," he laughed.

"True," Sophie replied, recalling the barren bread shelves and milk aisles at the grocery store when snow had been forecasted as a kid.

"Great! I'll text you my address. See you at six," Brad said, before hanging up.

"See you at six," Sophie replied into the empty room,

as she removed the phone from her ear and stared at it in her hands. *Brad probably didn't realize how rude he'd been just now*, she thought. *Why was she making excuses for him? He should have waited for her reply.*

At four o'clock, Sophie and Ellen locked up and headed home. As she drove, Sophie peered occasionally at the sky. The clouds were definitely growing and getting darker. Their smoky-gray hue gave the ominous impression that a storm was looming and undoubtedly coming. Arriving at the farm, Sophie saw that Grant was home early too. *Was everyone in town overreacting, or was it possible they really were in for one of the state's big storms?* Sophie hung her keys on the key-rack and then headed towards the kitchen. Grant was still wearing his coat and drinking a cup of coffee.

"Good, you're home early too," he said, sounding relieved as he set his mug on the counter. "We need to get the cattle in the barn before the storm arrives."

"Oh, of course," Sophie sputtered, embarrassed that she had forgotten about the herd.

"When you're ready, we can head out," Grant remarked.

"We can go now," Sophie replied. "We need to be done before six."

"Is that when they're now expecting the storm to hit?" Grant questioned.

"No, but that's when I'm supposed to be at Brad's," Sophie remarked.

Grant's eyes narrowed. "Brad expects you to drive to his house when there is a snowstorm coming? A *gentleman* would never ask a lady to do such a thing," he blurted, his words dripping with disdain.

"Brad *is* a gentleman," Sophie rounded defiantly. "He would not ask me to drive tonight if he really thinks the storm is going to be as bad as the weathermen are implying."

"No," Grant retorted. "A gentleman would not ask a lady to drive to his house, knowing very well, that she will get stranded by the snow and be forced to stay the night."

Sophie's cheeks reddened at the implication of Grant's assessment of Brad's character and her apparent lack of such a realization. "I have known Brad *forever*. You have no right to judge the people I chose to spend time with," Sophie rounded angrily.

Grant opened his mouth to reply, then closing it again, shook his head instead. "I'll be outside when you're ready," he muttered, then turned and walked out the door.

Sophie stood, fuming a few moments longer, before she retrieved her coat from the closet and went outside. The wind was certainly starting to pick up. Her hair swept across her face, and she hastily stuffed the loose strands beneath her hat. *Maybe she should call Brad and reschedule. No,* Sophie thought, with annoyance, *if she did that, Grant would assume she had agreed with his ridiculous judgments and she most certainly was not going to give him that satisfaction;* as much as she did not want to admit it, Sophie knew her pride had definitely been bruised.

When Sophie had left work, Ellen had told her the storm was not expected to arrive until later in the evening. *If she left Brad's by eight, she was sure to get home before the roads turned hazardous*, she reassured herself. As they began rounding up the cattle and steering them towards the barn, Sophie felt small ice-drops begin to pelt her cheeks. Looking up at the sky, she watched as the faint droplets began to descend more steadily. Sophie turned towards the barn nearing in the distance, and caught Grant looking at her. Refusing to meet his gaze, she continued working to guide the cattle forward. She was not about to let Grant see the worry that was slowly forming within her.

When they reached the barn and the last of the cattle had been guided in, Sophie sprinted towards the house. The ice that had been increasing in its furry, had now become mixed with large whipping snowflakes, that swirling around Sophie as she ran, made it hard for her to see. *It is just a little bit of snow*, Sophie told herself. She had been up east the past five years and driven through her fair share of winter weather. Driving in this should not be anything she could not handle. *Still…* Sophie could not shake the sense of uneasiness that was slowly beginning to creep within her.

After a quick shower, Sophie dressed in a pair of jeans and a sweater. Hurrying down the stairs, she grabbed a scarf and gloves, then pulled on a pair of boots and her hat. It was 5:40. The sun was almost setting and the snow, instead of letting up, had begun to fall with more force. Grabbing her phone and purse, Sophie braced herself for the arctic blast as she pulled open the door and darted towards her car.

Starting the engine, Sophie rubbed her gloved hands together then turned on the heat. As the windshield wipers slid back and forth across the glass, she saw that the road was already covered with a light layer of snow. Putting the car in drive, Sophie slowly stepped on the gas and began making her way down the driveway. She heard the soft crunch of snow and ice beneath the wheels, but their traction seemed to be okay. She hesitantly turned onto the road, and turning up the wiper speed, continued driving. *Why was she being so crazy? Was it because she felt like she had to prove a point to Grant? Prove that Brad was a good and decent man and that she was a good judge of character? Why was she so determined to make things work with Brad and not give Grant a chance? What was she afraid of?*

Sophie had driven about five miles, when her heart jumped within her chest. She was turning the bend, when she felt the wheels slipping and the car begin to hydroplane! Holding tightly onto the steering wheel, Sophie clenched her fingers against its leather, and fighting with all her might; tried to hold the car steady. But it was no use. She was sliding uncontrollably! She couldn't hold the wheel steady. The car turned, and she was sent spinning to the side, careening straight towards a ditch! Sophie closed her eyes. *This was it; she was going to die!* She was jolted forward as the car slammed to a halt. Opening her eyes, Sophie stared around her. *She was okay! Her car was not, but she was miraculously okay!*

Cutting the engine, Sophie pulled out her phone.

"Hey, Soph," Brad sounded on the line.

"Brad, I'm so sorry, but I'm not going to be able to make it tonight," Sophie said, her voice and body shaking with adrenaline.

"Really? Soph, I'm sure the roads are still okay now. Besides, if they get too bad, you can always stay the night at my place," Brad offered.

"That's exactly what Grant said you would say," Sophie blurted, before she could stop herself. She heard silence on the other end of the line.

"Just what else did *Grant* say?" Brad replied, his voice filled with resentment. "Is that why you're canceling Sophie? Because some guy, you hardly know, suggested I'm some ill-intentioned scoundrel? Why I..."

"No, Brad, I'm canceling," Sophie stated, feeling a bit aggravated, "because I'm currently sitting stuck in a ditch five miles from my house."

"You know, the more I think about *Grant*, the more I don't...wait, what?" Brad uttered; his voice suddenly filled with concern. "Are you okay? Are you hurt?"

"I'm fine," Sophie replied, putting a hand to her forehead. "My car's not, but I'm okay."

"I'm glad to hear that," Brad breathed in relief.

"Thanks," Sophie murmured. "I'm going to have to let you go, I've got to try and hike back before the weather gets any worse."

"Are you sure that's the best thing to do?" Brad asked, worry filling his words.

"Well, I can't very well stay here all night," Sophie declared.

"Okay, true. But if I don't hear from you in an hour, I'm phoning the police to come get you," Brad said protectively.

"I'll text you when I'm back home," Sophie promised, before hanging up.

Getting out of the car, Sophie shivered. The temperature had dropped since the sun set, and the snow was falling even more rapidly than before. Using the flashlight on her phone to guide her, Sophie prayed its battery would last, as she began her cold, long, trek back towards the farm.

Chapter 18

Grant had watched Sophie leave. He had tried to convey his concern for her but had unfortunately chosen the wrong method. Now, pacing back and forth across the living room, he turned on the television and watched the weather report.

"Motorists are being advised to stay off the roads unless absolutely necessary," the meteorologist urged. "With ice initially falling, and snow now accumulating rapidly, roads are quickly becoming hazardously slick. As gusty winds continue to blow from the north and mix with the falling snow, conditions are sure to cause perilous whiteouts. Current projections of accumulations are..."

Grant turned off the television and stood looking out the window. He could barely see the driveway. *If this was what the driveway looked like in only a few short hours*, he thought anxiously, *he could only imagine the condition of the roads*. Grabbing his keys off the hook, he quickly pulled on his coat and headed out into the storm.

As he slowly drove along the road, Grant looked for Sophie's car. *He shouldn't have let her go; he should have tried better to convince her that it was too dangerous. If anything happened to her, he would never forgive himself.* Grant was trying not to think the worst, when his eyes caught sight of an image that made him breathe a thankful sigh of relief. There, walking towards him along the side of the road softly illuminated by the flashlight on her phone, was Sophie!

Grant parked his truck in the middle of the road, and without turning off the engine, jumped out of the vehicle and bounded towards Sophie. He was so grateful she was okay, that without carrying what she might say, he lifted her up in his arms and carried her back to the truck.

Sophie's teeth chattered, as leaning against Grant's chest, she felt the soft beat of his heart and his warmth wrapping itself around her. She braced herself for Grant to chide her for being stupid and stubborn and was shocked when instead she heard him whispered softly into her ear, "I'm so glad you are not hurt." As Grant opened the cab door and gently set her in the seat, Sophie watched him, sure she was dreaming, walk in front of the truck and climb into the driver's seat beside her.

"How did you know I needed help?" Sophie asked, finally finding her words.

Grant turned towards Sophie and held her gaze, the concern and relief in his eyes vivid, but there was something else present, something Sophie was sure she was imagining. *She must be mistaken. Grant could no possible feel what she thought she was seeing, could he?* Looking into his eyes, Sophie suddenly felt like she was glimpsing a part of his soul, and what she saw was compassionate, honorable, and good.

"I heard on the news that motorists were being advised to stay off the roads. I was worried about you," Grant replied, afraid that if he took his eyes off Sophie she would no longer be sitting beside him.

"Thank you," Sophie murmured softly, her heart fluttering. *Why did Grant make her feel so flustered?* Then she heard a small voice remind her, *hearts never lie.*

Driving cautiously, Grant got them back to the farm safely. Gazing upon the outline of the house, its frosty windows twinkling with light, Sophie was never more relieved to be home. Grant got out of the car, and opening the door for Sophie, helped her down. Sophie had just begun to warm up on the drive, and the cold winter air instantly sent chills coursing through her body. Dashing as quickly as they could, Grant and Sophie trudged up the front steps and burst through the front door. Quickly slamming the door behind them, they stood, covered in snow, looking at one another with thankfulness and relief.

"Why don't you go and sit by the fire and warm up," Grant suggested, removing his coat and shaking the snow from its sleeves. "I'll go make us some hot chocolate," he added.

Sophie nodded and began unbuttoning her jacket. "That sounds marvelous," she agreed, her teeth chattering as she pulled her hands from her gloves and felt her fingers begin to thaw.

After Grant excused himself to the kitchen, Sophie

made her way into the living room and sat down on the hearth. The fire was crackling lively in the grate, and as she rubbed her hands together in front of it, she felt its warmth begin to radiate throughout her frozen body. The heat felt so wonderful. *If Grant had not set off to find her*, Sophie shuddered, *who knew how much longer she would have had to endure the freezing temperature*. Sophie heard the wind began to howl against the windowpanes, and she was grateful to be warm and safe inside.

Pulling her phone out from the pocket of her jeans, Sophie remembered she needed to text Brad so he wouldn't send a search and rescue party out looking for her. She only had to wait a minute, before she felt a soft vibration signaling Brad's response. Glancing at the screen she read, *"Glad you made it back fine. You had me worried. How does rescheduling dinner the day before Christmas Eve sound?"* Sophie's fingers moved nimbly across the keyboard. *"Works for me,"* she typed, then returned her phone back to her pocket.

"One piping mug of cocoa," Grant smiled, walking into the room and handing Sophie a brimming mug topped with marshmallows. "I thought you'd like it right away, so it's made with instant mix instead of melted chocolate. I hope that's okay."

"Thanks," Sophie smiled, wrapping her hands around the mug and bringing it up to her lips. "Oh," Sophie breathed happily, feeling the beverage's heat trickle down her throat and warm her chest. "This hits the spot!"

"I may have also added a little bourbon to it," Grant grinned, taking a sip from his mug. "I thought after walking in the cold, you might need it."

"You thought right!" Sophie exclaimed, her smile animating her entire face.

"Cheers to being safe and warm," Grant said, clinking his glass against Sophie's.

"Cheers," Sophie echoed.

"If the snow keeps up," Sophie remarked thoughtfully, taking another sip of her hot chocolate, "we might end up with a white Christmas after all."

"That would be nice," Grant replied.

"Speaking of a white Christmas, have you seen the movie? You know, with Bing Crosby?" Sophie asked.

"Don't judge me too harshly, but no," Grant admitted.

"Oh, I'm definitely judging," Sophie laughed. "How on earth have you not seen it?"

"Musicals aren't really my thing," Grant replied honestly.

"Well, we are just going to have to rectify that blasphemy and change your mind," Sophie continued, rising from the fireplace and heading over to the television. "Here we are," she smiled, holding up the film and opening its case.

"If I'm going to be *forced* to watch this…," Grant chuckled, feigning torture.

"Oh, you are," Sophie interrupted, her eyes sparkling.

"At least give me a second to get us something to eat," he added, a smile filling his face.

"That sounds great! I'm starving!" Sophie replied, smiling as she felt her stomach grumble. "Give me a second, and I can help," she added, popping the movie into the player.

After making turkey sandwiches and broccoli and cheddar soup, Grant and Sophie returned to the living room, ready to enjoy their meal.

"Just so you know, I'm going to be singing along with all the songs," Sophie warned with a grin, as she sat down on the couch. "When I hear the song, *White Christmas*, it reminds me to never give up hoping for a white Christmas," she declared, her face beaming with hopefulness. "You're going to love the film. I just know it!" she added, before taking a bite of her sandwich.

"If you say so," Grant chuckled, raising an eyebrow as he sat down beside Sophie, his heart beating happily within his chest. *Yes, he would undoubtedly love the movie,* Grant smiled to himself, *because spending time with Sophie was all he had been hoping for.*

Chapter 19

When Sophie awoke in the morning, she lay in bed smiling. Watching *White Christmas* with Grant had been so much fun. Grant even admitted that he enjoyed the movie and it was better than he had expected. *Seriously,* Sophie laughed to herself, *how could anyone watch White Christmas and not love it?* Forcing herself to abandon her warm jumble of quilts, Sophie slid on her slippers and headed excitedly to the window. She could not wait to see how much snow had actually fallen! She knew it was silly, but every time it snowed, she still experienced the same jubilant excitement of a kid hoping for a snow day. Gazing through the frost strewn casement, Sophie's mouth dropped open. What had appeared overnight was not merely a few inches of snow, but rather a winter wonderland like those created only on the fronts of Christmas cards!

Everything lay covered as if by a soft down blanket, tranquil and sparkling in the soft morning light. As the sun rays danced across the frosted earth, the snow suddenly gave the appearance that thousands of diamonds and glittering quartz were hidden within its drifts. *Enchanting. Simply enchanting,* were the only words Sophie could think of that could adequately describe the scene before her, as a smile spread across her face. Snow held a magic all its own. Its frozen serenity beckoned to the hearts of young and old alike, holding them spellbound in fanciful wonder, for snow had a way of always bringing out one's inner-child no matter how old they were.

It was as she continued staring at the alluring landscape, that Sophie felt the sudden urge that she needed to get outside and become a part of the winter wonderland as soon as possible. Hurriedly dressing, she bounded down the stairs, feeling as light as a feather and as happy as a kid on Christmas morning. She would grab something quick for breakfast, something she could eat as she pulled on her coat. Right now, what was most important was to not miss a second of such a picturesque snowfall! After feeding the cows, she was going to plop down and make a snow angel, then maybe a snowman, and then maybe go for a sled ride! As Sophie rounded the corner of the stairs and burst into the kitchen, the smile that illuminated her face was unearthly.

"Good morning," Grant greeted, Sophie's smile holding him captivated. *How did she manage to look more lovely each time he saw her? Her chestnut curls...her deep-brown eyes...her smile...*What Grant had been thinking only moments ago, lay completely forgotten by Sophie's presence.

"Good morning!" Sophie exclaimed brightly, helping herself to a muffin from the basket Grant set on the table.

"Someone's very happy this morning," Grant said, managing to find his words and hoping they sounded casual and did not give away how much he was beguiled.

"Have you looked out the window?" Sophie replied with a grin.

"Yes," Grant smiled, taking a sip of his coffee. "It looks just like it did in the movie last night."

"Well, I'm going to grab my coat and gloves and head outside," Sophie remarked, popping a piece of her muffin into her mouth. "Thanks for the muffin, by the way. It's delicious," she added, turning to leave the kitchen.

Grant stared at Sophie, shocked. "If I knew snow would get you out of the door before me, I would have prayed for it days ago," he teased.

"Ha ha, very funny," Sophie laughed, popping her head back around the corner and smiling. "I'm planning on making snow angels and sledding after feeding the cows," she added.

"I'm right behind you," Grant replied, getting up and following Sophie to retrieve their coats.

"Really?" Sophie remarked astounded.

"I'm not going to let you have all the fun," Grant grinned.

The first steps out into the snow were always Sophie's favorite. Standing on the porch, staring in front of her, Sophie breathed in the crisp air, and watched the wispy vapors of her breath as she exhaled. All around her, the world lay peaceful and undisturbed. It was almost too serene to disturb, and to do so must surely be a sin. But seeing the snow, seeing it dazzling white and unmarred by footprints, also beckoned to the adventurer within her. It was time to embark upon a quest, time to take the first step onto snow which had never before been trodden upon by foot. It was time to become a part of the winter wonderland that called to her very soul. Lifting a boot, Sophie descended the porch steps, and watched as she left the first tracks to be seen. Snow was the frontier of the inner-child... the dreamer... the pilgrim embarking on a journey.

Grant watched, as the smile that had never departed Sophie's face, spread beyond what he thought was possible. "What are you thinking about?" he asked, hoping she would grant him the gift of sharing her thoughts.

"I'm not sure I can find the words to convey what I'm thinking. I feel like any I choose would not describe it justly," Sophie admitted honestly.

"Try?" Grant persisted with a smile.

Sophie looked at Grant, her eyes searching his face. *Would he understand? Did she really dare to express her thoughts and hope he would empathize with the feelings she was experiencing? His eyes...*staring into Grant's eyes, Sophie saw not only hope, but longing. A longing to be included in her confidence, a longing to share in the intimacy of her mind. It was his eyes, and what she read within them, that compelled Sophie to finally speak.

"I was thinking that stepping onto fresh fallen snow for the first time is like embarking upon an unknown adventure; and that it is like you are able to become a part of the winter wonderland that lays before you. That's silly, isn't it?" Sophie uttered embarrassed, as she quickly averted her gaze to the ground. She felt Grant's eyes resting upon her, the warmth of their gaze causing her cheeks to flush.

"No," Grant said, his voice sincere. "I think that's a beautiful thought." He watched as Sophie turned and looked up at him, her face glowing from his compliment. *Her words were not all that was beautiful*, he thought. *Sophie was beautiful in all the ways that mattered most.*

While they fed the cattle, Grant continued to ponder upon Sophie's words. *The way she thought, the feeling and depth of emotion she experienced from something as simple as snow was a rare treasure, a rare expression of character. Sophie was truly special, and she deserved someone who saw and valued the worthiness of her person. If,* as much as the thought pained him, *Sophie was truly happy with Brad, Grant only hoped Brad realized just how exceptional of a woman Sophie was.*

"You seem like you're deep in thought," Sophie stated, interrupting Grant's brooding. "What's troubling you?" she asked, curious to know if Grant was also as willing as she had been to share his thoughts.

"Nothing," Grant lied. He knew by the glare Sophie shot him that she did not believe his words.

"Only a few moments ago I shared with you what I was thinking about, and now you have the nerve to not share your thoughts with me. That's completely unfair!" Sophie shot.

"Alright, I wasn't thinking about nothing. It's just...I'm not sure it would be appropriate for me to share my thoughts," Grant murmured.

"And why not?" Sophie inquired determinedly.

"Fine. If you must know," Grant expressed, dropping his guard, "I was thinking that finding someone who has such emotion and depth of thoughts about something as simple as snow is a rare find." It was part of what he had been thinking, but now was not the time to share the full breadth of his thoughts.

"Oh...that's...that's nice of you to say," Sophie murmured quietly. She had not expected Grant's thoughts to have been about her.

"It's the truth," Grant returned with a smile. "The way you describe ordinary things turns them into something extraordinary. Now, let's get finished feeding these cows so we can have some fun," he added, before he decided to share anymore of his thoughts.

As they continued walking towards the barn, Sophie's heart beat happily within her chest. Knowing that Grant had been thinking about her was flattering, but knowing that he was thinking about her when she too thought about him often, was a pleasing thought indeed. Feeding the cattle did not take too long, and once they had finished, Sophie was about to turn and leave the barn to retrieve her old sled from the shed, when she saw Grant heading towards the wall where her Grandpa had always hung his tools. "What are you doing?" she asked perplexed. Grant had said he wanted to head out into the snow, and the direction he was going was definitely not outside.

"I was thinking, since Christmas is in a few days," Grant replied, turning to face Sophie with a smile, "today would be a perfect day for us to go chop down a Christmas tree." He then turned and removed a hatched from its hook on the wall.

"But *everything* is covered in snow," Sophie uttered mystified.

"Which makes it the perfect time to go hunting for a Christmas tree," Grant remarked, his grin beaming. "Where is your sense of adventure you were just talking about?" he added, his eyes twinkling.

"Alright! Let's do it!" Sophie exclaimed excitedly. She had chopped down Christmas trees on the farm many times before, but she had never actually gone looking for one in the snow. Grant was right, this was the perfect opportunity for an adventure; the perfect chance for her to continue trudging through the pristine snow-covered landscape on a purposeful quest! Besides the hunt for a Christmas tree, who knew what other adventures might await them in the winter wonderland. Sophie's eyes glowed with the childish prospect, that escapading through the snow laden woods, would be exactly like the setting the Pevensie children encountered in *The Lion the Witch and the Wardrobe*. Recalling her favorite book from her childhood, somehow made the snow seem even more tantalizing!

Trudging through the snow, with Ivy playfully bounding up and down like a snow-hare, Sophie felt like she was in a painting of a picturesque Christmas scene. The woods around them were quiet. The bare trees, their branches laden with snow, stood majestic, like the tall masts and billowing sails of ships; and the evergreens that dotted the frozen whiteness with their lively greens, reminded Sophie that everything, though it appeared to be sleeping, was still alive. Sophie gazed up at the sky and was just about to say something to Grant, when she felt her foot slip. Then losing her footing, she suddenly found herself lying on her back in the snow.

"Sophie, are you alright?" Grant asked, coming over to where she lay sprawled in the snow.

Laughing, Sophie brushed Ivy's licks off her cheeks, and looking up at Grant's face, watched as his worry was replaced with a grin. "I'm fine," she smiled. "I should have been watching where I was going. Now that I'm down here, though, I might as well make a snow angel," she added kicking her feet out to the side and lifting her arms up above her head.

"Well, I can't let you have all the fun," Grant laughed, plopping down in the snow beside her. "I haven't made one of these in years!"

Sophie looked at Grant kicking his legs and moving his arms wildly beside her. *The way his face was lighting up...the smile that engulfed his features emitting pure happiness...* As Grant turned his head and Sophie's eyes locked with his, her arms suddenly faltered. Gazing into his eyes, seeing the twinkling delight pouring forth, caused her heart to beat loudly and a knot to form within her throat. Being in Grant's company was so easy...so *natural*. Sophie continued staring into Grant's eyes, their deep-green hue, shimmering like an emerald, holding her entranced. She opened her mouth to speak, to tell Grant, what exactly, she did not know. Sophie's heart was racing; her eyes longing to continue searching Grant's face, when the sudden vibration of her phone caused her eyes to reluctantly break contact. Sitting up, she pulled her phone from her pocket. Brad. *She was being so foolish!* The text knocked Sophie back to her senses. She was "dating" Brad. She could not keep thinking about Grant! She stared at the words on the screen. *"I cannot believe how much snow we got! So glad you are safe at home. Downtown is in utter chaos! Meeting with snow removal personnel to work on getting things cleared up. I'll call you tonight."*

"Is everything okay?" Grant asked, his gaze concerned.

"Yes. Everything is fine," Sophie replied, quickly typing a reply then putting her phone back in her pocket. *What was wrong with here? Why had she deliberately left*

Brad's name out of her reply? Did it matter?

"Good," Grant declared, sitting up and rising to his feet and offering Sophie his hand. "Making snow angels was great! I don't think I've had this much fun since mudsleding!" he added, his face glowing with delight.

Dusting off their pants, Grant and Sophie looked down at their snow angels, the wings connecting as if they were holding hands. As they continued staring in silence at their imprints, Sophie had the sudden sensation that fate was quietly whispering through their snowy figures.

"Not too shabby," Grant said quietly, his fingers touching Sophie's ever so slightly.

"Yes, they do look pretty good," Sophie agreed, her heart fluttering at Grant's touch.

"We should probably continue looking for our tree," Grant remarked, turning to face Sophie.

"Uh huh," Sophie mumbled, her words abandoning her as Grant smiled.

"You've got a bit of snow on your hat. May I?" Grant asked, lifting his hand and dusting the top of her knit cap. "There," he smiled, his eyes lingering on Sophie's face. Clearing his throat, Grant continued, "It looks like there is a small grove of evergreens not too much further ahead." He forced himself to turn away from Sophie and point a few hundred feet in the distance.

As they set off walking again, Sophie prayed Grant would not hear how loudly her heart was beating. *Spending time in Grant's company was enjoyable*, she reflected. Even though she had not known him that long, Sophie did not feel the need to try and be anything but herself around him. Grant was relaxed and easy going, and after spending several years in a big city, Sophie found this characteristic of his quiet refreshing. The snow began falling lightly around them, as they continued walking, and as Sophie looked up, catching the frozen flakes in her eyelashes, the stillness and soft sound of falling snow made her realize just how romantic her outing with Grant had suddenly become.

"What about this one?" Grant asked, coming to a stop and pointing at the snow-covered pine before him.

Sophie gazed at the tree, forcing herself to stop thinking about the dreaminess of their adventure. *It did look nice. All of its branches, even the ones that stuck out in odd angels, seemed sturdy as they bore the weight of the snow.* Comparing it to the few other trees that stood beside it, Sophie noticed it was slightly rounder, which she liked. It seemed to have a personality of its own, and that was exactly the kind of quality that a Christmas tree should possess.

"It's perfect!" Sophie piped with a grin.

"Great! If you'll hold it right here," Grant instructed, lifting Sophie's hand and placing it on the trunk halfway up the tree. "I'll start chopping it down."

As Grant worked on bringing down the tree, Sophie could not help but smile. She had forgotten how much she loved hiking through the farm looking for the perfect

Christmas tree. It was a tradition she had not experienced since she had left, and a tradition she had not realized just how much she missed.

"Timber!" Grant hollered, cupping his hands around his mouth like a lumberjack.

Sophie let go of the tree, and they watched as it landed with a soft thud upon the snow.

"Now, for the hard part," Grant chuckled. "Towing it home."

Hoisting the trunk between them, Sophie and Grant headed back to the house pulling the tree behind them, while Ivy wagged her tail ahead of them, glancing back every so often with a canine look of encouragement.

"We've got to look hilarious," Sophie panted, watching the greenery on the tree limbs leaving swirling lines upon the snow. "We should have grabbed my old sled from the shed."

"Now you tell me," Grant laughed.

"You didn't ask," Sophie grinned.

"We're not too far away. We can make it," Grant grunted, shifting the weight of the tree to his other arm.

When they finally arrived back at the house, panting and exhausted, Sophie plopped down in the snow.

"Hey, no time for resting," Grant teased. "We've got to get this tree inside."

Rolling on to her side, Sophie scooped up a handful of snow and threw it at Grant. "I thought you said you wanted to have some fun," she grinned mischievously.

Grant's eyes glinted brightly. "Now, it's on!" he exclaimed, bending down and grabbing an armful of snow as Sophie, laughing, jumped quickly to her feet.

"You've gotta catch me first!" Sophie yelled, darting away as fast as the snow would allow, with Grant in pursuit.

Sophie ducked, as one of Grant's snowballs shot towards her, and quickly grabbed another handful of snow. Grant was gaining on her! He was about to chuck another snowball in her direction, when Sophie saw his feet fly up from under him and Grant fall tumbling to the ground. She stood laughing, but noticing that Grant had not jumped back up and that Ivy was whining by his side, suddenly stopped.

"Grant! Are you alright?" Sophie hollered, concern filling her voice. He did not answer. "Grant!" Sophie dropped the snowball she was holding and ran over to where he lay. "Grant!" she shook his shoulder.

Grant's eyes flashed open. Then smiling mischievously, he reached up and dropped a snowball on top of Sophie's head, causing Ivy to bark and bounce around excitedly.

"Hey! No fair!" Sophie yelled, as she brushed the snow from her hat.

"Caught you!" Grant chuckled, sitting up and looking at Sophie beside him.

"I thought you were possibly really hurt," Sophie said seriously.

"I'm sorry," Grant replied, forcing himself to stop laughing. Gazing into Sophie's dark-brown eyes, he saw genuine concern. *Did she have feelings for him after all, or had she only been worried that he might really be hurt?*

Holding Grant's gaze, Sophie felt her heart racing. There was a tenderness in Grant's eyes when he looked at her, a tenderness she had not seen in Brad's. She watched as Grant's lips parted, and her heart began to race even faster. *Was he going to kiss her? Did she want him too?*

Standing up, Sophie quickly began brushing the snow off her pants. "We should probably get the tree inside," she said, refusing to meet Grant's gaze. *She could not look at him any longer, or she might possibly fall in… love?* Her heart continued racing, and she hoped he couldn't hear it.

"Of course," Grant replied, getting up and wiping the snow from his clothes.

Watching Grant, as he turned his attention back to the tree, Sophie was sure she saw a look of disappointment flash within his eyes, and her heart began fluttering wildly again. *Why was she afraid to let him kiss her?*

Chapter 20

"**M**e either. Sounds good!" As he read the words from Sophie's text, Brad felt his heart sink slightly. Sophie's reply had not been the heartfelt response he had been expecting. It was short and concise, almost as if replying to him had been an afterthought. Roughly continuing to shovel the snow off the driveway, Brad's dejection was soon replaced with frustration. *This stupid snow had ruined his evening with Sophie, and it was continuing to ruin his chances of ensuring that she fell in love with him! Now,* he gruffed, *this inconvenient white powder had effectively snowbound Sophie and Grant together! First, Grant had insinuated that he was not a gentleman since he had offered Sophie lodging, and now Sophie was trapped in the company of Grant for who knows how long!* Stewing with this horrible thought, Brad continued shoveling. *There was no way he was going to lose Sophie, the woman who would be his perfect political companion, to this bothersome Mr. Bakesfield!*

It took Brad over an hour to clear his driveway, and by the time he was satisfied with his work, his mood had still not improved. He had racked his brain but had been unable to figure out how he was going to remove Grant from the playing field. This, along with the thought of Sophie and Grant together, continued to plague his mind, and the fact that the snowplows had yet to drive down his street further added to his annoyance. If only he could get out of the house and do something about the situation! Pulling off his gloves and boots, Brad left them, along with the shovel, in the garage then headed inside. *Maybe, Sophie had sent him another message,* he thought hopefully. But reaching the kitchen where he had left his phone, Brad's hopes were quickly dashed as he scanned the multitude of messages and missed calls. His phone had been blowing-up while he had been outside, but only by city council members and other local government personnel. *Well, at least some people find me important,* he muttered dryly to himself.

It was as he was reading the texts he had received, that Brad's face suddenly lit up with something he remembered. "Of course!" he exclaimed. He had completely forgotten about her. He had been so blinded by jealousy, that he hadn't remembered his initial plan. Karah and Grant had become acquainted at the basketball game. *What if he could help them become better acquainted?* he thought with a smile. *Blast this horrible snow! It was putting everything on hold. He couldn't just sit around waiting until tomorrow hoping that the roads would be clear enough that he could swing by the flower shop. No, he needed to get in contact with Karah now, but how? He couldn't just text Sophie and ask for Karah's number, cause what if Sophie interpreted the motivation of his request incorrectly? No, he would just have to get Karah's number another way.* Scrolling through his contacts, Brad read over the list of names. One of his contacts had to be friends with or related to Karah. He tapped his thumb impatiently against the side of the case as he scrolled further down the list. Then...*Finally!* He only had to wait a moment before he received a message with Karah's number. Copying Karah's number, Brad quickly typed a message and then hit send.

****

Karah stared happily out the frost covered glass door sipping her cup of tea. The amount of snow that had fallen made her backyard appear like a frosted confection! Gazing at the serenity outside, her heart felt content as she listened to the soft melodies of Christmas carols drifting merrily in the background, before taking another sip of tea and heading over to the couch. Sitting down and resting her feet on the ottoman, Karah gazed around at her surroundings. The twinkling glow of soft white lights from on top of her mantel and Christmas tree, the subtle aroma of spiced apple wafting from the candle she'd lit, and the splendid view of snow was even more than she could have hoped for this close to Christmas, but sitting here all alone with no one to share this perfectly cozy atmosphere, made her heart begin to ache.

Before she had time to further contemplate her loneliness, however, Karah heard the soft sound of jingle bells notifying her that she had received a text message.

Setting her cup of tea on the end-table beside her, Karah rose from the couch and went to retrieve her phone. Her heart momentarily ceased beating when she read the message. *She had to be dreaming. This had to be some kind of a joke!*

"Hey, Karah, it's Brad Devanston. I got your number from your Uncle Jerry. Sorry to bother you on your snow day. Would you mind if I gave you a call?"

Karah stared blankly at the message reading and rereading it over and over again. *Brad. Brad Devanston wanted to call her! She shouldn't allow herself to get her hopes up. He was surely just calling to ask her something about Sophie. Oh, gosh!* Karah thought in panic. How she hoped Brad was not calling to get her advice about how to propose to Sophie. Even though she had decided not to allow her feelings about Brad to be made known, Karah was sure having to hear Brad ask her advice on that subject would surely kill her. *It's much too soon for something like that,* Karah tried to reassure herself. *Maybe...maybe Brad really does want to talk to you...?* She felt ashamed by the thought, like she was betraying Sophie, but Karah could also not deny her hope. Texting her response, Karah hesitated for a moment before hitting send. She only had to wait to read that the message was delivered when her phone began to vibrate.

"Hello, Brad," Karah answered, trying to mask her excitement.

"Hi, Karah," Brad returned, his voice sounding delighted.

Hearing Brad's reply sent Karah's heart fluttering. *What was wrong with her? This was not the way someone who was trying to quell her feelings should be acting. She was Sophie's friend, and was not going to destroy her happiness.* Karah's mind raced, as her heart continued beating loudly within her chest.

"Sorry again to bother you," Brad said brightly. "It's just what I need to talk to you about can't wait."

"It's no problem," Karah replied intrigued, wondering what was so urgent that it was causing Brad to fret. *It could not be business related. If he was ordering flowers for Sophie, surely those could wait until the snow was cleared.* Forcing her voice to remain casual, Karah continued, "What is it you need to talk about?"

"It's this *Grant* fellow," Brad began. Karah could hear the resentment dousing his words. "I just don't think it's proper that he's staying at the farm with Sophie. And then there's this *supposed* contract," Brad continued. "I still have yet to see it."

"Brad," Karah said reassuringly. "You know Sophie's character. If she's made her feelings clear to you, then stop worrying." *It was jealousy that had motivated Brad's phone call,* Karah understood sadly. *But at least she wasn't being regaled with his affections towards Sophie or being asked her advice on proposing. That at least was some consolation.*

"I know Sophie is a respectable woman...I just don't know about Grant's intentions... I guess that's the reason I wanted to call you," Brad rambled. "Sophie said you met him at the basketball game. Surely, you can tell me more about him. And then I was thinking that you..."

"Yes. I met Grant at the basketball game," Karah interrupted. "But, Brad, that's the only time I've spoken to him. You can't really expect me to judge someone just on one encounter, can you? That would be unjust."

"I have a proposition to run by you," Brad continued, ignoring Karah's response. "I need to make sure Grant doesn't have any interfering intentions, and to do that, I'm going to need your help."

"Need my help?" Karah sputtered.

"Yes! I need you to spend time with Grant, you know, keep him away from Sophie," Brad said matter-of-factly. "Then, you and I can meet up and you can tell me what you've learned about him and if he has any designs on Sophie..." Brad felt his annoyance rising just thinking about such a possibility. "I mean, Grant could be trying to take the farm right out from under Sophie for all she knows," he continued. "I mean, why else would he stick around now that Charlie is gone?"

"Brad, I'm not sure I'm comfortable with this idea. It feels deceitful," Karah uttered, her stomach feeling queasy. She felt conflicted. *On one hand, if she helped Brad carry out his plan, she felt like she would be going behind Sophie's back, but on the other hand... if she did go along with it, she would get to spend time with Brad...Oh, she must stop thinking about her own feelings! But was Brad only thinking about his feelings and not Sophie's?*

"Come on, Karah. Do you want Sophie to fall for someone who might be only interested in her newly inherited estate?" Brad asked.

"When you put it that way…" Karah murmured. "Okay. I'll see if Grant will meet up with me, but I'm only…"

"Thank you!" Brad interrupted. "Karah, you are absolutely terrific!"

But as she hung up the phone and stared distractedly at Brad's name on her received calls list, Karah felt far from being terrific.

Chapter 21

“T here!” Sophie declared, as Grant placed the Christmas tree in the corner next to the fireplace. “That looks absolutely perfect!”

Stepping away from the tree, Grant surveyed the room. The tree did indeed look perfect standing round and full in its new location. “Wait here. I've got a surprise for you,” he said excitedly, leaving the room and heading into the kitchen.

As Sophie stared after Grant, wondering what he might be up to, she decided to grab the tree lights from the hall closet. After the year the ornaments had been tossed out accidentally, she and her Grandpa had decided to find a better storage spot. Pulling the worn carboard box down from the top of the closet, Sophie brought it out into the living room and set it on the ground in front of the tree. Sitting down on the floor beside the box, she lifted the lid and froze. There, staring back at her, was an envelope with her name written across it. She slowly pulled the envelope off the shoebox it was tapped to and opened it, her heart pounding happily.

My Dearest Sophie,

If you are reading this letter, then I was unable to give you these in person. I know how much you love reading old letters, so I thought I would share one of the best love stories I know; and now that I'm gone, I'm no longer embarrassed for you to see my letter writing skills. You can laugh, it's okay. I hope as you read the letters your Grandma and I wrote to one another, years ago when I was in the Navy, that they will bring you as much joy as they brought us. I hope one day you will be able to find your own love story and make it the best one ever written. Merry Christmas my little Sophie.

Love,
Grandpa

Folding the letter and putting it back in the envelope, Sophie brushed the tears from her cheeks as she lifted the shoe box, with anticipation, and set it on her lap. Inside the box, a stack of twenty or so letters, worn by age and love, waited to be read. Untying the faded crimson ribbon that held them bound together, Sophie carefully picked up the letter on top and slowly opened it.

June 11, 1952

My Darling Grace,

Since I have arrived in Korea, the thought of you sustains me. Thinking of your smile... your laughter... your kind heart...fills me with a strength to endure what I must, and a mission to make it back home. When I think back to the first time I laid eyes on you, in English class only a couple of years ago, I remember how I knew instantly that you were special. You had just moved to town, and even though I didn't know you, my heart fluttered every time I saw you. When I asked you to the fall dance a week later, I felt like I must be dreaming when you said that you would love to accompany me. Then, when we shared our first kiss...I knew, without a doubt, that you were the one— the woman I was to love for the rest of my life. A kiss speaks more than words; a kiss speaks for the heart. I pray that this war will soon come to an end, so that I can return to you, my dearest Grace, and that we may finally marry. Until I am able to hold you in my arms, know that you are always in my heart and that when you are thinking of me, I too am thinking of you.

With all my love, your,
Charlie

A kiss speaks more than words...a kiss speaks for the heart... As Sophie pondered her Grandpa's wisdom, she realized his words echoed with truth. The way he had described his love for her Grandma...it was the way she had always hoped to feel when she met the man destined to be her better-half. *If her Grandpa could so easily know, and so easily verbalize his feelings, why then couldn't she? Surely, there was something genetic that should have been passed down to help her understand her own heart.* Caught up in her thoughts, Sophie did not hear Grant approaching.

"Are you ready for your surprise?" Grant asked excitedly, walking into the room.

"Yes," Sophie replied, quickly setting the letter back in the box and closing the lid. Even though Grant had known her Grandpa, Sophie wasn't quite sure she was ready to share his letters with him, at least not right now. "What have you been up to?" she asked, rising from the floor.

"You'll see," Grant ginned. "Now, if you will please follow me," he continued, turning and walking towards the kitchen.

Shaking her head good-naturedly at Grant's mysteriousness, Sophie followed him out of the living room wondering, all the while, what he could possibly have waiting as a surprise.

"After you," Grant grinned, stepping aside to let Sophie walk into the kitchen ahead of him

As Sophie entered the room, her face lit up in a radiant smile. "Grant, you did not have to do this!" she exclaimed, in wondering disbelief. As Sophie's eyes darted happily about the room, the joy she felt within was bubbling and nearly overflowing.

"Yes, I did," Grant said, his tone conveying the

essentialness of his actions as he stood smiling next to her. "I hope I have got everything we need. I've never made salt-dough ornaments before," he admitted, with a shrug of his shoulders. "I had to look up a recipe online."

Spread out across the kitchen table, Sophie observed that Grant had compiled mixing bowls and cookie cutters, along with flour, salt, and water.

"Shall we get started?" Grant asked, turning towards Sophie, his eyes gleaming with excitement.

Sophie nodded enthusiastically, as she picked up a spoon and began measuring flour into a bowl. "I haven't made these since that Christmas I told you about," she confided, as she dumped a cup of flour into the bowl.

"Well," Grant replied gently, "I hope you enjoy making them as much this year as you did then."

Sophie put down her measuring spoon and smiled at Grant. *How was it that he was able to speak to her heart? And how did he seem so often to know her better than she knew herself?* "Thank you," she said, her words full of sincerity. "You do not know how much this means to me."

"You're welcome," Grant nodded knowingly. Watching Sophie smile at his words before turning back to add the remaining ingredients to the bowl, caused Grant to feel something stir within his heart. When Sophie smiled at him, it was as if her smile had drawn back the curtains that had sought to shield his heart from the hurt which had been inflicted upon it. With her smile, Sophie had awakened feelings within him which had long been dormant. With her smile, Grant knew he was not crazy for falling in love with her from mere words of her description. With her smile, Grant felt hope that maybe Sophie too could fall in love with him.

"I can't believe you never made salt-dough ornaments before," Sophie said, as she kneaded the dough between her fingers.

"Well, as a kid, if the dough I was making wasn't cookie dough, I didn't want anything to do with it," Grant laughed, as he spooned a glob of dough onto the table and rolled it back and forth with the palm of his hand.

Once the dough was mixed, they rolled it out on the table and began using the cookie cutters to cut out shapes. Candy canes, snowmen, stars, gingerbread men, Christmas trees, and snowflakes soon began taking form across the tabletop.

"Okay," Grant said, pulling a star that was sticking off the cookie cutter. "How do your shapes turn out so perfect and mine come out looking like *turds*?"

"Yours don't look like turds," Sophie laughed, eyeing Grant's row of misshapen ornaments as Grant raised an eyebrow. "Okay," Sophie admitted. "They might look a little…"

"Turdish," Grant chuckled.

"No, I was going to say *unique*," Sophie offered with a smile. "Here," Sophie continued, lifting a spoonful of four out of the jar, "if you sprinkle a little flour down first, and then don't roll the dough out so thin that will help."

Grant spread the flour around with his hands, and then flattened a ball of dough onto it with a rolling pin.

"Okay, perfect. Don't roll anymore," Sophie directed. "Now, try cutting out a shape."

Grant picked up the Christmas tree cutter and sliced it into the dough. Lifting it up, he stared at the shape he had cut still laying on the table. "Wow! For someone who has not made these in a while, you sure know how to get them to turn out," he declared in admiration.

"It's just like baking cookies," Sophie remarked, pleased by his compliment. "You just have to get the right thickness."

They proceeded to cut shapes out of the rest of the dough, and then using a straw, made holes in each ornament so after they baked they could attach the string.

"Okay," Sophie remarked, putting the trays of ornaments in the oven and setting the timer. "While these bake and cool, how about we put the lights on the tree and string some popcorn for garland?"

"That sounds great!" Grant agreed. "It's a shame we don't have any white and red pipe cleaners. We could have also made the candy cane ornaments you told me about."

Sophie's eyes brightened. "Hold that thought," she exclaimed, dashing from the kitchen and heading up to her room.

While he waited, Grant began making the popcorn, and when Sophie returned, she was beaming from ear to ear.

"I've always kept a stash of art supplies in my room. You never know when they might come in handy," Sophie remarked happily, setting an assorted bag of Christmas colored pipe cleaners on the table. "Here is red, and white, and green. We can make candy canes, and then if we want to get adventurous," she added with a grin. "We can try making some green and red Christmas wreaths too."

"This is going to call for some hot chocolate," Grant smiled, dumping the popcorn into a bowl and retrieving two mugs from the cupboard.

While Grant worked on making mugs of hot cocoa, Sophie gathered up the popcorn and pipe cleaners and took them into the living room. Setting them down on the fireplace, she turned on some Christmas music and began stringing popcorn.

"Your beverage, Madame," Grant smiled, handing Sophie her mug of hot chocolate. "I can start on the lights," he offered. Taking a sip of his hot chocolate, Grant set his mug on the mantle then pulled the Christmas lights out of the box.

As Sophie worked on stringing popcorn, she found her eyes could not help but wander onto Grant. Watching him walk the lights around the tree, occasionally humming or singing along with the carols, Sophie found herself mesmerized. Grant was a conundrum who continued to surprise her. Ever since she had met him, he had treated her with kindness even on occasions when she had been impolite or undeserving. Grant made her breakfast every morning, had driven her to town to meet up with another guy, went searching for her in a snowstorm...and now, he had helped recreate her fondness Christmas memory. Sophie's stomach fluttered with butterflies, as Grant caught her watching him. Grant's eyes locked onto hers, and he smiled. Sophie quickly averted her gaze. Turning her attention back to the popcorn, she felt Grant's gaze lingering upon her, and found she rather liked it.

Chapter 22

"T here!" Sophie exclaimed, her voice pleased, as she hung the final ornament on the tree. Stepping back, Sophie and Grant admired their handy work. The tree, twinkling with soft white lights, looked dazzling and enchanting! Decked with homemade ornaments and entwined in strings of popcorn, it appeared enchanting and as though it had waltzed right off the stage of a performance of *The Nutcracker*. Simple and old fashioned in its splendor, the tree beckoned warm and inviting, wrapping the entire room in cozy contentment.

"I don't think I have ever seen a tree this pretty," Grant said softly, his eyes roving across the greenery of its branches and taking in its peaceful elegance.

"It is something to behold," Sophie agreed, as she sat down on the couch and gazed admiringly at the tree's soft glow. "We still have one more decoration to put up though," Sophie said, rising to her feet and enjoying that she now got to be the mysterious one, as Grant gave her a questioning look.

Heading back to the hall closet, Sophie stood on her tiptoes and lifted another cardboard box down from the top shelf. This was her absolute favorite Christmas decoration to put up each year. Sophie remembered, as a child, the first time her Grandparents had gifted her with this decorating task. Her fingers had trembled as she had gently unwrapped the white tissue-paper afraid she might break one of the precious figurines. Coming back into the living room smiling, Sophie could not wait for Grant to see her favorite decoration and heirloom.

"What do you have there?" Grant asked curiously.

"This," Sophie replied brightly, "is my favorite Christmas decoration."

"I'm intrigued," Grant smiled, watching Sophie as she set the box on the coffee table and gently pulled back the top.

Holding one of the figurines in her hand, Sophie gently unwrapped the tissue- paper surrounding it, and smiled as a painted ceramic shepherd gazed up at her. "This is the nativity set my Grandmother made," Sophie shared, as she walked over to the fireplace and set the shepherd on the mantle.

"Your grandmother made this?" Grant uttered in disbelief, as Sophie unwrapped a tiny sheep and added it to the mantle.

"Yep!" Sophie declared proudly. "She took a ceramic class a year after she and my Grandpa were married and used molds to make each figurine. She then hand painted each figure, and even glued little jewels on the wise men. Would you like to help me set it up?" Sophie asked.

"I'd love to," Grant remarked. Unwrapping the

figurine Sophie handed him, Grant carefully placed a ceramic camel next to one of the wise men. Each figure he unwrapped amazed him even more than the last. The time... the detail... the love that Sophie's Grandma had poured into making such a beautiful display, was a gift in itself. "Your Grandmother was very talented," he murmured, placing the figures of the Blessed Virgin Mary and Saint Joseph beside the empty manger.

"Yes, she definitely was," Sophie agreed, as she stood back smiling and admiring the mantle.

"Just one more piece," Grant said happily, as he pulled back the tissue-paper revealing baby Jesus in the palm of his hand. Lifting the porcelain babe gently with his fingers, he reached his hand towards the empty manger.

"Wait!" Sophie exclaimed, startling Grant, his fingers inches from the manger. "It's tradition. You can't put baby Jesus in the manger until Christmas Day."

"Well, where else do you expect me to put him?" Grant asked bewildered.

"We can put him in one of the stockings," Sophie suggested, reaching for baby Jesus.

"That just seems wrong," Grant said, closing his fingers over baby Jesus before Sophie could pry him away and stuff him in a stocking.

"Do you have a better idea?" Sophie inquired; her eyebrows raised.

"Yes, as a matter-of-fact, I do," Grant smiled,

reaching into the box that had held the Christmas decorations and retrieving a small red velvet ornament box. "We'll put him in here and place him under the tree like a present, then open him up on Christmas morning. There you go, little fellow, I won't let you wait in some old sock," he said, gently placing baby Jesus in the box and setting it beneath the tree.

It should simply be impossible that Grant could continue to amaze her, but as Sophie watched him carefully set baby Jesus beneath the tree as if he were setting down the greatest treasure he had ever held, she felt a warmth within her heart that was more tender than she believed possible. Grant was a genuinely good and faith-filled man; and the more she unwrapped of his character, the more she was beginning to realize that men like Grant did not appear every Christmas.

"There!" Grant declared, straightening back to a standing position and giving Sophie a smile.

Sophie felt her cheeks glowing as she returned Grant's smile. The way he looked at her was unlike any other look she had ever received. As Grant's eyes beheld her, the gaze which kept her own eyes transfixed, was one which seemed to see inside her; to look past her outward appearance and really see her for who she was as a person. Feeling flustered, Sophie quickly took a seat on the sofa to regain her composure. "This room looks like it belongs on the front of a Christmas card," she gushed, in hopes that her words would distract her from her feelings. "Everything looks so wonderful."

"There is only one more thing to make this room look even more perfect," Grant remarked. Walking over to the hearth, he proceeded to build a fire. "There," he smiled, sitting down beside Sophie. "Now, it feels like Christmas is getting even closer."

With the fire crackling merrily in the fireplace and Christmas music playing softly in the background, Sophie was beginning to feel like this entire day was becoming her new favorite Christmas memory. *How strange it was*, Sophie thought, *that decorating for Christmas, with a man she had not known very long, was now to become a treasured memory.*

"Grant," Sophie said, turning and looking at him. "There is something I want to show you." Getting up from the couch, she retrieved the box of letters her Grandpa had given her and sat back down.

"What's in there?" Grant asked, his interest piqued.

"When you were setting out the ingredients for making salt-dough ornaments, I found these with the Christmas lights," Sophie shared, removing the lid and displaying the folded pieces of parchment. "These are letters my Grandpa and Grandma wrote to one another while my Grandpa was in the Navy," she explained, carefully removing the letter she had read earlier and unfolding it.

Grant watched as tenderness traced the features on Sophie's face while she continued to stare at the letter within her hands. "A gift as priceless as this, is worth more than any other Christmas gift," he whispered softly.

Sophie nodded. "I'm glad you got to know my Grandpa," she smiled.

"He was a good man," Grant remarked. "And he raised a strong and good woman."

Sophie blushed at Grant's complement. "I would like to share this with you," she said, handing Grant the unfolded letter. "I read it earlier. And since you knew him...well, I thought you might also appreciate this."

"It would be a privilege," Grant remarked.

Taking the letter within his hands as Sophie sat quietly beside him, Grant began reading. With each word he read, Grant felt his heart hammering louder within his chest. Charlie's words were so honest and truthful. He had never been one to read love letters or for that matter write love letters, but reading these words upon the page...*Did Sophie feel this way about him? Was that the real reason she wanted him to read this?* Then with a sinking heart, Grant quickly realized the true reason why Sophie wanted him to read this letter. *He was being such a fool! It was so obvious now. When he had witnessed Brad and Sophie's kiss after the parade...By sharing this letter, Sophie was merely trying to politely tell him that Brad was the one for her, and she knew it from their kiss.* Grant felt his heart sinking further into the pit of his stomach as he finished reading the letter. "Thank you for sharing this with me," he mumbled. Then folding the letter, he handed it back to Sophie, unable to meet her gaze.

Grant's words had not been the reaction Sophie had been expecting, and the tone in which they were delivered... *Had she done something wrong? She had thought...never mind what she had thought, it did not matter now, because she had clearly been mistaken. Was there anyway she could salvage the rest of the evening? Today, spending time with Grant and decorating for Christmas had been an unexpected delight, and when Grant had refused to meet her gaze...* Sophie felt as if the gift she had just been given was slowly slipping away.

"Today has been one of the best days I've ever had," Sophie voiced assuredly, looking at Grant and hoping he would meet her gaze. "You hardly know me, yet you go out of your way to make sure I'm happy. Why?" she asked. *Maybe asking a question would make Grant at least acknowledge her.*

Grant turned towards Sophie and forced himself to look into her eyes. *Was that a glimmer of relief he saw flash across her almond eyes? Had he been incorrect in the conclusion he had drawn? Should he answer her question? Did he dare tell her why he wanted her to be happy? She was sure to find him ridiculous, but he could not refuse to say anything.* "Because," he uttered, forcing his voice to remain steady, "after all the stories your Grandpa told me about you; the way he spoke of you, your kindness, your heart, you as a person, I...I fell in love with you without ever meeting you,"

Grant fumbled quickly. *There. He had said it. Even if Sophie was in love with Brad and not with him, at least he had told her the truth.*

Sophie stared at Grant, taken aback by his words. *Had she heard him correctly? Did Grant just say he was in love with her? How was that possible? You don't just fall in love with someone from what you have heard about them, do you?* But Sophie could not deny that her own growing infatuation was just as *impossible* of a notion.

"Please say something," Grant uttered, afraid of what Sophie might say, but even more afraid she might say nothing at all. Grant could not believe he had just told Sophie that he was in love with her. *He had just read her Grandpa's letter, for goodness sake, and he knew she was in love with Brad. He was such an idiot! Maybe, if he wished hard enough, he would be able to take back his words.*

"How could you possibly fall in love with me from what my Grandpa told you?" Sophie stammered in disbelief. *Sane people don't fall in love with someone from stories. That was simply preposterous…?*

Grant felt a weight lift from his chest. Sophie had said something, she had not laughed at him or declared him some kind of stalker, *at least not out loud,* he thought; nor had she told him he was wasting his time. *Was there still a chance that he had misinterpreted her intentions about the letter? That Sophie was actually interested in him and had instead felt something different in Brad's kiss?* Grant scolded himself. He was acting like a boy who had just sent the girl he had a crush on a "Do you like me?" note.

"I guess," Grant ventured, before he lost his nerve, "over the course of four years, hearing about you on a daily basis made me feel like I already knew you. And what I learned about you, made me like you as a person, and then that *like* eventually turned into *love*. I know, it sounds ridiculous," he added, catching sight of Sophie's doubtful expression.

"Grant...I...," Sophie stammered, feeling her heart flutter. *Could it be just as possible that she had fallen for him in the short time she had known him, and that was the reason why her heart was feeling so conflicted? Didn't that seem just as unfathomable?*

"Forget I said anything," Grant mumbled, his expression looking hurt, as he turned his face to stare at the fire crackling in the hearth.

Sophie's heart was pounding within her chest. *This was absolutely crazy! She must be crazy. Things like this did not happen in real life. Things like this were the serendipitous events that only happened in books and movies. But if that was true...why then did she feel the way she did?* Sophie heard the song, *I'll Be Home for Christmas*, begin to quietly play in the background, as the words from her Grandpa's letter began echoing within her mind. *She had to know. She had to be sure...*

"Grant," Sophie said, her heart pounding as he turned

and looked at her once more.

Then before she lost her nerve, Sophie leaned forward and kissed him!

Chapter 23

Sophie felt Grant's initial shock as her lips met his, but his shock quickly melted into happiness as his lips moved tenderly against hers, deepening their kiss. Sophie felt Grant's arms, strong and secure, wrap around her; and as she folded herself against his chest, feeling his hands holding her softly against the small of her back, Sophie felt like nothing else in the world mattered except this moment—this moment where Grant was kissing her back!

Sophie felt Grant's hands slide softly along her back and entwine themselves in her hair. *"Then, when we shared our first kiss...I knew without a doubt that you were the one— the woman I was to love for the rest of my life..."* The words she had read in her Grandpa's letter echoed softly within Sophie's mind, and suddenly she felt terrified by this realization. *Could a person possibly discern something as important as finding the love of their life from just one kiss? Was not the idea of such a thing just a fanciful romantic notion? She had felt nothing when Brad had kissed her,* Sophie recalled, *but now, kissing Grant...*

"I'm sorry," Sophie blurted, pulling away from Grant's embrace. Then, with her face as red as Santa's coat, she collected the shoebox of letters and darted upstairs, before she lost all sense and fell head-over-heels in love with a man she barely knew when she was technically courting another.

Grant, entirely shocked by what had just transpired, watched as Sophie disappeared up the steps. Putting a hand on his chin, he remained staring in disbelief. *Sophie had kissed him.* And when she kissed him, he had felt the spark he had always believed was just a myth. *Was it possible that Sophie had felt it too? If so, why had she run away?* Alone in the living room, Grant's mind raced in confusion.

Shutting her bedroom door quickly behind her, Sophie flopped down on her bed and touched her lips. *What had come over her? Had she merely been caught up in the moment, all romantic in its Christmas decor, or was there some other reason, some other motivation at work she had been trying to deny?* Sophie felt dizzy. Laying back against her pillow, she stared blankly at the ceiling. Her heart was thundering and felt as though it would gallop straight out of her body and race circles around the room. She had been caught up in the moment, that was the logical explanation. Tomorrow she would be thinking more clearly. *But tomorrow,* Sophie thought, feeling her stomach turn somersaults, *how could she possibly face Grant? Had he felt something in their kiss too?*

Sophie's mind continued to whirl in thought. *What was she trying to do? Playing with the hearts of others was not a game. Brad... Grant... herself...they could all end up getting hurt if she was not careful, if she did not figure out the feelings of her heart soon...But she could not go back downstairs, not now. What would Grant think of her running away? Yet, she could not stay upstairs forever either. What was she going to do? Did she tell Brad she had kissed Grant? Brad! She had known him forever; she loved Brad. But what if she did not love him romantically? She was such a mess! Why couldn't she just understand her own heart?*

Running her hands through her hair as she lay sprawled upon her bed, Sophie heard her phone start to ring. Bolting to a sitting position, her heart continued pounding loudly. *It had to be Brad calling. He had told her he would call. If she answered, he would know there was something wrong with her from her voice. But if she did not answer...* She quickly snatched her phone off the nightstand.

"Hi, Brad," Sophie answered, hoping her voice sounded casual and not as shaky as she believed.

"Are you alright? This snow is ridiculous! I don't see why anyone loves it. All it does is ruin plans," Brad replied agitated.

"I'm fine," Sophie acknowledged. "I rather enjoyed my snow day. I..."

"Alright, Soph, what's wrong?" Brad asked.

"Nothing," Sophie quickly replied.

"It's not nothing," Brad persisted. "Your voice just went up an octave like it did when you said you were fine. Did Grant do something? If he did anything I'll..."

"No, it was me," Sophie blurted. "I kissed him." She could not lie to Brad, she had to tell him the truth even if it hurt him.

"You...you did *what*?" Brad sputtered. "Why?" he asked, the shock in his voice coated with disbelief.

"We had been having such a great day. We made salt-dough ornaments, cut down a Christmas tree, put up my Grandma's nativity set...I read a letter my Grandpa wrote to my Grandma... I guess I...I just got caught up in the moment. Brad, I think I...," Sophie rambled.

"Don't say it," Brad interrupted. "This was exactly what I was afraid might happen. Being snowed in with *him* at the farm... I knew he would try and take advantage of the situation and turn your thoughts to him," he ranted.

"I was the one who initiated the kiss, not Grant," Sophie uttered. "It's not his fault, it's all mine. Brad, I'm so sorry. I didn't mean to hurt you."

"Soph, I know it wasn't *your* fault." Regardless of what Sophie said, Brad knew where the real fault lay. *Why couldn't Grant see that Sophie was his girl? Hadn't he made that explicit the first time he had encountered the man?* Brad thought peevishly. "Don't worry, Soph. Once the roads are clear enough to drive, we will get together and sort out this mess. I will give you a call tomorrow." *Once the roads were clear, with Karah's help, he would put his plan in motion*, Brad promised himself.

Everything was a mess, Sophie realized, as she set her

phone on her nightstand. And she was the reason for all the mess. *Was she going to ruin Christmas for everyone?* Maybe Brad was right. Maybe she could sort out the mess she had created. Praying that the roads would be drivable in the morning, Sophie climbed into bed; and pulling the covers up around her, hoped the solution she sought would be clear in the morning.

Chapter 24

Sophie had set her alarm even earlier than usual. Now, tiptoeing down the stairs, she was relieved to see that the kitchen light was still off. For once, she had gotten up earlier than Grant. Pouring herself a bowl of cereal, she quickly ate and then dressed to feed the cattle. Shivering from the frosty chill, Sophie made her way to the barn, and once inside turned on the overhead light. She couldn't avoid Grant forever, she knew, as she piled armfuls of hay into the feeding troughs, but at least she could avoid him a little while longer.

Recalling her conversation with Brad, Sophie felt a knot twist within her stomach. She had been about to tell Brad that she believed she was in love with Grant, when he had interrupted her. *Why had she not just told him what she was feeling regardless of his interruption? And then there was the whole "run away from Grant incident" after she kissed him, because she felt guilty for kissing him while "dating" Brad. So, was she really then in love with Brad? But then her heart had fluttered when kissing Grant and not when Brad had kissed her...* Sophie's mind was an indecipherable vortex! All she knew for sure was that she needed to get away from the farm to clear her thoughts.

When she was finally finished with her chores, Sophie knew she could no longer prolong the inevitable and headed back towards the house. There was still about a foot of snow on the ground, but the sun had made the roads at least appear to be drivable. Pulling off her gloves and hat, Sophie slipped her boots off and left them by the door. She heard the sound of coffee brewing and knew Grant was awake.

"You're sure up early today," Grant said with a smile, as Sophie entered the kitchen.

"I just wanted to get an early start," Sophie replied, avoiding Grants eyes. "I think we might be able to go into work today. The roads don't look too horrible."

"I'll give you a lift," Grant offered. "And I can see about getting a tow for your car."

"Thanks," Sophie replied, finally looking at Grant. His eyes were just as pleasant as always, and his lips...*she could not look at his lips or she was sure to kiss him again. What was wrong with her!*

"It's no problem," Grant smiled. "The distillery is still without power, so I've got a pretty free day."

Sophie felt a sinking feeling inside. Grant had still not mentioned their kiss. She had been sure he would have said something. But to be fair, she had not mentioned it either. Sophie did not know what was worse, being afraid to talk about the kiss or not talking about it at all. Leaving the kitchen, she donned her hat and gloves and headed outside, Grant following behind.

As they slowly made their way into town, it seemed

to Sophie that Grant had decided their kiss had never happened. Throughout the drive, Sophie sat on the edge of her seat waiting, but much to her frustration their tender embrace was never brought into the conversation. *Was Grant waiting for her to mention it? Or was he simply trying to forget about it?* Sophie wondered. *If he was trying to forget about it...then maybe Grant had decided he really was not in love with the woman he'd said he had fallen in love with through the stories he'd heard. If that was the case, then she should not allow herself to fall for him...but was she already too late?* Sophie's mind and heart were even more confused than they had been last night. Gazing out the window, trying to distract herself, Sophie noted that the roads were still fairly bad, and it was actually a miracle that she and Grant had managed to arrive at the museum without incident.

"What time would you like me to pick you up?" Grant asked, pulling up to the curb.

"Five please," Sophie replied, with a smile she hoped masked her anxiety.

"Your chauffeur will be waiting," Grant declared, returning Sophie's smile as he helped her from the cab.

"Thanks," Sophie acknowledged, as she took Grant's hand, her heart fluttering wildly as she returned his smile. Then standing on the sidewalk, she watched as Grant drove away before heading inside.

"Good morning, Ellen," Sophie greeted brightly, as her fellow coworker looked up from the front desk at the sound of the door being opened.

"Good morning, Sophie," Ellen returned cheerfully, her face wearing a warm smile. "How did you fair out on your farm?" she asked interestedly.

"We managed okay," Sophie replied. "We didn't lose power, and everything is still in one piece."

"Well, you're mighty lucky," Ellen said, her face emitting signs of awe. "We lost power again, if you'd believe it," she continued, shaking her head. "But not to worry," she added, catching sight of Sophie's concerned expression. "We braved the roads and have been staying with my sister. Now, more importantly, who is this *we* you're referring too?" Ellen inquired, her eyes brimming with curiosity.

"Oh," Sophie uttered, a little taken off guard. Brad and Karah both knew about she and Grant's situation, but she had not explained it to anyone else. *That's all I need,* Sophie thought. *The facts getting misinterpreted and spinning out of control until the whole town thinks I'm allowing some strange man to live with me.* "Just a friend my Grandpa was letting rent a room while I was away," Sophie shared, hoping her answer would suffice.

Sophie watched as Ellen opened her mouth. *Nope. She had been wrong*, Sophie thought. Ellen was not going to be satisfied by such a vague response.

"And does this *friend* have a name?" Ellen asked with a grin, her eyes conveying to Sophie that by leaving out a name, the *friend* was most certainly of the male persuasion.

"His name is Grant Bakesfield," Sophie conceded, knowing she had no other choice, for lying would just make things worse.

"And how long will this *Mr. Bakesfield* be staying with you?" Ellen persisted. "I know it's not really any of my business," she continued, "but it seems like Mayor Devanston has been stopping by a lot lately, and I'm quite sure it's not for a history lesson," Ellen added, her eyes implying the weight of her words.

"Brad is a dear friend," Sophie replied. "He's only stopped by a few times so we could catch up." *Would Ellen believe this partial truth?* she wondered.

Ellen raised an eyebrow. "Honey, I wasn't born yesterday. It's quite obvious that Mr. Devanston has other motivations than just catching up. What does he think about this *Grant* fellow staying with you?"

Sophie blushed. She really did not feel like discussing the confusing love triangle that was forming within her life. *Yes, she knew Brad had feelings for her and that she had agreed to try dating him, believing she might also have feelings for him; but now...she felt like she might have feelings for Grant, and until this morning, she had believed Grant had feelings for her too.*

"Just be careful," Ellen began, understanding Sophie's silence. "When hearts are involved, it's easy to end up hurt." She patted Sophie's hand tenderly, and then proceeded to make them both cups of tea.

While Sophie sipped her cup of peppermint tea, she thought long and hard about Ellen's words. *If she really analyzed her heart and believed the words from her Grandpa's letter, then she knew she was in love with Grant. And if Grant had changed his mind and decided he was not in love with her after they had kissed...Well then, so be it. She should allow her heart to get hurt.* Sophie knew she could not keep stringing Brad along when she knew her love for him would never grow into the love he deserved. *She could not hurt Brad by continuing to date him just because she was afraid of getting hurt by Grant. That was selfish, and Brad deserved much better than that. He deserved to be with someone who was head-over-heels in love with him; to be with someone who would help bring out the best in him. He deserved someone who would love him unconditionally. It's decided then,* Sophie concluded, *she would end things with Brad even if it meant she would lose his friendship.* Setting her empty teacup on her desk, Sophie began working on archiving the latest estate collection that had arrived and dreading her conversation with Brad.

Chapter 25

Whenen Brad looked out his window in the morning, he was thrilled to see that the streets had been plowed enough for him to make it into the office. Grabbing his phone, he sent a quick text to Karah inviting her to lunch. He had to get his plan rolling, and even though he had discussed it with Karah on the phone, he still felt like they needed a better game plan. *How was he going to get Karah and Grant to meet one another again for one thing?* he thought. Looking at the text he had just received, Brad smiled, grateful that Karah had agreed to meet up with him.

Driving into work, Brad was surprised at the state of the roads. From his window, the roads had appeared to be suitably clear, but driving slowly he soon realized his view had been deceiving. The ice that lay beneath the snow hindered the traction of his tires, making the roads in actuality in really poor condition. He was even going into work late, hoping the sun would cause more melting, but even that had not helped. As Brad carefully rounded the corner and passed by the history museum, he clenched his jaw. There, parked along the curb, was Grant's black truck! Seeing Grant's truck, caused a wave of jealousy to wash over Brad; yet its full impact was not felt until, with a swirl of brown curls, he spied Sophie taking Grant's hand and climbing out of the cab!

Seeing Sophie standing on the sidewalk smiling at Grant, caused Brad to tighten his grip on the steering wheel. *Was he being a fool? He had cut Sophie off on the phone last night afraid she was going to tell him she had feelings for Grant. But that was utterly ridiculous! Sophie and he had history. They had known each other for practically half their lives. Surely, Sophie couldn't really fall for some guy she barely knew in merely a few short days...* So caught up was Brad in his thoughts, that he was surprised to find that he had arrived outside City Hall. Parking his car and cutting the engine, he pocketed his keys and opened the door. *How on earth was he ever going to concentrate at work today?*

The hours until one o'clock seemed to drag by miserably slow. More than half of the people he usually worked with had been unable to make it in today, and Brad found it nearly impossible to complete the work he had hoped to accomplish. With a sigh of relief, he looked up at the clock that hung on his office wall. It was finally a quarter till one. Coming into work today had been basically useless. At least his lunch would prove to be more fruitful, he thought happily.

When Brad arrived at *The Sugar Plum Bistro*, he was relieved to find the restaurant open. He had been so busy with trying to come up with a plan and getting a hold of Karah, that he had forgot to question the good chance that the restaurant too would be closed due to the storm. Scanning the sparse crowd in the dining area, Brad quickly spotted Karah. *Was it his imagination, or did Karah look extremely lovely when she looked up from her menu, her bright blue eyes sparkling at the sight of him?* Brad thought, astonished by his assessment. Smiling at him, her short brown hair pulled slightly to the side and framing her face, Brad found himself suddenly unable to move. *Had Karah always been this charming? Had he just been so mesmerized by Sophie that he had never really seen Karah? This was not good!* Brad chided himself. *He was in love with Sophie— the woman he wanted to marry— the woman who was going to help further his political career. But did Sophie love him?* a small voice asked. *Hadn't she in fact kissed Grant? Hadn't she been about to tell him something last night on the phone that he didn't want to hear?* Regaining the use of his legs, Brad smiled back at Karah as he made his way towards the table.

"I don't know about you," Karah said brightly, as Brad took his seat, "but I'm starving!"

"I'm pretty hungry myself," Brad remarked, finding it impossible to look anywhere but at the woman sitting across from him. *What was happening to him? Had he completely lost his senses?*

"Why are you staring at me like that?" Karah asked, her gaze holding Brad's eyes intently.

"Am I? I'm sorry," Brad uttered embarrassed, as he hurriedly averted his gaze towards the menu; yet not before he glimpsed a faint smile flash across Karah's lips before quickly disappearing. *Were they both embarrassed to be in one another's company? Were they somehow embarrassed for different reasons?* Brad wondered.

"Did the storm knock out your power?" Karah asked, a sense of concern in her words. "Luckily, I didn't lose power," she shared. "But I've heard half the town is without it."

"No, I'm also one of the lucky ones who still has power," Brad shared. "I've been on the phone all morning with the electric company, snow crews, and residents about when they expect downed wires to be fixed, and unfortunately it sounds like it is going to take a couple of days before all power is restored."

"That's awful, especially with it being so close to Christmas," Karah uttered sadly. "What's being done to help those without power? Has anything been set up for them to keep warm and receive meals?"

Brad saw the genuine worry and care expressed on Karah's face. "I contacted the local food pantry and some of the town's churches, and they are working together to get hot meals ready and offer temporary shelter to those who need it," Brad explained.

"Oh, that's wonderful!" Karah exclaimed. "You're such a good mayor, Brad. I hope you know that," she smiled.

Brad smiled at Karah's compliment. There were days when he sometimes wondered if he was actually making a difference. It wasn't easy work helping to run a town. Sometimes people were even downright mean when things didn't go the way they wanted. *It was nice*, Brad thought, *to hear someone acknowledge that she believed he was doing a good job. It was nice to know that Karah believed in him.*

After they had placed their orders, Brad turned his attention back to Karah. "Shall we get down to business?" he asked. Hopefully, turning their attention to the reason for their rendezvous, would force him to stop thinking about how enchanting he was suddenly finding Karah. *The way she smiled... the way she looked at him when he spoke... Karah's kindness and civic-minded heart... He needed to be careful. Sophie was the woman for him, remember?* Brad reminded himself.

"Yes," Karah murmured, the brightness within her eyes flickering. "Brad, I've been giving it some thought, and I really don't think I can go along with your plan. I mean, Sophie is my friend, you're my friend... If I try to go on a date with Grant just because you want to keep him away from Sophie, it just seems well...*dishonest*," she finished quietly.

Hearing Karah put the reason for his plan so bluntly, caused Brad's insides to squirm. Deep down he had always known his plan was derived out of jealousy, but he had convinced himself that he was somehow protecting Sophie from a man with dubious intentions just to get rid of his competition. *What kind of a person was he becoming? Was* he even really in love with Sophie or just in love with the idea of her because of some high school crush which had been rekindled?

"If you really love Sophie, Brad, then you should want her to find happiness. You need to let her trust her heart even if you might get hurt," Karah elaborated.

"You're right," Brad admitted, ashamed of his behavior. "I've been acting like an envious jerk."

"I wouldn't go that far," Karah said with a smile. "You're a nice guy, Brad. And your heart, I'm sure, was in the right spot, even if it was a tad misguided." Looking at Brad, his expression and everything about him attractive as he sat attentively across from her, Karah's heart began to ache. *Why did she always have to be such a good friend? Would Sophie be as good of a friend as she was trying to be for her sake? Why,* Karah continued silently, *did she feel the need to suppress her own feelings for someone else's happiness? If only Brad would realize how much she loved him. If only...* Karah sighed, suddenly feeling disloyal for thinking such thoughts.

Gazing across the table at his lunch companion, Brad's mind began to wander. *Was he really more concerned with getting rid of his competition, that he was failing to read Sophie's heart? Was he even deciphering the feelings of his own heart correctly? Karah had suggested that his heart had been in the right spot even if his actions had been misguided, but had his heart really been in the right spot?* Brad wondered. *Karah's heart sure seemed to be. She was loyal to Sophie and had seen right through his selfish motivations...There really was more to Karah than met the eye,* he realized.

"Thank you, Brad, for lunch," Karah said smiling, after they had finished eating.

"It was my pleasure," Brad replied. Lunch with Karah had indeed been enlightening. "What are you going to do with the rest of your day, seeing as half the town is still snowbound?" Brad found himself asking.

"I think I'm going to head over to the food pantry and see what I can do to help out," Karah replied brightly. "Now that I know there is somewhere those without power can go for help, I'd like to see if I can offer a hand."

Why had he not thought about offering to help out? Brad thought, feeling disgusted by his lack of concern. *As mayor, it was his duty to be of service to his fellow citizens, and as a person— it was his moral obligation to help those in need. He and Sophie used to volunteer together in high school... Had he really lost sight of what was important in his desire to further his career? Had he focused so much on bolstering his own image, that he had forgotten the promises he'd made to those who'd helped put him in his position? Had he really forgotten to help his most vulnerable fellow neighbors?* "Would you mind if I came along with you?" Brad asked, hoping the newfound light within his heart was not too late.

Karah stared at Brad in surprise. *Had she just heard him correctly? Brad, wanted to go to the food pantry with her...* "Of course!" she exclaimed quickly, before Brad had a chance to change his mind.

"Great! Shall we get going?" Brad asked with a smile, as he stood up from his chair and donned his coat.

As they walked towards the door, even though she knew Brad was only going with her so that he could also be of assistance, Karah could not suppress the fluttering of her heart and her feeling of delight. *She was going to get to spend even more time in Brad's company! Was she being disloyal to Sophie for being happy by such a prospect? For now,* Karah decided determinedly, *she would put that thought from her mind. For now, she would just enjoy her good fortune.*

Chapter 26

"I have to admit," Brad remarked, turning to Karah with a grin, "I really enjoyed helping out at the food pantry this afternoon."

"I'm so glad," Karah replied, as she returned Brad's smile, seeing the happiness upon his face. Watching Brad walking, his steps light, Karah knew he realized that he had spent his time doing something extremely worthwhile. He had helped the citizens he served in an entirely new capacity, and the knowledge that Brad was aware of this, warmed Karah's heart.

"I had forgotten what it's like to really help those in need— to really serve my fellow neighbors," Brad uttered, his heart pounding in delight. "Thank you for helping me realize that again," he added. *The way Karah was smiling at him, her gentle kindness... She truly was an enchanting woman,* Brad realized, suddenly feeling self-conscious about his appearance. "What are you doing the rest of the day?" he asked, finding himself not wanting to bid Karah farewell.

"It's going to sound entirely childish, but I was planning on going sledding in my backyard and then making some homemade Christmas cards," Karah admitted.

"I don't think that sounds childish at all," Brad replied with a smile. Then stopping beside the passenger door of his car, he turned towards Karah. "Would you mind if I join you?" he asked. *What was he doing? Wasn't he in love with Sophie...? Hopefully, Karah, would have the sense, he was apparently lacking, to tell him he could not join her.* Brad felt his stomach twist, knowing his *hope* was a lie, that he really hoped Karah would say, "of course, you can accompany me." *Why did he find himself wanting to spend time with Karah? There was nothing wrong with spending time with her. Karah and Sophie were friends, after all. Sophie wouldn't mind him spending time with her. It wasn't like he was planning on kissing her or anything,* Brad reassured himself. *Why had the thought of kissing Karah even crossed his mind? That was ridiculous, right? Sophie was who he was meant to be with, not Karah...*

"I'd love that," Karah replied, before she had a chance to change her mind.

"Excellent!" Brad heard himself exclaim, as he opened the car door for Karah.

"Do you mind if I turn on some Christmas music?" Karah asked, once Brad was seated. "I just can't seem to stop myself from listening to them twenty-four-seven after Thanksgiving."

"Sure," Brad replied with a chuckle. " I've been too busy at work to really listen to any."

"There's more to life than work, Brad. If you're not careful, you'll miss out on living," Karah remarked quietly.

Brad felt his cheeks burning with embarrassment. *Was he upset that Karah had said such words, or was he really upset by the truth they held? It was true,* Brad knew, *that he worked a lot, but there were goals he wanted to achieve. Was it possible to find a balance? To still achieve one's goals and also have time for recreation and leisure?* Gazing at Karah, Brad felt the flush of his cheeks subsiding. Karah was right. If he was not careful, he was going to join the pages of literature as another *Ebenezer Scrooge*. Forcing the thought of being haunted by the three spirits of Christmas and regretting the path he'd taken when he became an elderly man, Brad opened his mouth to speak. But before he had a chance to utter the words he was about to say, Karah interrupted.

"I'm sorry, Brad. I shouldn't have said anything," Karah remarked. The expression in her eyes displaying the regret she felt at delivering her wisdom so bluntly.

"No. Don't be sorry. You're absolutely correct," Brad assured her, the softness of a smile spreading across his lips. "What you said was a truth I needed to hear."

"Really?" Karah asked, smiling hesitantly.

"Yes," Brad replied. "I'll be the first to admit that I'm no longer the best at having fun, and if I'm being honest, probably not the best at celebrating Christmas either. There's another truth for you," he shared.

"I'm not sure I believe that," Karah returned.

"And why not?" Brad inquired, feeling happy that Karah saw him differently than he saw himself.

"Because, not only did you help ensure that the town's annual Christmas parade and bazaar were able to take place, but deciding to come help at the food pantry and serve those in need, *to give instead of receive*, well, I think that shows you're doing a great job of opening your heart to the hope, peace, joy and love of Christmas," Karah replied knowingly.

Brad smiled. What Karah was able to see in him was more than he had been able to see in himself. *How was it possible that Karah seemed to know him so well?* Listening to Karah give him directions to her house, Brad continued to ponder the intuitiveness of his delightful companion.

"We're here!" Karah sounded, pointing to a little brick house appearing, warm and cozy, against the snow.

Brad pulled into the driveway and turned off the car. Looking out the windshield, he noticed Karah's Christmas decorations. White lights twinkled warmly around the pillars on the porch, a wooden snowman holding a *Merry Christmas* sign stood by the door, and the peppermint striped wreath pulled everything together in a warm welcome. "Your decorations are classy," Brad said. "If it didn't take so long to put them up, something like this would look really nice at my house."

"Oh, putting them up is the fun part. The time is of no importance," Karah laughed brightly, as she unfastened her seatbelt.

Brad smiled. He wished he had Karah's kind of mindset. Growing up, his family had never decorated that much. They usually just put up a pre-lit tree a day or two before Christmas and then took it down after they opened presents on Christmas Day. In doing that, Brad now wondered, *had he and his family turned Christmas into nothing more than an interruption in the routine of their daily lives? Had they ever really stopped to appreciate the reason for the holiday? Was it possible to start appreciating it now?*

"Are you ready to go sledding?" Karah asked, her face alight with excitement.

"Yes! Let's go sledding!" Brad exclaimed, a smile engulfing his face as he opened the car door.

It only took Karah a few moments to retrieve a pair of saucer sleds from the garage. As Brad stood, watching Karah bounding towards him through the snow, the red and green plastic sleds fluttering out from under her arms as if she'd grown wings, the smile he wore upon his face grew even larger. Karah's pure joy, her childish delight, was absolutely radiant!

"What are you thinking about behind that grin?" Karah asked, arriving at Brad's side and offering him a sled.

"You'd probably think I'm stupid," Brad uttered, hoping that would suffice, but Karah raised her eyebrows.

"I will not think you're stupid. I promise," Karah said.

"Alright," Brad began, clearing his throat. "I was just thinking how I wish I had the same jubilant childlike excitement that you have."

"So, you wish you were a big kid too?" Karah laughed, her cerulean eyes twinkling merrily.

"You're not offended?" Brad uttered in amazement.

"Of course not. I know I'm a big kid when it comes to Christmas, and I'm perfectly happy with that," Karah replied, the smile she wore expressing her satisfaction. "Now, let's go sledding and bring that inner-child of yours back to life. Race you to the hill!" she added, then darted off as fast as she could through the snow.

At Karah's words, Brad tightened his grip on his sled and began chasing after her, feeling his steps becoming lighter as he opened his heart up to having fun. He reached the top of the hill just as Karah was climbing onto her sled. Throwing himself down in belly-flop fashion, Brad felt the cool air whipping through his hair as flecks of snow sprayed up hitting his face. He held his legs straight behind him, inches off the ground, and felt the sled beginning to swirl beneath him in a circular motion. Spinning faster and faster down the hill, Brad heard a whoop of delight escape his lips. He had not had this much fun in who knew how long! He heard Karah's bright laughter and giddy squeals as he caught sight of her spinning past him. Landing at the bottom of the hill, Brad rolled off his sled and lay on his back looking up at the gray, wintery, sky; his heart pounding blithely within his chest.

"Are you okay?" Karah asked, her voice slightly worried as she stood gazing down at Brad.

"Yes! Let's do that again!" Brad exclaimed. Looking up at Karah… *Karah, with her warm blue eyes and soft brown hair… Karah, with her bright smile and slightly flushed cheeks… Karah, the woman who had helped him to have fun again, the woman he wondered why he had never really seen before,* Brad felt a strange sensation. *Had his heart just fluttered? No, surely he must be mistaken. His heart belonged to Sophie. It had and would always belong to Sophie…?* Rising to his feet, Brad picked up his sled and followed Karah back up the hill, wondering why he suddenly felt like butterflies had made their home within his stomach.

"I'm freezing," Karah said with a shiver, after riding her sled down the hill a few more times. "How about some apple cider?" she asked.

"That sounds delicious," Brad replied. "I just need to send,

Soph, a quick text about dinner." *It was Sophie who was causing the butterflies in his stomach*, Brad tried to convince himself. *He just wanted to see her so badly, that he was unconsciously misplacing his feelings on Karah, Sophie's friend. What kind of fool was he? He was infatuated with Sophie. Karah was charming, but it was Sophie he...* Brad scolded himself, running his free hand through his hair while he texted. Relief flooded through him when Sophie's text confirmed their plans.

As Karah watched Brad texting Sophie, she felt guilty for wanting to spend more time with him. She had resided herself to the fact that Brad was Sophie's, but even so, she could not ignore the pain it caused her. *If only she had been brave enough to tell Sophie of her true feelings when Sophie had asked. If only she had not felt the need to sacrifice her own heart and happiness. Would it be wrong of her to ask?* Karah wondered. *Was it really any of her business?* When Brad pocketed his phone and turned his attention back to her, Karah uttered the words before she changed her mind.

"Brad, why do you love Sophie?" Karah watched the stunned expression appear on Brad's face as he was caught off guard by her words. *Would he answer her? There was really no reason why he should. Would he...*

"I've known Sophie forever. I liked her all through high school, and now she's finally given me a chance," Brad replied, not exactly answering Karah's question. *Did he really love Sophie? He thought he did, he told himself he did... but was he sure that what he was feeling was love? When he had kissed Sophie, he had enjoyed it, even though he had a feeling Sophie had not. Was he blinded by the desires that Sophie had finally given him a chance, and that he believed her to be his perfect match, that he was confusing friendship love with romantic love?*

Brad's words had conveyed more than Karah had expected. *Maybe, he was not really in love with Sophie, but rather in love with the idea of Sophie. Was it wrong of her to feel happiness at this discovery?* Karah wondered, as she stood gazing a Brad. Brad's explanation had not been full of romantic descriptions or adulations, but rather shallowness. *If she didn't know any better,* Karah thought, *Brad was behaving like Jane Austen's Mr. Darcy before he fell in love with Elizabeth Bennet; concerned with ensuring he married a woman he deemed a proper match instead of a match made out of love. Brad needed time to figure things out on his own. He and Sophie needed to determine their true feelings for one another, and she was not going to mingle any further.*

"On second thought," Karah said, resting a hand on her forehead. "I've got a slight headache and I think I need to lie down. Thanks for the ride home." Then before she changed her mind and invited Brad inside again for apple cider, Karah took both sleds and headed inside.

Brad watched as Karah shut the front door behind her. The entire last five minutes had been strange. *Why would Karah invite him in for apple cider, ask him why he loved Sophie, and then say she had a headache? Why did everything have to be so darn confusing?* Walking towards his car, Brad remained lost in thought. Maybe dinner with Sophie tonight would give him the answers he needed.

Chapter 27

As she sat in the front passenger seat staring out the window, oblivious to the passing landscape, Sophie's stomach twisted and turned with the fluttering sensation of biking down a hill too fast.

Brad had texted her while she was at work to reschedule their dinner plans for tonight, and instead of feeling elated, Sophie felt miserable. She could not keep putting off the conversation she needed to have with Brad, no matter how much she dreaded the prospect. To further add to her misery, Grant, having picked her up from work at five just like he had promised, still had not mentioned their kiss during the entirety of the car ride home! When they pulled up to the farmhouse, the butterflies in Sophie's stomach lessened as she was distracted by the sight of her car parked out front.

"You were able to get it towed!" Sophie exclaimed in surprise, thankful for the momentary distraction. "With the roads as bad as they still are, I wasn't sure if you would be able to."

"I wasn't sure I was going to be able to at first either," Grant admitted with a grin. "But things ended up working out."

"Thank you so much!" Sophie exclaimed, her smile matching the glow that filled her eyes.

"You're welcome," Grant replied.

A glimmer of confliction raced across Grant's eyes, and Sophie felt her heart begin hammering loudly within her chest. *Did Grant regret kissing her? Was that why he had not spoken about it yet; why his gaze seemed to be fighting with the prospect of speaking or remaining silent? Why did the notion of Grant's rejection suddenly hurt so much?* Then before another doubt or worry could pass across her mind, Sophie observed Grant's lips part, and her heart gave a hopeful flutter.

"I'll be inside in a sec," Grant uttered. "I have something I need to do first," he added, his voice a bit mysterious.

"Okay," Sophie remarked, feeling the hopefulness in her heart begin to sink as she stared at him perplexed. Those had not been the words she had been anticipating. *What could Grant possibly have to do, out in the cold snow, before he came inside? Was that simply an excuse to continue avoiding talk about their kiss?* Sophie didn't know what bothered her more, the fact that Grant had not mentioned the kiss, or the fact that he seemed to be averting any discussion of it.

Determined to not let her annoyance or curiosity get the better of her, Sophie headed inside. Removing her coat and opening the closet door, she found an envelope taped to the hanger where she normally hung her coat. *What could this possibly be?* she thought, pulling the envelope off the metal hanger. Examining the envelope in her hands, Sophie saw her name scrolled across its front in handwriting that was unfamiliar. Slipping her coat onto the hanger, she closed the closet door and took the envelope with her into the living room. As she sat down on the couch, the glow of the Christmas tree illuminating the room in a soft golden light, Sophie's excitement bubbled within her, and she hurriedly tore open the envelope and pulled out the letter. Feeling her heart flutter as she unfolded the stationary, she slowly began to read.

Dear Sophie,

After sharing that I've fallen in love with you through the stories your Grandpa told me over the course of the past four years, you must think me a complete jerk for not saying anything to you about our kiss last night. For giving you that perception, I sincerely apologize. You see, last night I just did not have the right words to fully express my feelings. So, not wanting to say something wrong or foolish, or something that might offend you, I decided not to say anything until I had time to collect my thoughts and compose them in written form. I know that must sound silly in today's time of speedy text messages and tweets, but I guess I'm just a little "old fashioned" in the ways of communication. So, here it goes. I hope when you read this letter it sounds as articulate as it did in my mind when I was writing it.

Sophie, kissing you was more than I could have hoped for or could have ever imagined. You might think me a sentimental fool, but kissing you felt right— like it was somehow meant to be. I have always believed the notion of feeling a spark or something along that nature to be a myth, but that myth was proven true by you. Maybe I'm the only one who felt anything, and maybe you will never look at me the same after confiding this to you, but I had to convey to you what I experienced. All I can say is, Sophie, I have been waiting for something my entire life; something I thought I had once found when I lived in Nashville, but then circumstances made me no longer believe it to be real. Kissing you, however, brought my belief back; because in our kiss, I found that something for which my heart had always been searching—love—the spark of unconditional love.

There, now I've said it and will not have to live with the regret of remaining silent. Sophie, my heart is now yours to do with as you wish.

> *Hopefully yours,*
> *Grant*

Sophie read and reread the letter she held trembling between her fingers. *Grant had felt something... She was not the only one! He was interested in her and did have feelings for her after all. Love...The spark of unconditional love...*

264

Sophie's heart was pounding with nervousness and excitement. *Grant was in love with her...* She had initially tried to deny it, but Sophie knew she was in love with him too! *Unconditional...Could Grant really feel that strong of a love from just the one kiss they'd shared? From just the short time they'd known one another?* The thought of such a strong revelation both scared Sophie and filled her with an abounding sensation of joy! *For Grant to indeed feel for her a love so strong...* Sophie prayed her love for him was just as strong. Reeling in elation, Sophie was thinking of what she was going to say to Grant when he came inside, when she felt her phone vibrate within her pocket. Glancing at the screen, Sophie's heart dulled, and the joy she had just experienced now felt like a rock slowly sinking within her stomach.

"Looking forward to dinner tonight!" Brad had texted. *"I have had such an interesting day. Can't wait to tell you about it over a delicious dinner at my place!"*

Sophie felt horrible. After reading Grant's letter, she had instantly forgotten she had told Brad she would have dinner with him tonight. She could not just cancel last minute, even if she was dreading how ending things with Brad tonight would make him feel. Sophie knew she had to end things with him in person, not over text message. Brad deserved that kindness. To not do so, would be cruel and utterly unfair. *Now that Grant had admitted he was still interested in her...Now that he had told her that last night he had fallen in love with her...*Sophie had to be honest about her feelings and her discernment of them; she had to express her heart.

"I've had an interesting day too," Sophie texted back, her fingers moving stiffly against the keys. Seconds after she sent her reply, Sophie felt her phone vibrate against her fingers. *"Great! See you in an hour!"* she read, before returning her phone to her pocket. *Why was she being such a coward? She needed to pull it together. Ellen had warned her, that if she was not careful, hearts would get hurt. Oh, how she wished she could just wiggle her nose or point a finger and magically make things turn out fine.* Wrestling with her thoughts, Sophie heard the front door open and looking up, saw Grant standing in the door frame smiling at her handsomely.

"I see you found my letter," Grant stated, his voice both hesitant and hopeful as his eyes surveyed Sophie's expression.

"Yes, I did," Sophie breathed, feeling butterflies begin to once again take flight within her stomach.

"And what did you think about it?" Grant asked, taking a step into the room.

"I found it very *enlightening*," Sophie answered, her eyes holding Grant's gaze as she took a step in his direction.

Before Sophie could take another step, Grant closed the space between them, and gathering Sophie into his arms, kissed her with a tenderness even more loving then the kiss they had shared last night. The passion and wonder Sophie felt in Grant's kiss, mirrored the feelings she felt within her heart. *How could she initially have been so blind? Why had it taken her so long to see what her heart had seen from the very beginning?* Sophie wrapped her arms around Grant's neck, feeling the strength of his shoulders beneath her hands. She was just beginning to pull him closer and felt Grant take a step towards her, tightening their embrace, when Sophie felt her phone again vibrate. Grant felt her distraction, and as his lips pulled away from hers, Sophie saw in his eyes that she was losing him. Despite her efforts to regain their connection, Grant released her from his arms.

"What is it?" Grant asked, his eyes questioning and concerned as he held Sophie's gaze.

"It's just... I'm supposed to...I'm supposed to have dinner tonight with Brad and..." Sophie watched as looks of hurt and betrayal flashed across Grant's face.

"I'd hoped...after all your Grandpa said and the faith I had in your character. I never imagined you would pretend just like *her*," Grant declared dejected, then stormed from the room leaving Sophie crushed and confused.

Chapter 28

Sophie's heart ached as she watched Grant retreat from the living room. He had not even given her a chance to explain. *She couldn't just cancel on Brad without giving him an explanation in person; he was her friend and she owed him at least that much. Breaking it off with Brad was going to break his heart. Grant should have understood. He should have let her tell him why she had to go to dinner tonight instead of just storming out of the room. But Grant...*Sophie thought, feeling her heart shattering into pieces, *he had been so quick to judge, so quick to accuse her of "pretending like her;" a her whose story she did not even know.* It was entirely unfair! Sophie felt a tear silently begin rolling down her cheek. *How could Grant have reacted that way? How could he have been so insensitive after all the previous sensitivity he had shown her?* Then hurriedly wiping the tear away, Sophie felt her cheeks flush in anger. *If Grant was going to be like that, maybe she didn't need to give him another thought. Maybe, Brad had been right about him all along and Grant was nothing but a man of poor character! If Grant was so prideful that he was willing to pass an instant and uninformed judgment upon her, maybe he did not deserve her. Maybe, he didn't even really love her!* Heading upstairs, Sophie tried to mask her hurt with indifference, but even though she swore she would guard her heart much better from now on, she could not ignore the pain she felt at present.

It was a quarter to five, when Sophie descended the stairs wearing a maroon sweater dress and brown leather boots. As she tugged her arms through the sleeves of her coat, feeling both relieved and upset that she had not encountered Grant, Sophie was surprised to find another envelope with her name on it lying beside her purse. Sitting down on the bottom step of the stairs, Sophie opened the letter as Ivy came over, wagging her tail, and sat down in front of her. As Sophie pulled out two folded pieces of paper and began scanning the first page while scratching Ivy behind the ears, her heart quickly sank. *"Here is the contract. Maybe you can find a way to dissolve it. Grant."* Hurriedly flipping the paper over, Sophie's eyes sought for a glimmer of ink hoping there was more Grant had written. It was pointless. Grant's words were as stark as the white blankness of the stationary in her hand. Feeling the ache of her heart growing, Sophie turned her attention to the other slip of paper and read:

"Marten's Farm and Cattle: Work and Lodging Agreement.

I, Charles "Charlie" Marten, being of sound mind and body, do hereby permit, Mr. Grant Bakesfield, to lodge at my residence in exchange for his services carried out around the farm. Mr. Bakesfield will continue to tend to the

cattle and perform all other necessary farm responsibilities,
until the first of the year. Mr. Bakesfield is, therefore, entitled
to remain in his lodgings until said time.

> *Signers:*

> *Charlie Marten— owner of Marten's Farm and Cattle*

> *Grant Bakesfield--- lodger."*

As Sophie held the slips of paper in her hands, her
fingers crinkling the edges as she tightened her grip, it was
clear to her that Grant no longer wanted anything to do with
her. Rising from the steps, Sophie shoved the papers roughly
into her purse and turned to Ivy. "I really don't know why
you like him," she said glowering, as Ivy wagged her tail
happily in reply. Then grabbing her car keys, Sophie turned
and headed out the door. Maybe Brad could finally have a
look at the contract. *Yes! That was exactly the course of
action she should take! After all*, Sophie recalled, *Brad had
told her he was interested in seeing the contract.*

While she drove, Sophie continued to mull over the
events of the past two days. *Was Grant playing some kind of
game? His words had seemed so genuine...his letter, so heart
felt...Where had she gone wrong in her interpretation of him?*
So consumed was she in thought, that Sophie was surprised
to find she was already driving into town. Her mind was
definitely distracted. *She probably shouldn't be driving in
such a state*, she chided herself.

A few minutes after she'd driven through town,

Sophie turned into a neighborhood filled with rows of cookie-cutter-style construction. Consulting her GPS, she began searching along the closely packed houses scanning for Brad's address. Slowing down, Sophie gazed at the GPS on her phone. *She had to be almost there. She was practically on top of the dot identifying her destination*, she thought with frustration. She proceeded to drive along the street a little further, and then quickly slammed on the brakes. Peering out her window, Sophie saw that she had arrived. Silhouetted by the snow, Brad's home stood before her like an undecorated gingerbread house. Looking just like the home two doors down, the house's sand colored brick and brown sided build appeared stark and... Sophie thought for a moment trying to find the right words to adequately describe it. The house was not homey, but stark and almost...*impersonal?* Brad's house was a complete contrast to Karah's, and to her own for that matter. There were no rocking chairs on the front porch, no wreath upon the door...There was absolutely nothing highlighting the personality of its occupant. *Maybe,* Sophie thought, giving her friend the benefit of the doubt as she took her foot off the brake and drove into the driveway, *Brad has not been living here long.*

Stepping out of her car, Sophie walked along the shoveled sidewalk and up the cement-pebbled steps onto the front porch. She had barely raised her hand to knock, when the front door was thrown open and a cascade of light flooded the front porch.

"Sophie!" Brad exclaimed with a grin. "Come on in." He opened the door wider, allowing her to step inside. "Did you have any trouble finding the place?" Brad asked, as he took Sophie's coat and hung it in the closet.

"No," Sophie replied with a smile. "I just typed your address into my GPS, and it brought me straight here."

"Good," Brad said jovially. "How about a tour?" he offered, gesturing for Sophie to follow him.

"Sure, that would be great!" Sophie replied with genuine interest. *She was bound to find more of the homeowner's personality within the house's walls,* she thought hopefully. The house Brad had grown up in, although fairly posh, had always felt homey, Sophie remembered. Surely, Brad's home would be just as comfortable and display some of his interests. As she began following Brad out of the foyer, Sophie found she was also eager to see how Brad had decorated for Christmas!

But following Brad throughout the various rooms, instead of meeting her assumptions, made Sophie feel sorry for her friend. With each new room they entered, the term *impersonal* continued to echo within Sophie's thoughts. It was not that Brad's home was completely spartan in its decor, *everything was put together rather nicely,* Sophie admitted. It was just...well, all the rooms looked like they had come straight out of a catalog and were never actually lived in. At her home, Sophie could tell a story about every piece of furniture, and every decoration hanging upon the walls.

Everything in her home, Sophie realized, said something about the family member who had bought it our hung it up. *Where was Brad's personality? Where was the glimmer into him as a person?* The Brad she was currently seeing, as they continued to traipse throughout the house, was not the Brad she remembered from high school. *Had she and Brad really changed so much?* Sophie wondered.

"Well, that just about concludes the tour," Brad said businesslike, as they began approaching the kitchen. "What did you think?" he asked, turning and gazing at Sophie.

Not only was she going to crush his heart tonight, Sophie thought sadly, *but now she was going to have to tell Brad she wasn't a fan of his decorating…She couldn't just lie, though…* "You're decorating is…umm…nice," Sophie began, "but I just feel like something is missing…"

Brad stared at Sophie, but instead of looking upset he smiled. "It doesn't really look like me, does it?" he admitted.

"You see that too?" Sophie uttered, taken off guard by Brad's response.

"Truth be told," Brad replied with a shrug, "I'm at my office more than I am here and have never really been good at decorating, so I gave my mom some money and let her decorate the place."

"Where are your Christmas decorations?" Sophie asked, unable to stop herself. *Brad would have at least put those up, wouldn't he?*

"You're not going to like my answer," Brad began,

"but honestly, I'm not a big fan of putting up a lot of decorations," he shared, leading the way towards the kitchen. "People spend so much time putting them up, only to have to take them down a few weeks later."

"Oh," Sophie murmured, unable to keep the astonishment from her voice. "Don't you find not decorating well... *sad*?" she asked, the expression on her face as shocked as her voice. "I mean, when you put up decorations, you get to remember decorating with family members... reminisce about the meaning behind each ornament... talk about what Christmas means as you anticipate the birth of..."

"Sorry," Brad interrupted and shrugged. "I guess I'm just not that sentimental. Growing up, my family always just put up a small pre-lit tree a few days before Christmas, and then we took it down after opening presents Christmas morning. Surely, you remember that?" he added, turning towards Sophie.

Sophie stopped walking. *Christmas was the most profound time of the year! When sacrificial and merciful love took human form. How could Brad just shrug it off so nonchalantly?* Thinking of Brad's words, Sophie had a vague recollection of The Devanstons' treeless home the day after Christmas. *But did they really take it down Christmas morning after opening presents? That just seemed so...so wrong! Christmas Day was just the beginning of the Christmas season.*

Brad read the shock in Sophie's eyes, and continued.

"Don't worry, I have a small pre-lit tree in the kitchen. It will give us a nice romantic mood for dinner," he smiled. *It wasn't that he hated Christmas decorations*, Brad thought, *he had actually really liked the way Karah had decorated her home--- it was warm...inviting... He had to stop thinking about Karah! Maybe it was laziness, or maybe it was because of the lack of a family decorating ritual, but he just did not like decorating. He enjoyed the decorations when they were up, but he just didn't want to be the one to put them up. In his ambition to excel in his career, had he really become that much of a "Scrooge?" That much of a "Grinch?" Was he really forgetting to truly appreciate the Christmas season for all that it was? The way Sophie was looking at him now...Was that pity he saw in her eyes?*

Sophie shook her head and continued following Brad. Brad was totally missing the meaning of Christmas. Christmas was not just about setting a romantic mood; it was so much more than that. When they arrived in the kitchen, Sophie saw the tree Brad had been talking about. Brad had definitely not lied about not liking to decorate, Sophie realized in disbelief. There was not a single ornament on its branches!

"How can you not like decorating a Christmas tree?" Sophie asked, her eyes unable to tear themselves from the barren tree limbs. "My Grandpa and I always had such a fun time decorating. We always waited to put our tree up a few days before Christmas so it would last through Epiphany. We would talk and laugh, make hot cocoa while we worked, and when…"

"I'm sure it doesn't seem like work when you have someone to help," Brad interrupted. "But when I come home from the office, I just can't bring myself to spend time working on something that I'm only going to have to take down in a few short weeks. Don't get me wrong, Soph, I *do* love a nicely decorated tree and home and the warm atmosphere it creates, I just currently don't find decorating to be all that *fun*. But if I had someone in my life who enjoyed decorating… I don't think I would mind helping with some of the decorations," Brad mused, as visions of Karah's festively decorated porch and then Karah speeding past him on her sled laughing happily, danced across his mind. *He had to be certain. He had to know for sure, without a doubt, if Sophie was in love with him and if he, for that matter, was truly in love with Sophie.*

What if Sophie was in love with him, and he was not in love with her like he had believed? Brad wondered. *Would he be able to forget the way his heart had felt when he was with Karah? But he had already made his intentions known to Sophie; had insisted that he was interested in her… If Sophie was indeed in love with him…* Brad knew he could never hurt her, that he would be a gentleman and stay by her side.

Sophie stared at Brad, continuing to process the words he had just spoken. When she had dreamed about her future, she realized, she had never imagined getting married to a husband who did not help her decorate for Christmas. Such a thought had never even crossed her mind! Sophie had always just assumed that she and her spouse would do things like that together...assumed that one day, if they were lucky enough to have children, that they would decorate as a family, like how she and her Grandpa had always done. When she had made ornaments and decorated the tree with Grant...*Was having a decorating tradition something she had taken for granted?* The way Brad was talking, he would never go looking for a Christmas tree out in the snow, Sophie realized, suddenly feeling extremely sorry for him. *Maybe, her conversation with Brad was going to prove easier than she had expected... Maybe, he could be brought to understand that they were entirely too different to work... Maybe, Brad's heart would not be broken*, Sophie thought with hopefulness.

The awkwardness of unspoken words seemed to fill the air, Brad thought, as he smiled politely while pulling Sophie's chair out and helping her into her seat. He then walked over to the counter and retrieved two wine glasses and a bottle of wine. *How on earth was he going to start his conversation with Sophie?* he wondered, feeling his stomach twist nervously as he worked on uncorking the wine. *He couldn't just open with— "Sophie, do you love me?"—now could he? If Sophie was in love with him, saying something like that, something that sounded so much like the beginning of a breakup, was bound to make her cry....And making Sophie cry, was something he had no desire to do.* The soft pop of the cork sounded, and setting the corkscrew down on the counter, Brad slowly began pouring the glasses of wine wishing, but knowing, there was no way to avoid the conversation.

"Can I help you with anything," Sophie offered, taking the glass of pinot Brad handed her.

"No, everything is under control," Brad replied, pulling a pasta casserole out of the oven, and setting a basket of rolls on the table.

"Wow!" Sophie exclaimed, smelling the enticing garlic and alfredo aroma as she gazed at the bubbling dish. "That chicken alfredo casserole smells marvelous! When did you become such a cook?"

"Well, unfortunately I can't take credit for it," Brad admitted. "I know my initial plan was having us cook dinner together, but I don't really enjoy cooking. Plus, if we cooked then we would probably end up spending most of the evening washing dishes instead of talking. So, I decided to ask a friend from work if I could pay her to make this for us. It does smell good, doesn't it?" Brad remarked, grabbing a serving spoon from a drawer and sticking it into the casserole.

There was absolutely nothing wrong about not cooking a meal yourself, Sophie told herself. She had enjoyed her fair share of ready-made entrees, and still partook of them since she was not the best cook herself. But even so, she couldn't help thinking how much she enjoyed talking with Grant while he made her breakfast, or when they had made dinner and then watched *White Christmas*. Brad was a great guy, a great friend. But the more time she spent with him, Sophie realized, they had less in common then she remembered. *Please let Brad understand...please let him realize he deserves someone who truly loves him,* she prayed.

"Here you are," Brad said, setting a plate of steaming casserole in front of Sophie, then taking his seat. "Here's to wonderful company and to old *friends*," he toasted, raising his glass of wine. How he hoped Sophie had heard the way he'd enunciated the word *friends*. *Sophie was beautiful. She was charming, and he truly enjoyed being in her company. Ever since she'd returned to town, he had believed her to be his perfect match,* Brad recalled, gazing at Sophie as she sat across from him. *But Karah...Karah had helped a side of him that had been dormant come back to life. Karah had helped him to have fun again... had made his heart feel like it never had before... Karah had helped bring out the best in him. There was no denying it any longer,* Brad realized. *He had fallen in love with Karah!*

"Cheers," Sophie replied, clinking her glass against Brad's.

"So, have you given any more thought about spending Christmas Eve and Christmas Day with my family and me?" Brad asked, as they began eating. *Maybe,* Brad hoped, *Sophie's response would help him determine her feelings.*

Sophie gently wiped her mouth with her napkin. "I don't know if that is such a good idea," she began. "You see, it's…"

Brad set his fork on his plate and looked across the table at Sophie. *The way she was looking at him, as if she was afraid to hurt him, as if she might regret her words… Could it be possible? Was Sophie not in love with him? Would he not have to forsake his feelings for Karah after all?* He had to be certain. He had to know if Sophie was in love with him, and if he was still bound to his honor as a gentleman. "Why on earth would it not be a good idea?" Brad interrupted, causing Sophie to shift uncomfortably in her seat. "My parents would love to see you. They have not seen us together since high school." *Now, to really determine what Sophie's feelings are for me,* Brad decided. Then holding Sophie's gaze, he added, "Plus, I don't want you spending Christmas alone, especially when we can spend *our* first Christmas together," he finished emphatically. *There. His words explicitly implied he was in love with her. If Sophie was in love with him, then he should see an extreme expression of joy fill her face. And if not…well then, things might be easier than he believed,* Brad thought hopefully. *Neither of them would end up getting hurt.*

Sophie's insides squirmed at Brad's declaration. Even though Grant had made it clear he no longer want anything to do with her, she could not continue to string Brad along when she knew she was not in love with him. When Brad had kissed her, it had been nothing like the way she had felt when Grant's lips met hers. *When Grant's lips had pressed against hers, their warmth and tenderness, the way her heart had raced...* Sophie shook her head. She had come here tonight to end things with Brad, so she needed to end things before she made the situation any harder.

Sophie still had not replied, and the look in her eyes expressed that she was experiencing a kind of inner turmoil, Brad observed. *If only she would give him an answer. Maybe he needed to set a more hypothetical example of their possible future together*, Brad thought. "If this Christmas is any indication of *our future*," he began, "we will be engaged, sell the farm, and be living happily married by next year! We will..."

As Brad continued talking, Sophie stopped listening. *Sell the farm! Was Brad crazy? Why on earth would he ever think she would be willing to sell the farm? Did he even know her?* Brad's feelings for her were more than Sophie had anticipated. Ending things was not going to be easy, but Brad had to know they were just too different. He had to know that she was not in love with him, that she was in love with Grant, even if the love she felt for Grant was now unrequited.

"Brad," Sophie interrupted, choosing her words carefully. "I like you; I really do. We were great friends in high school and seeing you again... it is almost like nothing has changed, and we have never been apart." Sophie saw Brad watching her and listening to her every word, his eyes bright with anticipation. She took a deep breath and continued. "But things have changed. *We* have changed. And no matter how much we might not want to acknowledge it, *like* and *love*, are not the same feeling. Brad, I would be lying to us both if I told you that I felt the latter," Sophie concluded, seeing the realization of her words sink in, as Brad's eyes flashed with not dejection but...*relief*? Sophie was confused by Brad's expression but continued. "You deserve someone better than me, Brad. You deserve someone who loves you without a doubt in her mind. A woman who helps you both bring out the best in each other." Brad shook his head and remained silent, a soft smile forming upon his lips, as Sophie felt her heart beating anxiously. "Please say something," she implored.

Brad reached across the table and placed his hand gently on top of Sophie's. His eyes held her gaze as he rubbed the top of her hand softly with his thumb. Deep down, when he had first believed he was in love with Sophie, Brad had known her feelings were not as strong as his, but he had hoped that they would eventually grow into love. Then, when he had become aware of his own misinterpretation of his feelings, he had believed Sophie's feelings for him might be stronger than he had initially believed. *And now, as it turned out, they both had been afraid tonight to break the other's heart*. Brad gave Sophie's hand a squeeze, and still looking into her eyes, smiled. "Soph," he said softly. "When I saw you at lunch with Karah, I felt like the same lovestruck kid I was in high school all over again, and I knew when you told me you would give me a chance, that you probably didn't feel the same way I *believed* that I felt about you; but since I always regretted not getting to date you high school, I was determined not to miss my chance again."

"Brad, I'm so sorry," Sophie remarked gently, her eyes filled with compassion.

"No," Brad continued apologetically. "I'm the one that is sorry. I'm sorry for being the one who always wants to turn our friendship into something more. I know now that we are just meant to always be friends. You did warn me to take it slow, and then when I kissed you...well, it was kind of obvious when you didn't really kiss me back, and I still ignored it. I was just so blinded by what I thought I felt for you that I didn't realize really until today that my feelings for you are not those of love," Brad laughed with a shake of his head.

"Wait, hang on, you're not in love with me?" Sophie asked, her voice full of shock. "And you knew I didn't feel anything the first time we kissed?" Sophie continued in disbelief.

"Really?" Brad replied with a chuckle. "I didn't know you felt *nothing*. I just knew the kiss did not make you feel the same way it made me. But I was so caught up in getting to kiss you and thinking what a great wife you'd make, that I didn't care and didn't take the time to really think about how I felt either. As it turns out," Brad continued with a smile, "I think I've actually fallen in love with someone else. But if you had told me tonight that you were in love with me, Soph, I promise I would have stayed with you. Knowing all this, are you still okay with us being friends?" Brad asked.

"Of course," Sophie smiled, giving Brad's hand a gentle squeeze. "On one condition, though. You've got to tell me who you've fallen in love with," she remarked intrigued.

Brad shifted in his seat. "I hope you won't be upset, but I've fallen in love with Karah," he said. "It wasn't intentional," he continued. "But with all the times we've been around each other, and then going to the food pantry and sledding with her today...it just happened. I promise, I'm not some kind of a scoundrel like Mr. Bakersfield implied," he added. "When you and I have been *dating*, my actions have been completely honorable. I made my intentions known to you, and I'm a man of my word."

"I know you are Brad," Sophie smiled softly. "You've always been a man of good character all the years I've known you."

"Thanks, Soph, that means a lot," Brad uttered, returning her smile. "I just wish I was a man who was better at perceiving other people's feelings," he laughed. "First, I made myself believe that I was in love with you and you in love with me, and now that I've admitted that I'm in love with Karah, well, I have no idea if she returns my feelings,"

Brad admitted.

"You're not the only one who wishes they were more perceptive," Sophie said. "I thought Grant was in love with me, but it turns out I'm the only one who fell in love. I was such an idiot! You tried to warn me from the beginning that I didn't know anything about him and that he might only be trying to somehow take the farm," Sophie ranted.

It was just like, deep down, what he had always suspected, Brad pondered. *He had known from the first moment he laid eyes on Grant that he was competition, and somehow,* Brad thought, *he had always known he had a good chance of losing. Maybe that was why he had forced himself to believe that he and Sophie were meant to be together.* "Soph, I did say something along those lines, but the words were spoken out of pure jealousy," Brad admitted. "The first time I met Grant, I could tell he was interested in you, chalk it up to a guy's intuition. I'm sorry. I was wrong in thinking that, and I'm sorry that he hurt you," Brad added, his words laced with compassion. "As a good *friend*," Brad offered, hoping to cheer Sophie up, "the invitation to come celebrate Christmas at *The Belle of Sugar Plum* tomorrow night still stands."

"Well then, as a *friend*, I happily accept the invitation," Sophie agreed. Brad truly was a good friend. "Especially, since the alternative would mean spending Christmas at the farm with a roommate who will be sulking around and angry with me." Even as she spoke the words,

Sophie could not ignore the sting of rejection that surged through her heart. *How could she have been so wrong about Grant?*

"I wish I could see that contact," Brad muttered. "I'm sure I could help you find a way to force him to leave."

But I don't want Grant to leave, Sophie thought sorrowfully. *He's the one who wants to leave.* "I have the contact," Sophie voiced instead, stifling her heartache, as a wave of agitation swept over her as she recalled the bluntness of Grant's words—*Maybe you can find a way to dissolve it.* "I'll go get it now."

Chapter 29

The entire drive home, Sophie repeated over and over what Brad had told her. *"Now that you are the owner of Marten's Farm and Cattle, the contact is no longer accurate, since your Grandpa is listed as the owning party. Also, since you stood to inherit the farm and were not included on the contact, all parties did not agree to the arrangement. Put all that together, despite the fact that the document is notarized, and the contract is, therefore, completely void. Simply tell, Mr. Bakesfield, all that, and then tear up the contact."* Sophie took a deep breath to calm herself. *She could do it*, she told herself, as the farm came into view. *She could tell Grant that the contract holding him here was not valid. She could let him go.*

Sophie's heart beat sadly against her chest, as she listened to the soft crunch of snow beneath her boots, while she walked towards the house. She didn't know why she was so nervous. Grant had practically thrust the contract at her in an effort to illustrate his desire to terminate it. *Why then was she so anxious?* As she stepped into the foyer, Sophie had expected to be met by some tantalizing aroma from something Grant was cooking, but instead her eyes rested on the small pile of packed suitcases that stood near the door. She felt her heart sink in somber understanding. Grant was leaving regardless of breaking his contract or not, and there was nothing she could do to keep him here. Sophie suddenly found herself wishing the contract could indeed be legally upheld in court. *Why was she being so ridiculous?* But as she felt the fractures beginning to tear within her heart, she knew why. *Oh, how things had changed since she had first laid eyes on Grant.* But she could not force him to stay; she could not force him to love her.

Gathering herself, Sophie strode into the living room prepared to encounter Grant, but as she stepped into the room, she found it vacant. The lights on the Christmas tree softly twinkled, offering a cheerful welcome, but Grant was nowhere to be seen. Slumping down onto the sofa, Sophie's eyes roved across the mantel, donned with boughs of holly and displaying the porcelain nativity. Ivy trotted quietly up to her, and giving Sophie's hand a gentle lick, laid her head on Sophie's lap. Running her fingers through Ivy's soft fur, Sophie stared at the handcrafted ornaments glistening upon the tree, as shards of light made contact with the paint. Grant had been so mystified, she recalled, when she had cracked an egg, and separating it, told him he was ready to paint. *"What do you mean? That's not paint, that's an egg,"* Grant had declared, as if she had lost her mind. But after Sophie mixed a drop of food coloring into the yolk and mixed it, he had been amazed at her ability to make a homemade tempera paint. Sophie continued to watch the tree lights softly bouncing off the ornaments' sheen, lost in thought. *It was not even Christmas yet, but Grant had already helped to make this Christmas happy and special, and just like that, after feeling spurned, he was taking away all that he had given her. It wasn't fair.*

Wiping away the tears that were silently trickling down her face, Sophie's eyes noticed something beneath the tree. There, resting under the fragrant evergreen boughs, was a medium-sized package wrapped in brown paper and tied with shiny red ribbon. Forgetting her tears for the moment, Sophie rose from her seat, her curiosity piqued. *If Grant truly despised her, why would he give her a Christmas present? Was she being foolish to grasp at such a small strand of hope?* Bending down on her knees, Sophie pushed a cinnamon curl behind her ear and leaned forward to read the tag. "To Sophie, from Grant." Now that she was up close, she also noticed there was an envelope on top of the present. "To Sophie, Love Grandpa. Do not open until Christmas," the envelope read. Sophie's heart began to race with excitement. She would honor her Grandpa's request and not open his letter until Christmas, *but since Christmas Eve was tomorrow and Grant was leaving...*Sophie pulled the package towards her and slowly began unwrapping it.

As she tore off the paper, the crisp parchment crinkling between her fingers, Sophie had no idea what could possibly be inside. *She had not even thought to get Grant a present*, she realized embarrassed, *and even though he now disliked her, he had still given her a gift*. As the wrapping paper fell away, Sophie's breath caught within her chest.

"Sophie's Christmas Treasures," she breathed aloud, as her hand traced the lettering engraved upon the wooden chest. *The deep cherry stain, the elegant etching... It was absolutely beautiful!* The time Grant must have spent carving such a heartfelt gift, caused Sophie's eyes to tear up in wonder. Moving her fingers along the chest's smooth edges, Sophie's fingers lifted the lid. A note lay at the bottom of the box. *"To store the ornaments, joy, and Christmas memories you make, so they will never accidentally get thrown out again. Merry Christmas, Grant."* *This was quite possibly the best gift she had ever received,* Sophie thought, her face glowing as she continued to gaze at Grant's handywork. *If only receiving it did not hurt so much.* A cough startled Sophie, and she turned and saw Grant standing in the doorframe watching her.

"I'm glad you like it," Grant uttered, his green eyes dull and void of their usual liveliness.

"Thank you," Sophie replied, holding his gaze. "The time and care...you didn't have to…," her words caught in her throat.

"I will be leaving tomorrow morning, after Midnight Mass," Grant remarked curtly, his hands resting in the pockets of his jeans.

Sophie felt her heart breaking. "The contract is void. You need not worry about breaking it. You are free to go," she murmured flatly, and watched as Grant nodded and started to leave the room. But as Sophie watched him turn away from her, a tiny voice inside her began demanding to be heard. *She was undeniably in love with Grant, and love is something that is not easily found. Why on earth was she not fighting for it? If she let Grant walk away without letting him know her feelings, without letting him know that he had misjudged her reason for keeping her dinner plans with Brad,* Sophie realized, *she would regret it for the rest of her life!*

"Wait!" Sophie blurted, removing the chest from her lap and rising to her feet. She watched as Grant slowly turned and faced her, his eyes wary and uncertain. "You are being entirely unfair!"

"I hardly believe…," Grant began, his voice flat and eyes flickering with betrayal.

"No, let me finish," Sophie interrupted. "When I told you, I was having dinner with Brad tonight," Sophie ignored the look of deceit Grant cast at her and continued, "you never gave me a chance to explain. I had agreed to have dinner with Brad before you and I kissed, but after that…when I finally realized the feelings of my own heart and my unfairness to Brad, I knew that I had to go to dinner tonight to end things with him in person."

Grant's expression softened at Sophie's declaration, and his eyes could not hide his confusion. Sophie's words had not been what he had been expecting. *Had he so horribly misjudged her? Was it possible? Did he dare continue to hope?*

"Grant," Sophie declared firmly, her hands on her hips. "I have undeniably fallen in love with you, and up until recently, I was quite certain you were in love with me."

Sophie stared at Grant, hearing the sound of her heart echoing within her ears. *Why wasn't he saying anything? She had just professed her infatuation with him, and he was being silent...* Sophie continued watching Grant nervously, her heart pulsing faster against her chest, as she observed a smile slowly pulling at the corners of his lips. Then, before she realized what was happening, Grant had crossed the space between them and scooped her up into his arms!

"I'm so sorry," Grant whispered, holding Sophie gently in his embrace and looking down at her face. "I was such a fool. I allowed a scar from my past to jade my views of love. Can you find it in your heart to forgive me?" he asked, brushing his lips softly against Sophie's forehead.

Sophie felt her hurt melting, as Grant continued to hold her tenderly in his arms. Even if she had wanted to hold a grudge, Sophie knew she never could. Feeling warm and safe in Grant's embrace... watching him gaze lovingly into her eyes... took away all her selfish desires and left only one thought in her mind. "Of course, I can forgive you," Sophie whispered softly. "I only wish I understood your accusatory words," she added.

Grant stepped back and looked at Sophie, her warm chocolate eyes holding his gaze like a mug of hot cocoa, and he found himself wishing he could remain forever a marshmallow floating within them. "You have every right to be owed an explanation," he said, unable to tear his gaze from Sophie's face. *Sophie was different. She was nothing like the her he had so wrongly accused her of being like. How could he have ever thought of Sophie to be one to pretend like that?* Grant scolded himself. Sophie was kind, smart, intriguing, sentimental, and exciting. Spending time in her company was like being given a wonderful gift. Sophie was, without a doubt, the woman he had always hoped to meet. His heart, having once tasted betrayal, had been guarded for too long. Seeing Sophie looking at him so tenderly, Grant felt his heart throb joyfully against his chest. He had not been erroneous to entrust his heart to her; he had been wrong to judge her so quickly, but he had not been foolish to fall in love with Sophie. "Let's sit down," Grant said gently, steering them both towards the couch.

Once they were seated, Grant ran a hand through his hair. He had not spoken about what had brought him to Sugar Plum since he had told his friend, Jack, four years ago. But Sophie needed to know, she needed to know why he had acted the way he had, even though it did not excuse his actions.

"When I was living in Nashville," Grant began, "I was engaged." He saw the surprise on Sophie's face, but instead of interrupting him, Grant watched as she continued to hold his gaze, waiting for him to continue. He cleared his throat and proceeded. "My fiancé, Delilah, and I started dating when we were juniors in high school. We ended up going to college together, and Delilah, who was a talented singer, began pursuing a degree in music. After graduating from college, we got engaged and had hopes of her signing with a recording studio. To make a horrible story short," Grant continued, "if I had not been so blinded by what I thought was love, maybe I would have seen the signs sooner. The girl from high school had changed in college, and I refused to see the change. And even though, Delilah, professed her unconditional love for me, she chose fame and its lifestyle over us."

"Grant, I…I'm so sorry," Sophie said, seeing the pain Grant's story still caused him wash across his face. "After you and I kissed, and I told you I was going to dinner with Brad… I can see now how you thought I was pretending to love you," Sophie remarked understandingly.

Grant nodded his agreement, but his eyes were filled with guilt. "It was completely unfair of me, though, to judge you so quickly. From what I knew about you, Sophie, and the time that we've spent together... I never should have judged you so harshly. It's just, living here with your Grandpa for the past few years and hearing him speak of you... I had finally started to believe in love and its ability to be unconditional again, and then when you…"

Now it was Sophie's time to nod. "You don't have to say anymore," she smiled tenderly, causing Grant to breathe a sigh of relief. "Grant, what I'm about to tell you is going to sound entirely cheesy, but I'm being completely honest with you," Sophie began. "When I tell you that *I love you*, I truly mean it. I'm an old soul trapped in a modern world, and as hopeless of a romantic as you can possibly get. That is probably why I love history so much," Sophie admitted with a laugh. "I believe in lifelong love, the kind where a couple grows old together; and I believe in writing a history, all our own, with the man I love." Sophie's eyes were dancing with happiness, as she gazed admiringly at Grant and continued. "I've read numerous letter correspondences between couples in my years of study, wishing someone loved me as much as the writers of the past loved one another. Then meeting you... experiencing your kindness towards me and your chivalry, even when my behavior did not deserve it... reading your letter… Grant, I have been looking for a man like you my entire life," she smiled, snuggling up to him. "*You* are the man I love, the man I have been searching for, for so long."

Grant wrapped his arm warmly around Sophie's shoulder and pulled her closer to him. "And I love you, Sophie Marten," he murmured affectionately. "The woman who taught me what love truly means, and that it does indeed exist, even when we have given up believing." As Grant gazed at Sophie snuggled beneath his arm, *not even the sparkling Christmas tree, glittering nearby, could outshine the smile upon her face*, he thought. The way Sophie was looking at him, the way she was seeing him for who he truly was, was more than Grant felt he deserved. He made a vow, then and there, that he would spend the rest of their days together showing her that she had not been wrong in giving him a second chance.

Chapter 30

Rolling over, Sophie looked at the alarm clock on her nightstand. *Was she dreaming? Had she and Grant really professed their love for one another last night?* Smiling happily, Sophie folded her arms behind her head and continued to lay upon her pillow. *Snuggling with Grant on the couch last night… her heart had felt at peace*, Sophie recalled. How she had wanted to remain sitting there all night with him, even if they merely sat there in silence not speaking. *Just continuing to be in Grant's presence would have been enough*, she thought. *But sleep was inevitable, no matter how long they had tried to resist it*, Sophie recalled with a laugh, thinking of how she and Grant had almost fallen asleep on the sofa. Their bodies had finally given in to the gentle caress of slumber and caused them to bid each other goodnight. Sighing with love-filled contentment, Sophie closed her eyes, her mind racing with thoughts of thankfulness.

The lowing of the cattle waiting to be fed, however, caused Sophie to open her eyes again. No matter how long she wished to remain in bed recalling last night, she needed to get up. A farm didn't run itself on its own. But as she pushed her quilt back, Sophie was suddenly struck by another thought. *Today was Christmas Eve!* Jumping out of bed with the same jubilant anticipation the spirit of Christmas never failed to keep alive within her, Sophie peered out the frost covered window. It had been cold enough that the snow, which had fallen a few days ago, was still laying softly across the landscape. Although the sun had melted it mostly from the roads, the fact that the snow still blanketed the rest of the ground, gave Sophie hope that Sugar Plum might actually see a white Christmas this year! Christmas Eve was indeed full of hope, Sophie mused delightedly. And this Christmas, at first having been wrapped in unhappiness, was miraculously transforming into one of the best Christmases she could have possibly imagined! It was as Sophie was reflecting on the change of events, that her thoughts suddenly froze on today's date. *It was Christmas Eve...that meant... Tomorrow was Christmas, and she didn't have a gift for Grant!*

After hurriedly dressing, Sophie made her way down the stairs, and grabbing her keys, was about to dash out the door when...

"Whoa!" Grant exclaimed, from the living room as he saw Sophie darting by. "Where are you going in such a hurry?"

"No time to explain," Sophie replied, hurriedly grabbing her purse. "Tomorrow's Christmas!"

"I know," Grant chuckled, causing Sophie to shoot him a playful glare.

"I won't be long. I promise," Sophie remarked, opening the door.

"Good," Grant smiled. "Because I've got Christmas Eve plans that include your presence. Oh, and don't worry about the cattle, I'll feed them while you're gone," he added.

"You're a saint! Thank you so much!" Sophie gushed. "Don't start those Christmas Eve plans without me," she added, shooting Grant a smile before darting out the door.

Driving into town, Sophie racked her brain for gift ideas to get Grant. *He had given her such a thoughtful gift... Honestly, he'd already given her so much! How she wished she could think of something just as heartfelt to give him.* Sophie had just turned onto Main Street, when she spotted *All Thymes and Occasions. Maybe Karah would be able to help her think of something*, she hoped, parking along the curb and heading towards the shop. The bell above the door softly jingled as Sophie stepped inside, and she was delighted to see Karah standing behind the counter, working on a festive arrangement of red-and-white flowers.

"Karah!" Sophie exclaimed excitedly, as she walked towards her friend with a smile. "I need your help."

"Sophie! Merry Christmas Eve!" Karah replied brightly, returning Sophie's smile. "What can I help you with?" she asked.

"I need help finding a gift. I know it's really last minute," Sophie added embarrassed.

"What kind of gift are you looking for?" Karah asked, setting the vase of flowers she had been working on aside.

"Well," Sophie began, "I received a very thoughtful gift that was related to a memory I had shared, and I was hoping to find something that might be just as meaningful," Sophie finished hopefully.

"I see," Karah nodded thoughtfully. She glanced discreetly at Sophie's hand, and a sigh of relief she felt slightly ashamed of, fluttered within her. *Brad had not given Sophie an engagement ring! But he had still given Sophie something*, Karah knew, *but at least her heart was not yet entirely broken.*

"Grant got…," Sophie began.

"Wait… *Grant?* Don't you mean Brad?" Karah asked flabbergasted.

Sophie stared at Karah's confused expression. She had never confided her feelings for Grant to Karah, she realized. *How could she have though when she had not really understood her own feelings until recently?* "Brad and I have agreed it's best for us to just remain friends," Sophie explained. She watched as the confusion on Karah's face changed into one of amazement. *Was that a glimmer of relief she detected?* Sophie wondered. *Maybe her original hunch about Karah's feelings towards Brad had been correct despite Karah's assurance otherwise. If that was so…Brad had told her last night*, Sophie recalled with a smile, *that he had fallen in love with Karah but that he was unsure of Karah's feelings towards him. Was it possible that Karah was in love with Brad? Could two of her good friends end up this Christmas as happy as she and Grant? Was it too much to hope for?*

"Sophie Marten," Karah said, her eyes filled with disbelief. "Have you fallen in love with the man your Grandpa allowed to lodge at the farm?"

Sophie shook her head in confirmation and smiled in delight. "Yes. I didn't intend to, but I most definitely have fallen in love with him," she confided, still somewhat mystified.

"Then you're…you're absolutely sure you're not in love with Brad?" Karah asked, her heart pounding. *She needed verification. She needed to hear Sophie speak the words before she would allow herself to hope.*

"I'm sure," Sophie replied. "Brad and I both realized we were trying to force something that wasn't there. Besides, he and I are both in love with someone else," she added. Sophie watched Karah's expression. How she hoped Karah was in love with Brad.

Karah's heart began to pound faster at Sophie's words. *Brad was in love with someone else...What did that mean? The only other woman she'd seen spending time with Brad was...* Karah felt as if she were floating. *Was it too wonderful to believe? Was Brad actually in love with her?* She felt her cheeks growing warm and a smile spreading across her lips. "Well then, let's see what we can find as a gift for Grant," Karah said happily, her steps becoming lighter by the minute as she walked out from behind the counter.

As Sophie followed Karah, watching the joy radiating from her friend, she smiled to herself at the confirmation of Karah's feelings. *Now, if only she could find a way to bring Brad and Karah together...?*

"What did Grant get you, if you don't mind me asking?" Karah asked, as they continued walking around the shop.

"He made me a hand carved box to keep my Christmas ornaments in," Sophie shared, still in awe by Grant's heartfelt gesture.

"I know the perfect gift!" Karah remarked brightly, a smile spreading across her face, as she stopped in front of a Christmas tree display. "Give Grant Christmas ornaments that remind him of *this* Christmas," she suggested. "And write him a note that says something like, *here are a few ornaments to start our Christmas ornament collection.*"

"That's a brilliant idea!" Sophie declared, gazing at the ornaments on display.

"There's a reason I work in a flower and gift shop," Karah grinned. "I'll be up front when you're ready," she added, leaving Sophie to peruse the ornaments on her own.

Walking around the Christmas trees, Sophie gently turned and examined the various ornaments. There were wooden sleds, gingerbread men, and snowmen... she would surely be able to find something reminiscent of their time together. Sophie stopped walking and reached her hand towards a white angel with sparkling silver snowflakes on her gown. This would be a perfect tribute to when they made snow angels, Sophie smiled, holding the ornament up and watching it glisten in the light. She then continued looking, hoping another ornament would strike her with inspiration.

It wasn't long before Sophie added a silver cookie cutter ornament, shaped like a snowflake, to her collection, perfect for remembering the snowstorm and Grant's thoughtful homemade ornament activity. And then she found a vintage truck. From the looks of it, Sophie laughed, she was definitely stretching it, but maybe Grant would be able to see it as being attributed to when he went out searching for her in the snowstorm and brought her safely home. Sophie was just about to turn her attention away from the display trees content with her finds, when a simple wooden ornament caught her attention. She drew in her breath. It was almost as if this ornament had been made specifically for her. Reaching forward, her fingers trembling, Sophie grasped the delicately carved silhouette of a man and woman with a Christmas tree in tow. This was the perfect gift! Simple in its design yet saying more than any of the others. With her heart beating happily, Sophie headed towards the counter.

"Oh, these are lovely!" Karah exclaimed, as Sophie set the ornaments on the counter. "I'll wrap them up nicely for you," she added, ringing them up and laying each one delicately on pieces of soft white tissue-paper.

"Thanks so much, Karah," Sophie expressed with gratitude. "I can't wait until he sees these."

"I'm sure Grant will love them," Karah agreed, folding the tissue-paper carefully around the first ornament and placing it gently in a box.

"Please tell your sister and parents Merry Christmas from me when you see them tomorrow," Sophie said, as Karah continued to place each ornament in the box.

"I would," Karah began flatly, "but my sister's family all came down with the stomach-bug, so we're unfortunately not going to be able to get together until after Christmas," she finished sadly.

"Oh, Karah, I'm so sorry," Sophie said, feeling truly sorry for her friend. "Would you like to come over for Christmas dinner tomorrow?"

"Thanks, Sophie, that's really kind of you, but I don't want to intrude on your Christmas plans with Grant," Karah replied, wrapping the box of ornaments and tying a red ribbon around it. "I'll be okay, though, honest," Karah remarked, causing Sophie to raise an eyebrow unconvinced. "I'll watch some old Christmas movies, have a glass of wine, and just relax," Karah added.

"Well, if you change your mind, *please* don't hesitate to come over. I promise, you won't be intruding," Sophie offered.

"Thanks, Sophie. But really, don't worry about me," Karah insisted, hoping her feigned smile appeared convincing. "We'll catch up after Christmas. I can't wait to hear what Grant thinks about your present."

"That would be wonderful! Thanks again for all your help, Karah," Sophie remarked cheerfully, picking up her gift box and turning to leave. "Merry Christmas!"

"Merry Christmas to you too!" Karah replied brightly.

Once she was outside, Sophie turned and looked through the window. Karah was gazing glassily at the vase of red-and-white flowers, her elbows resting on the counter and chin in the palm of her hands. The chipper expression her friend had been wearing only moments ago, was now replaced with somberness and shrouded in disappointment. Gazing at Karah, Sophie knew beyond a doubt, that Karah, the woman who was usually exploding with Christmas cheer, was truly upset by the cancellation of her Christmas plans. *If only,* Sophie thought, *there was something she could do to help her.* How she wished Karah would have taken her up on her offer for Christmas dinner. Then, as Sophie was about to turn away and head to her car, her face lit up in elation. *Why hadn't she thought of it sooner?* Reaching into her pocket, Sophie pulled out her phone, and quickly searching her contacts, pressed call.

"Hey, Soph," Brad answered brightly. "Did you have any problems getting Grant out of your house?"

"Actually," Sophie replied, feeling a bit uncomfortable. Even though she and Brad had agreed upon friendship, that still didn't make what she was about to say any less awkward. "It turns out Grant and I…"

"Don't say it," Brad interrupted. "I think I knew it all along," he added.

"What do you mean you knew it all along," Sophie replied bewildered.

"Come on, Soph, anyone could tell he was interested in you. Why else do you think I acted so jealously when I saw the way he was looking at you in the church parking lot?" Brad inquired. "Remember, I admitted my jealousy to you last night?" he reminded.

"Sorry," Sophie uttered. "I guess it just took me a lot longer to see it."

"Don't be sorry," Brad replied gently. "I'm happy for you, honest. Don't feel bad about not coming over tonight, either. I'll see you around. Have a Merry Christmas, Soph."

"Wait, Brad, don't hang up!" Sophie rushed. "I think I know someone who would love to spend Christmas Eve with you."

"What are you talking about?" Brad asked. He had told Sophie last night that he was unsure of Karah's feelings.

"Karah," Sophie replied, excitement filling her voice.

"Karah?" Brad questioned. "Don't be silly, Soph. Yes, I would love to spend time with Karah, but I'm not sure she feels the same way. She practically slammed the door in my face the other day after she'd first offered me apple cider," Brad recalled. "Besides, if Karah did like me, I'm quite sure she wouldn't have wanted to be a third wheel around you and I all the time," he added. *Really*, Brad thought, *he was just trying to convince himself that Karah was not interested in him. Was he really that afraid of getting rejected again? It was true he wasn't in love with Sophie, but he also wasn't sure he could survive getting shot down twice this Christmas. He may appear tough and self-assured,* Brad thought, *but he had feelings too.*

"Now you're the one who's not seeing it," Sophie laughed. "When we all had lunch together, I suspected Karah might have feelings for you by the way she kept looking at you, and although she denied it later, I wasn't entirely convinced. And just a little while ago when I was at *All Thymes and Occasions* and I told her that you and I are just friends... You would have thought I'd told her she had just won the lottery!"

"Really?" Brad asked, his voice sounding surprised.

"Trust me. Give Karah a call," Sophie suggested.

"Okay. Give me her number," Brad remarked enthusiastically.

After hanging up, Sophie watched as Karah answered her phone. The smile that spread across Karah's face and the delight she expressed as she began talking, was enough to let Sophie know that she had given her two friends the best Christmas gift possible. Tearing her gaze from the window, Sophie walked towards her car, her heart feeling joyful and abounding in the belief of Christmas miracles!

Chapter 31

Arriving home, Sophie stepped into the living room and placed Grant's gift beneath the tree. *Perfect*, she thought, standing up and smiling as the red ribbon sparkled in the tree light. Sophie's heart fluttered as she thought about Christmas morning. How she hoped Grant would see the symbolism behind his gift.

"So, that's what you've been up to," Grant said, his eyes sparkling excitedly as he walked into the room.

"I know I opened my present already, but you'll just have to wait until tomorrow," Sophie teased.

"Alright, I promise not to shake it," Grant replied mischievously, as he bent down to look at his gift. "But I didn't say I wouldn't lift it up," he grinned, picking the parcel up and weighing it. "Well," he laughed, "I'd say it's safe to say you didn't get me a lump of coal."

"No, I didn't get you a lump of coal," Sophie laughed. "Now, put your gift down and stop guessing."

"Okay, if I must," Grant conceded with a smile, setting the present gently back beneath the tree.

"So, what are these Christmas Eve plans you mentioned before I left?" Sophie asked, hoping to distract Grant as he continued to stare at his gift.

"Oh," Grant turned and looked at Sophie, his face thrilled by the reminder. "I hope you're as good at making gingerbread men as you are ornaments," he said, leading the way into the kitchen. "Then I thought after that, we could try our hand at making some homemade lasagna, and of course listen to Christmas music the entire time. What do you think?" Grant asked, his eyes twinkling merrily as if he were Saint Nicholas himself.

"It all sounds absolutely perfect!" Sophie declared, reveling in what was sure to become one of the best Christmas Eves of her life.

Listening to the Christmas classics playing softly on the radio, Sophie hummed along as she kneaded a mound of gingerbread dough between her hands. The dough's dark molasses color tinted her palms as she breathed in the aroma of its sweet cinnamon and allspice flavorings. *If she could capture the scent of Christmas in a jar,* Sophie thought, *it would smell of gingerbread and pine needles with just the slightest hint of peppermint. Yes!* she smiled happily; *a jar filled with such aromas would capture the essence of all her Christmas memories!* As Sophie watched Grant smashing his ball of dough with a rolling pin only to get the dough stuck to it, she laughed to herself. She had forgotten how fun it was to make Christmas cookies with another person. Grant continued to give her gifts even if he didn't know it.

Grant caught Sophie looking at him and shook his head. "Why does this dough hate me?" he asked with a laugh.

"It doesn't hate you," Sophie replied, setting her dough aside and walking over to Grant. "Just rub a little flour on your hands and on either side of the dough before you try rolling it," she advised.

310

"Now, hold the rolling pin like this, and gently push down," Sophie continued, putting her hands on either side of Grant's and helping him roll the dough. "There, now you try," she added, releasing the rolling pin and stepping back.

Grant continued to roll the dough a few more times before stopping and looking at Sophie in wonder. "Wow! It didn't stick, and it actually looks thick enough to make cookies. You are definitely a cookie baking guru!"

"Thanks," Sophie replied with a smile. "I've had my fair share of epic baking disasters, though, don't you worry. The trick is you just have to keep practicing."

"Let's start cutting!" Grant exclaimed excitedly, a grin enveloping his face as he handed Sophie a cookie cutter.

Once all the cookies were cut and placed on a baking tray, Grant and Sophie stood and admired their handywork.

"Not too shabby!" Grant declared, pleased with how his cookies had turned out. *There were definitely a few that were somewhat misshapen, but you could still tell they were gingerbread men,* he thought.

"I agree," Sophie seconded, as she sprinkled some decorating sugar on top of a few. "Let's get them in the oven and start on the lasagna. I hope you know how to make it, because I haven't the slightest idea. I've always just bought frozen lasagnas."

"Don't worry," Grant said, placing the tray of cookies in the oven. "Cookies might not be my forte, but lasagna definitely is. We're going to use my Grandma's recipe, the one I followed when I made lasagna with her every Christmas Eve for probably fifteen years," he added.

"With a history like that," Sophie replied, a smile spreading across her face, "I can't wait to try it!"

Grant beamed at Sophie; *she really was wonderful*, then proceeded to pull the recipe up on his phone. As they were prepping the ingredients, Sophie suddenly stopped and listened intently. Her face brightened with delight, and Sophie turned to Grant, her eyes just as luminous and enchanting.

"I love this song!" Sophie exclaimed, as the whimsical melody of *The Christmas Waltz* began playing merrily on the radio. "This song always makes me want to dance," she admitted, her eyes turning glassy at the thought of dancing in a beautiful gown at a fancy Christmas Eve party.

"Well then," Grant said, as he turned to Sophie with a smile, "may I have the pleasure of a dance?" he asked, offering Sophie his hand.

Sophie's face glowed, and smiling, she placed her hand in Grants, allowing him to lead her around the kitchen in a waltz. As she spun in his arms, Sophie was amazed at how well Grant danced. She followed his steps easily, and when he twirled her and brought her back into his arms, she felt graceful and weightless. As the song began to conclude, Grant slowed them down and Sophie felt herself dipping in Grant's strong and tender arms. Looking into his eyes as he gently pulled her back to a standing position, Sophie was speechless. *If her Grandpa had not insisted on making Grant sign that contract to stay at the farm,* she wondered in amazement, *then she might never have met Grant and that,* Sophie realized, *would have been horrible.*

"Thank you for the dance," Sophie stammered, butterflies bouncing once again inside her stomach. *Why did she suddenly feel so flustered?*

"It was my pleasure," Grant replied. Smiling at Sophie in his arms, he still couldn't believe it. *Should he pinch himself? Surely, he must be dreaming.*

"We should probably get started on the lasagna," Sophie remarked, her cheeks warm and heart pounding. *Maybe,* she hoped, *redirecting them to their task would hide the fact that she was blushing like a middle school girl falling for her first crush. It was so embarrassing!* Watching the smile on Grant's face as he silently began pouring cups of yellowish flour into a mixing-bowl, Sophie knew, however, that he had witnessed the impression he made upon her face.

"Have you ever made homemade pasta noodles before?" Grant asked, cracking an egg and adding it to the flour.

"No. I'm honestly not that great of a cook. Cookies I can do, but I just haven't taken the time to really learn how to cook anything from scratch," Sophie admitted.

"Well, it's never too late to learn," Grant said, as he added water and salt to the dough. "How about you mix this up, and then I'll teach you how to run it through the pasta machine," he added. He then went over to the island and retrieved a pasta machine and lasagna noodle attachment.

"I never knew there was a pasta machine in this house," Sophie uttered in shock.

"I brought it with me when I moved in," Grant said, as he set the pasta maker on the island. "There's nothing quite like the taste of homemade pasta noodles. Especially when you use Semolina flour like we're using."

Sophie continued mixing the dough together, impressed by Grant's pasta making knowledge. "Alright, I think the ingredients are pretty well combined," Sophie said after a while. "Now, what do we do?" she asked.

"Now, we're going to take the dough out of the bowl and knead it a bit by hand," Grant directed, as he divided the dough and handed half to Sophie.

They pressed the dough back-and-forth against the granite surface until they had made two rounded balls. "I think that's enough kneading," Grant remarked after a while. "Now, we need to divide the dough again until we have four even balls that we can run through the flattener," he instructed. Turning on the pasta machine, Grant picked up one of the balls of dough. "You then flatten it a bit between your hands, and then gently guide it through the flattener like this."

Sophie watched, as Grant pressed the dough against the flattener and continued feeding it through the flattening attachment, until an evenly pressed lasagna noodle came out of the opposite end.

"Now, it's your turn!" Grant declared, dropping a ball of dough into Sophie's hands and smiling.

"Okay, I've got this," Sophie said, determined to get it right. Grant had no idea about the time she had blown-up the kitchen in her attempt to make a homemade beef soufflé like she'd seen on a cooking show. *That had been the last time*, Sophie thought nervously, *that she had attempted making anything else besides cookies from scratch.*

"Your hands are shaking," Grant said, looking at Sophie with concern.

"Are they?" Sophie breathed, glancing at her quivering fingers. *Why did they have to give her away?* she thought flustered.

"It's just pasta noodles. You can't mess them up. And even if you do," Grant said gently, "they're made of dough. So, all you have to do is squish it and try again."

"You're absolutely right," Sophie replied sheepishly. "Okay, here it goes!" she said, as she began feeding the dough through the flattener; and then to her delight, watched as a perfectly formed lasagna noodle began taking shape.

By the time they made the sauce and finished assembling the lasagna, it was nearly five o'clock. Closing the oven door, Sophie stood up and wiped her hands against her apron. "I don't know about you, but I'm exhausted!" she laughed, removing a couple of gingerbread cookies from the wire cooling-rack and placing them on plates.

"Yeah," Grant chuckled. "Between cooking, cleaning, and dancing, I'm beat," he replied, taking the plate Sophie handed him and walking towards the living room.

"You're just such a good dancer, it would have been a shame to not dance a few more songs," Sophie proclaimed with a grin.

Grant smiled at the compliment. "I'd dance with you all day," he remarked.

"How did you learn to dance so well?" Sophie asked, as they sat down on the couch.

"My Grandma," Grant admitted, taking a bite of his cookie.

"Seriously?" Sophie asked, a bit surprised.

"Well, not exactly my Grandma, but through her generosity. Dancing was something she always enjoyed doing with my Grandpa, and she was convinced the modern generation was losing an elegant form of art. Her Christmas gift to me every year from age eight to eighteen, therefore, was a year of ballroom dance lessons."

"You liked ballroom dancing as a kid?" Sophie asked amazed. Grant was continuing to surprise her.

"Heck no! I hated it!" Grant admitted. "But my parents made me go since it was a present, and it wasn't until I was in college that I actually appreciated and was grateful for my Grandma's gift. When I went to my first college party and saw everyone dancing, I realized she had been right. Dancing, and all of its elegance and romance, really is a form of art each generation is losing little by little."

"I completely agree with your Grandma's assessment," Sophie acknowledged. "When I research people and times from the past, I sometimes envy the simplicity and style of them and the era in which they lived. I admit not everything was perfect in the past, and modern times have advancements and conveniences you wouldn't want to live without; but the kindness...the manners...and the elegant attires... of past generations are often forgotten. Sorry, there's the historian for you getting all historically sentimental," Sophie laughed. But Grant did not laugh, and Sophie smiled, knowing that what she had said to him held value.

Chapter 32

After pulling the lasagna out of the oven and setting it aside to cool, Sophie and Grant decided it would be nice to dress up for dinner since it was Christmas Eve. Now, as she examined herself in the mirror, Sophie could not believe she felt so nervous. She had told Grant she was in love with him, and Grant had told her the same, *so why then was she fretting so much over her appearance?* The long-sleeved red sheath dress she wore complimented her red lipstick. Her pearl necklace and earrings went well with her attire, and she had swept her long brown curls into an elegant twist. *Without trying to sound vain,* Sophie thought, *she looked very well put together from her hair to her nude heels. So why then was she so jittery?* Understanding finally hit Sophie. She and Grant had done things entirely backwards. Tonight, Sophie realized, was the first "date" she and Grant were having with each other. *You would think declaring your love for one another would make things less nerve racking,* she laughed anxiously, *but apparently not.*

Feeling her heart pulsing through her body as she descended the stairs, Sophie steadied herself on the banister. The smell of lasagna drifted towards her as Sophie neared the dining room, and she could hear instrumental Christmas music playing softly. As she entered the room, Grant rose from the chair he had been sitting in, and Sophie stumbled slightly at his undeniable display of chivalry.

Had she somehow been transported into the pages of Pride and Prejudice? Or of Sense and Sensibility? Was Grant possibly a modern rendition of the beloved Mr. Darcy?

"You look lovely," Grant complimented, stepping towards Sophie and offering her his hand as he helped her into her seat.

"Thank you," Sophie murmured softly, her nose catching the subtle spice of Grant's cologne. "You look very handsome yourself," she affirmed, continuing to gaze lovingly at Grant.

Grant most certainly did look dashing. His neatly tailored suit, in its charcoal-gray, fit him exceptionally, and his emerald-green satin tie complimented the dark-green hue of his eyes. Feeling her heart swoon, Sophie knew that if she had not already been seated, her legs would have buckled beneath her. She watched as Grant, unfolding a cloth napkin, gently laid it across her lap and then proceeded to pour them each a glass of wine. The care he showed her was more than Sophie could have imagined. It was not, she knew, that Grant felt her incapable of performing a simple task like resting a napkin on her lap, but rather that he genuinely found her deserving of all the affection he could offer. Sophie smiled, never in her life had she met a man who treated her so much like a lady.

"Your lasagna, Madame," Grant smiled, setting Sophie's plate before her then taking his seat.

The fragrant scent of marinara sauce and ricotta cheese bubbled against Sophie's senses as her eyes took in the finished product they'd made. She could not believe how amazing it had turned out! After pretty much making a mess of the entire kitchen putting it together, Sophie was very impressed with Grant's and her culinary skills.

"Merry Christmas Eve," Grant said, raising his wineglass into the air. "May this Christmas continue to be filled with wonderful moments."

"Merry Christmas Eve," Sophie seconded, her eyes sparkling as brightly as her crystal glass.

Lifting her fork, Sophie cut a bite-sized amount of lasagna and brought it to her mouth. *Were there even words to describe it?* she wondered. *She must go with her initial assessment.* Wiping her mouth on her napkin, Sophie looked at Grant sitting across from her. "Alright, this has got to be the best lasagna I've ever tasted," Sophie declared, then took another bite. Her mouth was bursting in amazement as each bite she took seemed to reveal a new layer of flavor.

"I'm glad you like it," Grant grinned, taking a breadstick from the basket and breaking it in half.

"You continue to surprise me, you know that?" Sophie posed, taking a sip of her wine.

"What can I say, I'm a man of *amazement*," Grant replied with a wink.

"Hey now, don't go getting a big head or anything, I didn't say *amazement*," Sophie laughed good-naturedly.

Grant chuckled. "Seriously, though, how do I continue to surprise you?" he asked.

Sophie set her fork down and looked across the table at him. "If I'm being honest with myself, I've been surprised by everything," she said. "When I first met you, you surprised me with your kindness towards me; and then you continued to treat me with kindness even when I was not the nicest acting towards you. You went looking for me in a snowstorm, even when I was going on a date with another guy, you really listen to me, you cook, you dance... the list could go on and on," Sophie admitted.

"If we're being *honest*," Grant remarked, reaching across the table and taking Sophie's hand in his, "you've surprised me too. The stories your Grandpa told me about you do not do you justice. You are even more wonderful of a woman than I had imagined. And the fact that you chose to fall in love with me, well that was the biggest surprise of all," Grant finished, looking deeply into Sophie's eyes.

Sophie felt her cheeks blushing. *Falling in love with Grant had been the biggest and best surprise for her as well.* Reading her thoughts, Grant smiled warmly and continued to hold Sophie's gaze. In their silence, more was spoken than words could ever have conveyed. In this moment, nothing mattered except the beating of their two hearts professing their unanimous devotion.

Full from dinner, Sophie and Grant loaded the dishwasher and then proceeded to get their coats. As a child, Sophie remembered her Grandpa taking her to Midnight Mass every Christmas Eve. *The hardest part*, she recalled, *was always going out into the cold.* After dinner, she was always warm and snug and ready to go to bed, but her Grandpa always made sure she was ready on time. She didn't appreciate being dragged out into the cold as a child, but now as an adult, she saw the wonder in the gift her Grandpa had given her in all those years. *While others were sleeping in waiting anticipation, she got to witness the arrival of Christmas*

Day! Sophie continued to ponder the wonderful gift she got to experience and the symbolicalness of it all, as Grant drove along in the darkness. Seeing the lights shining forth from the stained-glass windows as they pulled into the cathedral parking lot, Sophie felt tears of joy forming in her eyes. In going to Midnight Mass, her Grandpa would always be in her heart at Christmas.

The readings that were read, the carols that were sung, the joyfulness of the light radiating from the Advent wreath now completed with its burning white candle, lifted Sophie's spirit in wonder throughout the entirety of the Mass, so that by its conclusion, the joy-filled love and happiness of Christmas Day was upon her. As Grant helped her with her coat, the radiance Sophie emitted was that of a woman who had come full circle. She had been filled with sadness and regret upon first arriving home, allowed herself to open her heart to hope, and through the course of Advent, found peace, joy and love. *This Christmas*, Sophie realized, *was truly a gift— a Christmas blessing. Was there anything*, Sophie wondered happily as Grant and she stepped outside, *that could make this Christmas even more surprising?* As if in answer to her question, Sophie looked up towards the sky. Snowflakes had begun falling softly, and as one landed in her lashes, Sophie burst into smiles of happiness. Holding Grant's arm as they began walking down the cathedral steps, Sophie felt that, in this early hour of Christmas, the joy she felt was already more than she could have imagined!

Chapter 33

Sophie stretched her arms above her head as she continued to lay cozily against her pillow. Forcing herself to turn and peer at the alarm clock, she was happy to find it was only 8:00am on Christmas morning. Sophie yawned; Christmas was still young! Pushing back her covers with a smile, she stumbled out of bed and dressed. *Was it her imagination,* she thought in disbelief as she descended the stairs, *or was Grant actually still sleeping?* She did not smell any delicious aromas permeating from within the kitchen, and walking into the living room, she found the Christmas tree unlit. *Well,* Sophie smiled feeling amused, *it seemed she had another gift she could give Grant.*

After plugging in the Christmas lights and setting the radio to the instrumental Christmas station, Sophie pulled a bottle of champagne out from the wine rack. *Mimosas would be a nice touch,* she thought with a laugh, *especially since she wasn't quite sure how her breakfast was going to turn out.* She might be a decent baker, but cooking anything else always seemed to have a fifty-fifty shot at being successful. Rummaging around in the refrigerator, Sophie decided to try and cook to her strengths. Pulling out the butter and milk, she then went to the pantry and retrieved flour, sugar, baking powder and salt. Baking was something she could do, and with her newfound confidence from making lasagna noodles, she decided to try her hand at homemade biscuits. After mixing the dough, Sophie put it in the fridge to rest and then pulled out a package of breakfast sausage. Stirring the sausage occasionally as it browned, Sophie decided to try her hand at making pepper gravy. She put a saucepan on the stove and poured in milk, salt and pepper. Turning on the burner, Sophie began to slowly whisk in flour, causing the gravy to thicken as it cooked. Pleased with how her gravy had turned out, Sophie set it aside and after draining the sausage, mixed the gravy and sausage together and covered it.

Sophie then turned her attention to the biscuits. Folding the dough out on the floured island surface, Sophie kneaded it until it was no longer sticky. She then flattened the dough and cut it into circles using a biscuit cutter. Setting the biscuits on a baking sheet, she put them in the oven and turned the gravy on low. *Not too bad*, she thought, wiping a floured hand against her apron. The biscuits had about five minutes left when she heard Grant coming down the stairs. Hurriedly removing her apron, Sophie poured glasses of mimosa and smiled as Grant walked into the kitchen.

"What time is it?" Grant asked groggily, running a hand through his untidy hair.

Even with his hair disheveled and sticking up on end, Grant still made Sophie feel weak in the knees. "Merry Christmas to you too," Sophie laughed brightly.

"Oh," Grant murmured embarrassed. "Yes, Merry Christmas! Something smells amazing by the way," he added, grinning from ear to ear.

"Thanks," Sophie replied, pleased by his compliment. "I hope you like biscuits and gravy," she added cheerfully, as she pulled the biscuits from the oven.

"And you said you weren't a good cook," Grant remarked, shaking his head. "Those look delicious!"

"You haven't heard about my attempt to make a beef soufflé," Sophie laughed, as smiling she halved the biscuits and ladled gravy on top of them. Glimpsing Grant's curious expression out of the corner of her eye she added, "That's a story for another time."

"That bad, huh?" Grant chuckled, taking a seat at the table.

"Yes, that bad," Sophie confirmed, setting the breakfast laden plates on the table and handing Grant a mimosa. "Merry Christmas, Grant," she said, clinking her glass against his. Then taking a sip, Sophie smiled. The bubbles from the champagne were no match for the bubbles she felt every time Grant smiled at her.

Ivy nudged Sophie's foot. "Of course, I didn't forget about you," Sophie said, patting the pup on the head, then rising from her seat. "Since it's Christmas, I've saved you a special treat," she continued. Opening the refrigerator door, Sophie pulled out a bowl of browned sausage. "Here you go, Girl. Merry Christmas!" Sophie said, dumping the sausage into Ivy's bowl and scratching her behind the ears. Ivy licked Sophie's hand affectionately and then, wagging her tail, proceeded to devour her breakfast.

"These biscuits and sausage gravy really are delicious," Grant complimented, as Sophie returned to her seat.

"Thanks," Sophie replied. "I'm not sure I would have attempted making them if you hadn't given me back my cooking confidence," she smiled.

"Well, now that your confidence is back, can you make this

every morning?" Grant asked hopefully.

"I don't know… with your lodging contact expiring, I'm not sure every day is feasible," Sophie teased with a grin.

"Don't worry, I don't plan on going too far away," Grant replied, his eyes twinkling happily as he gazed at Sophie and watched her smile back.

After cleaning up breakfast, Sophie and Grant headed into the living room with Ivy at their heels. As Sophie watched Grant set to work building a fire, she felt her heart beating happily within her chest. Watching him prepare the kindling, seeing Ivy beside him trying to stick her head in the fireplace to see what he was doing...the simplicity of the moment... filled Sophie with a sense of joy and caused her to smile.

Once the fire began to crackle merrily within the hearth, Grant turned and saw Sophie beaming at him. "Why are you grinning at me? Do I have something on me?" he asked, checking his hands for soot before wiping them across his forehead in case he had a smudge of ash there.

"No, you don't have anything on you. I'm just happy, that's all," Sophie admitted, unable to keep her smile from broadening.

"I'm happy too," Grant confessed, a grin lighting up his face. "So, should we open these present or what?" he asked, walking towards the tree. Retrieving the velvet box with baby Jesus, Grant gently opened the lid and lifted the porcelain babe from the tissue. "Here you go, little guy," Grant said softy, placing baby Jesus in the manger. "I should have never doubted the existence of unconditional love," he added with a smile. *Christmas, when the divine chose to*

dwell among man, was by far the most profound truth about love,
Grant knew. Then walking back to the Christmas tree, Grant lifted
the gift from Sophie and the envelop and brought them over to the
couch. "Here you are," he remarked, handing Sophie the letter from
her Grandpa and sitting down beside her.

"There were two letters?" Sophie remarked in awe, as an
envelope with Grant's name was revealed beneath the letter
addressed to her.

"Charlie gave these to me when he knew you were not going
to make it home in time. He told me we weren't to open them until
Christmas," Grant divulged.

Sophie took the envelope he handed her and gazed down at
her name. "Let's open these after you open your gift from me," she
said.

Grant nodded in agreement. "I've been trying to guess what
you got me, and I can't come up with anything," Grant remarked,
giving the package a gentle shake.

"Hey," Sophie laughed. "How do you know I didn't get you
anything breakable?"

"Did you get me something breakable?" Grant asked,
stopping his shaking.

"No," Sophie admitted.

"Well then, don't take away the fun," Grant chuckled, gently
shaking the package again.

"You're such a big kid," Sophie declared.

"Yes, yes I am," Grant replied, a grin enveloping his face.
"Okay, I don't have any guesses. Time to just open it!"

Tearing off the wrapping paper, Grant lifted the lid of the box and pulled out a bundle of tissue-paper. Unfolding the paper, he smiled as the white angel, donned with silver snowflakes, appeared. He turned his eyes to Sophie and stared at her, unable to speak. No one had ever given him such a thoughtful gift. Seeing the angel ornament, he instantly recalled making snow angels with Sophie when they were looking for their tree. *Did the fact that the angel was an ornament also carry a different meaning? The meaning he was hoping it might?*

"To remember making snow angels with you," Grant said. "Thank you, Sophie. This means a lot."

"You're welcome," Sophie replied, the bubbles she felt inside feeling like they might pop with happiness. "Go on now, and open the rest," she added, unable to contain her excitement.

Unwrapping each ornament one-by-one, Grant's realization of Sophie's thoughtfulness continued to grow. The cookie cutter, the wooden silhouettes with the Christmas tree...they all meant so much to him! He had to have Sophie help him understand the meaning of the old truck, but once she revealed its meaning...Grant felt his heart beating like it never had before! He knew it seemed crazy, but he wanted to ask Sophie to marry him right now. *If only he had a ring.*

"Sophie, these are the most thoughtful gifts I've ever received," Grant confided, fighting to keep his voice from breaking.

"*You,* and every second I've spent with you, are my Christmas treasures," Sophie smiled. "And I want you in my life for the rest of my life."

Grant pulled Sophie into his arms and held her close. Feeling her heart beating softly against his chest, Grant felt nothing but elation. His hopes that Sophie's gift held a deeper meaning than just memories of this Christmas was true. Releasing her, Grant took his box of ornaments over to the tree, and with Sophie watching him lovingly, hung them gently on the branches where they rested perfectly nestled against the greenery.

"Shall we open our letters?" Grant asked, returning to sit beside Sophie.

"Yes," Sophie nodded. "We should open them together."

Sophie delicately tore open her envelope and unfolded the letter. As she began reading, a smile spread across her face.

My Dear Sophie,

I know this Christmas was not the Christmas we both had hoped for but knowing that you will be home, even though I will not see you, is the best Christmas gift you could have given me. Do not be sad. I know you loved me, and I lived a wonderful life. Having you, Sophie, in my life was one of the greatest blessings I could have ever asked for. On another note, I wish I could have seen your face, though, when you found out about the contract I made with Grant. Leave it to your old Grandpa to try and be a matchmaker! I'm hoping by now the two of you have fallen for each other, just like I fell in love with your Grandma. If not, give Grant a chance, Sophie. I never thought anyone was good enough for you until I met him. Over the four years I've known him, Grant has continued to surprise me. I've found myself, on numerous occasions, saying, "Wow! If only

Sophie were here. She'd love that about Grant!" There aren't many old souls in this world, but Grant is one of them. He compliments you, Sophie, in so many ways. Merry Christmas, Honey. I hope love has found you, and I wish you all the happiness in the world!

> *Love,*
> *Grandpa*

Sophie clutched the letter to her heart and smiled. Good-old Grandpa. He'd somehow always known her better than she knew herself. Turning her attention to Grant, Sophie's mouth fell open. In one hand Grant held his letter, but in the other...Sophie watched as the sunlight, dancing across the diamond on her Grandmother's engagement ring, cast shimmers of sparkling light about the room! The mystified expression on Grant's face matched her own, as he stared at the letter he held in one hand and the engagement ring in the other.

Charlie had always known, Grant realized in wonder. *But how was that possible?* Reading the letter, he'd been left, Charlie's words made Grant smile and shake his head in amazement. Charlie was a perceptive man who seemed to have known both his and Sophie's hearts before they understood them themselves.

> *Dear Grant,*

> *Call me crazy, but I'm pretty sure you're in love with my granddaughter. How do I know this, you ask? Well, for one thing:*

every time I talk about her, your eyes light up and you hang on my every word, and two: why else would you agree to such a ridiculous contract? I figured you might need this, so I've enclosed the engagement ring I gave Sophie's Grandma so many years ago. I was blessed to share fifty-three wonderful years with the love of my life, and I hope you and Sophie will be just as blessed. Take care of my little girl, Grant, there's no one else I'd trust her too. Now, do me a favor and get down on that knee of yours and ask her to be your wife.

    Welcome to the family,

    Charlie

    Having finished reading his letter, Grant again gazed at the engagement ring. The sides of the band, dotted with tiny diamonds, twisted and turned in a vintage design. Resting on top, the band cradled an elegantly cut diamond that shimmered more beautifully than he believed possible. Everything about the ring echoed Sophie's name. *The history... memories... family... classic design...* He could never have found a ring more perfect for her if he had searched for a hundred years. Tearing his gaze from the ring, Grant looked at Sophie. Her dark-russet eyes were sparkling brighter than the jewel he held in his hand, and as the sunlight brushed against her soft brown locks, Grant's heart raced as she smiled at him.

    Standing up from the couch, Grant dropped to one knee, and taking Sophie's hand in his, felt her warmth against his skin as he gazed into her eyes.

"Sophie, I know some might say we're rushing things, that we barely know each other, but Sophie, I feel like I've known you forever. From the moment you walked in the door with pepper-spray to now, I've continued to fall in love with you. Every second I've had the privilege of spending with you," Grant continued, looking deeply into Sophie's eyes, "has made me realize that you are even more amazing than the woman I fell in love with through all those stories Charlie told. So, seeing as I have a ring, and your Grandpa's blessing," Grant smiled, his green eyes twinkling, "Sophie Marten, will you do me the honor of becoming my wife?" He held her gaze and watched as tears of happiness began forming within Sophie's eyes.

"Yes," Sophie choked, through tears of joy, as she flung her arms around Grant's neck. "Being your wife, Grant Bakesfield, and spending the rest of our lives falling in love with each other over and over again, would be the best adventure in the world!" she declared. Releasing Grant from her embrace, Sophie watched breathlessly as Grant gently slid her Grandmother's engagement ring on her finger.

Taking Sophie's hands in his, Grant pulled her to her feet, and kissing her tenderly, held her close in his arms. And as the song, *I'll Be Home for Christmas*, began to quietly play in the background, he led Sophie around the room in a waltz, knowing they both were finally home.

Epilogue
One year later

As she stood gazing at her reflection in the mirror, Sophie's heart fluttered with happiness. It was hard to believe it had already been a year since Grant proposed. Turning her gaze to the engagement ring she wore on her finger, Sophie smiled. Today, she was marrying a man for more amazing than she could have ever dreamed. Standing here now, Sophie suddenly found everything to be surreal. *Was she dreaming? Should she pinch herself? The way she had met Grant was something that seemed to be dreamed up for a fairytale. Was she really about to have her happy ending? No,* Sophie corrected herself, *she was about to embark upon her happy beginning!*

Sophie's heart raced in anticipation with the knowledge that she was mere moments away from walking down the aisle to Grant. Twirling ever so slightly, Sophie gazed once more at her reflection. She had decided to wear her mother's wedding gown. Beautiful, soft, white, Chantilly lace covered Sophie's shoulders and continued down the length of her arms. The delicate Venice-style lace, trimming the gown's modest V-neck bodice, continued elegantly along her waistline, until it met the full, slightly ballgownish, tool skirt flowing out behind her in a long cascading train. Sophie's long brown curls were twisted in an elegant updo, dotted with pearls and a few sprigs of holly, leaving just a few curls softly framing her face; while a soft and sheer cathedral-length veil rested lightly on top of her head. Holding her bouquet of red roses and baby's breath, Sophie smiled. She was ready!

"You look *so* beautiful," Karah gushed, coming to stand beside her.

"Absolutely stunning!" Vivian confirmed.

"Thanks," Sophie replied, turning to face her friends. "You both look lovely too," she complimented, gazing at Karah and Vivian and smiling. The light-silver bridesmaid dresses they wore, trimmed in silver lace with a few sparkles, were very becoming on both of them.

"So, will I get to be your bridesmaid anytime soon?" Sophie asked Karah with a hopeful smile. Ever since last Christmas, much to Sophie's delight, Karah and Brad had become inseparable.

Karah's face lit up. "I wasn't going to tell you because I didn't want to take away from your day but," Karah continued brightly, extending her hand. "Brad and I are engaged! He asked me last night," she added, her face beaming with happiness.

"Oh, Karah! Congratulations! I'm so happy for you both!" Sophie exclaimed, hugging her friend.

"Thanks, Sophie," Karah replied excitedly, holding Sophie in her embrace. "I'm truly the happiest I've ever been," she shared, stepping back and looking at Sophie, her entire face glowing.

"I'm so glad," Sophie remarked with elation. "You and Brad are really great together."

"Thanks, Sophie," Karah said with a grin. "We truly bring out the best in each other. But enough about me. It's your wedding day. I've got something for you," she continued, shifting her holly and baby's breath bouquet to one hand and giving Sophie a letter. "This is from Grant," Karah shared. Then smiling, she extended the envelope towards Sophie.

"Oh!" Sophie exclaimed, taking the letter from Karah and gently unfolding it. Feeling the crispness of the paper between her fingers, Sophie's eyes rested on Grant's words.

My Dearest Sophie,

Words cannot begin to describe the elation I feel today. As I write this, I still cannot believe that I will soon be blessed enough to call you my wife. Today, you make me happier than I ever believed was possible. I hope that, as your husband, I too will be able to make you just as happy. I know as the years progress, there will undoubtedly be times that we will disagree or be cross with one another, but I know we will persevere and always work things out. As long as we remember the love we have for one another and why we fell in love with each other, I do not believe there will ever be a time we cannot weather. I love you, Sophie Grace Marten, with all my heart, and I will keep loving you until my heart no long beats. With you I will forever be home, and I will continue to fall more in love with you every day I'm blessed to walk beside you. My beloved, soon to be Mrs. Bakesfield, today as you walk down the aisle towards me, I will be waiting with a heart that is forever yours.

Love, your soon to be husband,

Grant

As she finished reading Grant's letter, Sophie's heart was filled with a joy more profound than she could have imagined. Even when she felt like she knew everything about him, Grant continued to surprise her. *The words he had written...the heart and emotion he had given her... Grant truly was a man worthy of her heart and love and she,* Sophie knew, *was a woman worthy of his.*

"It's time," Karah smiled, walking over to Sophie and fluffing her train. "Are you ready?"

"Yes," Sophie declared, without a doubt, her smile making her face appear even more lovely. Thinking of Grant waiting for her, Sophie knew she had never been more ready for anything in her life.

Folding Grant's letter against her bouquet, Sophie followed Vivian and Karah into the sanctuary. As she waited for Karah to begin walking down the aisle, Sophie felt as though she was floating. Her life had come full circle. Listening to the organ playing, Sophie smiled. She was getting married in the parish where she'd grown up, and gazing at the roses in her bouquet, she knew her Grandpa was here with her in spirit. Sophie heard the sound of the pipe organ switch to playing *Ave Maria*, and looking up, she began walking down the aisle gazing lovingly at Grant, whose deep-green eyes shone just as bright as the smile upon his face.

Made in the USA
Monee, IL
09 December 2019